ONE LAST KILL

Bobby Ress is a cop with a simple life. He loves his wife and his daughter. He believes in making a difference. He has a place in the world.

Then people start dying — a lot of them — in horrible ways. It's a case like no other. And, step by gruesome step, the simple and true things Bobby knows to be right and good begin to make less and less sense.

Because Bobby is learning about pain. He doesn't like to admit it, he doesn't like to know, but he's slowly coming to a realisation. If you hurt someone badly enough, for long enough, then there's nothing — absolutely *nothing* — you can't make them do . . .

SPECIAL MESSAGE TO READERS

THE ULVERSCROFT FOUNDATION
(registered UK charity number 264873)
was established in 1972 to provide funds for
research, diagnosis and treatment of eye diseases.
Examples of major projects funded by the
Ulverscroft Foundation are:

- The Children's Eye Unit at Moorfields Eye Hospital, London
- The Ulverscroft Children's Eye Unit at Great Ormond Street Hospital for Sick Children
- Funding research into eye diseases and treatment at the Department of Ophthalmology, University of Leicester
- The Ulverscroft Vision Research Group, Institute of Child Health
- Twin operating theatres at the Western Ophthalmic Hospital, London
- The Chair of Ophthalmology at the Royal Australian College of Ophthalmologists

You can help further the work of the Foundation
by making a donation or leaving a legacy. Every
contribution is gratefully received. If you would like
to help support the Foundation or require further
information, please contact:

THE ULVERSCROFT FOUNDATION
The Green, Bradgate Road, Anstey
Leicester LE7 7FU, England

217506821

website: www.ulverscroft-foundation.org.uk

FINN BELL

---◆---

ONE LAST KILL

Complete and Unabridged

AURORA
Leicester

First published in 2016
as *Pancake Money*

First Aurora Edition
published 2022

A catalogue record for this book is available
from the British Library.

ISBN 978–1–78782–907–7

BEFORE . . .

We're not close to done yet.

We're still in the middle somewhere.

He's getting hot and sticky.

Reddening skin turns slick, beading sweat that stinks more than it should.

He hasn't stopped shaking and crying. All this time.

Tears and thin snot mix into a slippery oil that makes it hard to keep my hand over his mouth. My gloves are already dripping and it's smeared up onto my sleeves.

I can feel the shuddering breath from his nostrils play a warm rhythm against my cheek.

He's still trying to fight, feebly clawing at me. But he's too weak to win now. Broken.

We both know it.

Through my hand clamped over his mouth I can feel him try to shake his head. No.

No. Again and again.

His face is turned up to mine. Close. Keeps trying to catch my eye.

So much hurt there. Pleading. Shock. Intimate.

He doesn't understand that we could be doing this. That this is us now.

He finally stops fighting me. I sense the moment he accepts it.

Then he slowly puts his hands on mine.

Gently now. Like he used to.

I can feel his lips move. I think he's trying to talk.

1

Say something to me, one last time.

I know he loves me. Even now.

Can't stop himself. Can't help it. Dear God.

Father Mucci told me once that when people are dying, right near the end, when they know it's coming for them, they become their real selves.

That their souls come out. That you can see them.

And right then, whether full of grace or covered in sin, every soul is beautiful.

I don't know if that's going to happen.

But then, we're not close to done yet.

We're still in the middle somewhere.

MONDAY . . .

1:20 a.m.

When Pollo gets really drunk, he gets sad.

Some people go that way.

Maybe it's a good thing. He's a big man. Knows how to handle himself. Could do a lot of damage.

But mostly, he just goes away. Down inside himself.

Talks about when he was young. Growing up on the islands in Samoa.

Sometimes, only sometimes, he talks about his family.

'My dad, Bobby. My dad got drunk,' Pollo declares to me in slurred tones. Staring down at the table between us as he nods his agreement to his own statement.

'Sundays after church he and the other men would go into the bush and drink until the sun went down,' Pollo says, and stifles the start of a sudden laugh before falling silent again.

'Only sometimes. Not every Sunday. But Mum, she always knew when he was going to do it. Knew before,' Pollo says, then takes another messy gulp of beer.

Then, after a long time, Pollo says, 'Pancake money. That's how I knew when she knew, see? Figured it out,' Pollo explains.

'Sunday mornings when we went to church. At the end of the service, we had to give the priest coins.

3

Mum gave us all coins before we went. Money for God,' Pollo says, sounding angrier now.

'But on the days when Mum knew Dad was going to go drink after church, she'd keep some of the coins back,' Pollo continues.

His eyes still tracing the wood grain of the table.

'She'd wait for sunset. For Dad to come staggering back, angry, out of the woods. Then she'd put a coin in every hand. One for each of us,' Pollo says, pausing to drink again.

'She'd send us down to Aunty Manaia's shop to buy each of us a pancake,' Pollo says.

'Pancake money. Me and my brother and sister,' Pollo says.

'Only Natia, my little sister, she wouldn't buy her pancake. She'd run to the church and put the coin by the front door and pray,' Pollo says.

'But then later, when she got older, she stopped doing that. Then she just threw the coin into the sea,' Pollo finishes and falls silent.

'What did you do?' I ask.

But I already know the answer.

Pollo looks up and meets my eye for the first time.

He looks young when he answers, 'I ate the pancake, Bobby.'

★   ★   ★

8:15 a.m.

It's still early in the too-bright-and-cold part of later that same morning when I blearily look up at the little old lady standing in front of the lecture theatre.

'What motivates behaviour?' Bowlby asks.

4

Then, after a beat, she says, 'What really makes us do things? What makes us act? Before you answer, let's clarify the question. Because we're not just talking about people. Not only human behaviour, but about the behaviour of all living things. Everything you can think of. That's us at the top, along with all the other mammals, reptiles, birds, fish, and insects, and beyond, all the way down to the simplest little microbes clinging to a rock somewhere under the ocean. Even bacteria.'

Okay, that changes things, I think.

The click and creak of her walking stick as she rounds the table is the only sound in the busy silence.

'Nothing? Okay, I'll give you more clues. There's only one answer. It's the same thing for all of us. There's one single thing that is universal across all living things. It's predictable and reliable. Works better than anything else. If you want to motivate the behaviour of any living thing, this is all you need. This is the go-to,' she prompts.

'It's everywhere. Even here in this room right now. All of you know it. Very well,' she says as she takes off her glasses to look around the room. A tiny old lady. Friendly, wrinkled face and grey curls in a flowery dress. With the mind of a serial killer.

Several of them, in fact.

'Oh, come on. Greatness courts failure,' she says when there are still no answers.

'Oxygen?' a doubtful voice calls out.

'And unfortunately, failure courts greatness right back,' Bowlby responds with a shake of her head.

'Love!' someone else calls out.

'Ah, love. That one always comes up,' Bowlby says with a smile.

5

'Profound but problematic. The first problem there is that most living things on earth don't use sex to make more of their kind. That being the case, what use do bacteria have for love? And how would they feel it? They just don't have the chemicals. And are also hindered somewhat by a complete lack of a brain to feel it in. The second problem is that it also doesn't always work for higher animals like us humans. I could show you a great many people who profess a deep love for their partners, their kids, and their God. Unfortunately, no amount of me appealing to that love is going to motivate them to do anything different. It's not going to make them lose weight. Or stop using drugs. Or stop being mean to their husbands at seventy. Despite everything we want to believe about love, it's just not that reliable. Sometimes it works. Mostly it doesn't. Truthfully, if you look at the world, it hardly ever changes our behaviour over a given lifespan,' Bowlby says.

'Choice?' another voice calls out from the front.

Because there's always someone in a group like this who won't let their complete lack of understanding get in the way of participation.

'Choice? No, dear. This is Forensic Psychology 702. So just, no,' Bowlby says as she kindly pats him on the shoulder, drawing some laughs from the room.

'Remember, I said one thing that works for all living things. Every time. Perfectly. If I want to motivate behaviour, all I need is this one thing. Doesn't even matter what behaviour. This can get me anything I want. Works on individuals. Works on groups. If you're alive and I want to make you do something, anything, this is my best bet,' Bowlby says.

Then, deciding she's given us enough time, she

relents and says, 'Very well. What motivates behaviour? What makes us do things? What single thing can change the behaviour of any living being? Every time?' she prompts.

'Pain,' she answers herself.

'If I want to change your behaviour, motivate you to do something, anything I want, really — whether you're a man or an amoeba — all I need to do is hurt you, long enough and bad enough. Works every time.

'In scientific terms there's a statement: 'The primary motivator of human behaviour is pain.' I'll say it again slowly, 'The primary motivator of human behaviour is pain.' You're going to want to remember that,' Bowlby says.

'But using pain to make people do things is wrong,' someone from the group comments.

'This is Forensic Psychology, people. We're not talking ethics, but effectiveness,' Bowlby retorts. She surveys the class.

'Right or wrong, pain works. If I want you to do something, to behave in a specific way, all I need to do is hurt you. Enough pain and I can motivate you to do anything I want. Works better than anything else. Why do you think we make war? Why do men beat their wives? Why do criminals use violence? Because pain works.

'Let's go back to the example of people. There are millions of people out there eating themselves to an early death. Despite all the diet plans and the gym memberships, the home fitness programs, and the self-help books. Despite all the pleading of their loved ones, and even against their own will. They can't stop eating. There's no changing them. We know it. They know it. Eventually they're going to kill themselves.

'But, suspending ethics for the moment, let's try the primary motivator. Pain. Let's say I'm allowed to go live with them. Full-time. Twenty-four hours a day. Just one little old lady. And a hammer. So on the first day I tell them exactly what I want. I want them to eat a healthy diet and follow an exercise plan. No cheating. That's it. Then I wait. And the first time that person puts something unhealthy in their mouth or goes to the couch instead of the gym, I take my hammer and break their arm. No talking. No explanations.

'Now, I'm reliably informed that bone breaks are some of the most intense forms of pain you can experience. So, the first time I do it, I guarantee you this person isn't going to keep eating.

'I know what you're thinking. Eventually they get back from the hospital and the painkillers and all the sympathy from friends and family dulls the trauma. And, after a few hours, that piece of chocolate cake starts looking pretty good again. This time, as soon as they reach for it, I take my hammer and hit them again. Same place. Same break again.

'Now on a case-by-case basis, there's some uncertainty at this point. Maybe I have to break your arm only once. Maybe a few times. But eventually, the only difference between people is time. I absolutely guarantee you that if I'm consistent, if I hurt you badly enough for long enough, I can make you do anything I want,' Bowlby finishes.

A woman at the front of the class speaks up. 'Okay, setting ethics aside. Professor, you said this was efficient. But it isn't really. You'd have to stay with that person the rest of their life. I mean, they can just go back to eating bad things as soon as you leave.'

'Good point. But still wrong,' Bowlby says. 'Let's

say I leave. Again there will be some differences among individuals but, as has been pointed out, there's nothing stopping them from eating badly now, right? So maybe with some it's right away, maybe others take a few days or weeks. But eventually, they'll revert to eating everything in sight.

'That's when my hammer and I come back and I break that arm again. No hesitating. No debate. Deaf to the angry pleading and promises. Only this time it's different. How?' Bowlby asks.

I know the answer. I don't want to, but I do.

'This time you only have to break it once and you can leave. Because they know how it works now,' I say.

'Ah, young Bobby Ress. Good to see you've finally woken up, and with a correct answer, too,' Bowlby says to me.

'Again, there may be some differences between people. One visit could be enough for some. Or maybe I have to return a few times. But few. At most it would be around five times if the pain is severe enough,' Bowlby says, looking directly at me.

'So quick. Why, you could be a changed person in a few weeks!

'Only five times. If I've used enough pain, then that change in your behaviour is going to be permanent. Enough pain and you will never be the same. Ever. It works on every living thing.

'If I want change, all I need is to hurt you badly enough for long enough. It's simple. It's fast. It's easy.

'So, if that's true — and trust me, folks, it is — then why don't we use it? Why bother with all this talking to people and encouraging and pleading? Why bother with rewarding good behaviour? Or doling out punishments that don't hurt enough? We already know it

9

seldom works. Why haven't we come up with a way to use severe pain to change people forever?' Bowlby asks.

'Because it's wrong,' someone answers.

'Really? Wrong? Surely a few broken arms are better than watching your father drink himself to death. Or your kid keep using drugs until she overdoses. But I can understand how it would be hard to imagine doing that to someone you love. Okay. Let's make it easier. What about a sex offender? A multiple rapist who has re-offended every time he's been released from prison. He's not sorry. In fact, he can't wait to get out there again. Still think it's wrong? After all, we're going to save all his potential victims, spare all their families the grief. And he wins because he won't be coming back to prison for another rape. All that for a few broken bones. Doesn't the pain we avoid outweigh the pain we cause?' Bowlby asks into the silence.

'Isn't the good we could do worth the sacrifice?

'But enough of that. Go ponder ethics and your illusions of a moral compass on your own time.

'We're not here to talk about the good people ought to do but the bad they actually do, and why. And more specifically, today we're talking about pain. My question still stands: If severe pain is so effective at changing behaviour, permanently and reliably, then why don't we use it?'

And as I gaze down at the table, for some reason I'm reminded of that look in Pollo's eyes last night and I say, 'Because you get more.'

Not really sure what I mean yet.

'Mr Ress. That's the second correct answer from you today. Maybe you should come to class hungover

10

more often,' Bowlby says as she looks over. Damn. She spotted that.

'Come on then. Share with the rest of the class,' Bowlby prompts me.

'You can use pain to get people to do what you want. That's true,' I say, trying to think it through step by step before I continue.

'And it works. You hurt people badly enough for long enough and they'll do anything, anything. We don't like to think about it, but it's true.

'But . . . you also get more. The pain. Too much pain can change people. In ways you don't know. Can't foresee. So you can get them to do what you want but there's a price; you also get other things. You can get more than you bargained for.'

★ ★ ★

10:05 a.m.

People don't look like people when they're dead. It helps.

What's on the floor between us used to be Father Aldo Mucci, a retired Catholic priest.

He's naked, but he looks all wrong.

Most bodies have several straight lines to them; arms, legs, shoulders, and so on. What's lying in a dis-organised heap of curves in front of us has none of these. It looks like literally every bone in his body has been broken several times, until his skeleton finally gave up the shape of a person. What's left is just a wet, tangled collection. Tubes of meat in a confusing jumble, twisting round and curling back over and into itself in a sad little pile.

11

There are bruises of varying depth, colour, and size everywhere. That's bad. Once the heart stops pumping, you don't bruise anymore. Hit someone after they've died and you still rupture the vessels, still damage the tissue, but the blood you release drains away. All of it slowly pooling at the lowest parts of your body. It means most of this was done to him before he died. It took time. His head is untouched. Stands out. Looks out of place. Tiny white crust marks at the corners of his eyes. The dried-up residue of too many tears.

'Scene guys have done the photos?' I ask.

Doing a good job of keeping my voice steady despite the pounding in my ears. I haven't actually got used to this part. Just got used to not showing it.

'Yeah, left about an hour ago,' Pollo answers in a flat tone. Still hungover from last night too. Maybe he never got used to it either.

I get down on my knees and, following a particular curved shape, try to gently shift some of it to expose his foot.

'Don't fuck with it, Bobby. Coroner's Office will get shitty again,' Pollo says to me, but kneels down next to me to get a closer look anyway.

'I just need to see his toes,' I answer, as I succeed in shifting what looks like part of a loop of arm over to expose a row of toes sticking straight up. They're heavily bruised and several of the nails are broken, split in straight lines along the curve.

'That's about top of the pile, right?' I ask. Trying to concentrate on what needs doing and shutting out the rest.

'About,' Pollo answers, leaning in beside me as he reaches out to press and roll the big toe between his thumb and forefinger.

Then nods and says, 'Yup,' before getting up and looking down at the body again.

'Okay, so maybe they started at the bottom, feet first, and worked their way up. Took their time. Enough for it to hurt. Bad,' Pollo says, patting his pockets. Then stops when he realises he can't smoke in here.

'They?' I ask, looking back up at him.

'Dunno why yet. Just they,' Pollo says, eyes still on the toes. I don't challenge him. Pollo is like that, tends to know things before he understands why.

'I don't get it,' Pollo states, starting to shake his head.

'Which one you thinking?' I ask.

'That's just it. None are fitting for me,' Pollo answers.

If you've done this for a while, you learn to cheat a lot.

The world isn't complex. We aren't all snowflakes.

People mostly do bad things for only three reasons:

Money.

Sex.

Power.

And really, that's just the specific shape of it.

The real reason is always the same:

More.

So you look at the bad thing and you try to figure out which of the three is behind it. Then you find the people wanting more.

'It's not money. He was a dirt-poor retired priest living off a tiny church pension in this shitty little house. I don't think this is sex either, because I just know there was more than one of them here. And by all accounts, the good Father Mucci was actually one

13

of the few Catholic priests who didn't bugger the altar boys. That leaves power, but again, he's been retired almost a decade. Lived alone here. Hardly saw anybody. If he had secrets worth all this, it would have to come from when he was still a priest and part of the world,' Pollo says.

'And then why wait ten years to come get it out of him?' I finish that line of thought.

'Maybe he saw something he shouldn't have,' I suggest. Pollo gives me an impatient look.

'Power again, Bobby? So for being a witness they do this? They would have just killed him quietly for that. What's the point of all this, then?' Pollo retorts, shaking his head.

'So we don't know the why yet, but we've got the how,' Pollo says.

'Okay, so what do we know?' I then ask.

'All the pageantry aside, factor in for movements, tools, timing, and method, I'd say well planned,' Pollo answers.

'Experienced too,' I add, looking down at the loops of flesh. 'They hit him hard enough to bruise, to crack, and to break, but not so hard that they broke through the skin. It's not split anywhere. Aside from his bones, he still looks intact. Who knows how to do that?' I ask.

'Dunno, but I reckon you'd need some practice. And control. Doing it this way, you'd have to be careful the whole time. No letting go and just hitting as hard as you can. I can't see someone getting that right first try,' Pollo replies.

'Okay, so it was planned and controlled, and the unsubs have experience,' I summarise. 'It could still be any of the three, really.'

'And when you can't see the reason . . .' Pollo

prompts with a tired sigh.

'It's because the reason is somewhere else,' I finish. That's not good either. It usually means more bad things we haven't found yet.

'Who found him?' I ask.

'Nurse who comes to give him his medication. Didn't see or hear anything. Ditto for everyone else in the neighbourhood,' Pollo answers.

'It's that kind of neighbourhood,' I remark.

'And I'm betting forensics comes back clean as well. I can't see 'planned and controlled' fitting with leaving prints or trace evidence behind,' Pollo continues.

You hear about modern forensics and the amazing clues and detective work cops use to catch some killer, and you'd think it's almost impossible to get away with it these days. But the truth is, people learn quickly.

Some disposable gloves, a hair net, and some plastic bags over your shoes, and we have very little to go on. Bring along some Spray & Wipe cleaner and be careful with your choice of weapon and what you touch, and we've got close to nothing.

'So someone takes the time to turn Father Mucci into what is basically a skin sack of puréed bone and guts, and we have exactly dick in terms of evidence,' I say.

'Well, maybe the press will turn something up,' Pollo answers.

'Ugh, come on, you're serious?' I ask.

'Nurse lady told us, then told her friend, who works for Channel 3. The clusterfuck will commence at the 6:00 p.m. news,' Pollo answers.

'You watch, within a few days they'll lead with

15

satanic ritual,' I say.

'Nah, paedophile priest. People aren't scared of Satanists anymore,' Pollo answers.

'Dead priests. It'll be nothing but this for days,' I say, still looking down at the body.

'You ever heard of anything like this?' Pollo asks in a pensive tone.

'No,' I answer, shaking my head, still studying the mess in front of us as I take out the cough medicine in my pocket and use it to swig down more pain pills.

'Still nursing that cold?' Pollo asks.

'Nah, just like my traumatic experiences to be honey-lemon flavoured,' I answer, smiling over my pounding headache.

'Should have skipped class this morning and stayed home,' Pollo says.

'You're the one who dragged me out for that 'one drink' last night, remember?' I counter. 'I'm going to look around,' I add as I get up from the body.

'I'll call the coroner,' Pollo says as he heads back to the front door.

Father Mucci left behind a gloomy, barren space. No pictures, no souvenirs, just the odd crucifix on a wall. Worn Bible by the bed. Or maybe dead people's homes just always feel this way.

It happens as I'm looking around the tiny bedroom.

Sometimes you just have that feeling.

I know it the moment I hear that crowded quiet of someone intentionally not making any noise. It feels different than actual empty silence.

I don't see it happen. Just hear Pollo yell out. By the time I'm back in the hall, Pollo is already down on his knees, cradling the side of his head, blood pouring through his fingers, yelling, 'Go! Go!'

16

I jump over him and run out the door straight down the road immediately. The shot of adrenaline burning away my flu symptoms. Hand automatically reaching for the gun I no longer carry as I yell out, 'Stop! Police!' Damn.

The big athletic shape accelerating away only paces ahead of me looks fit, young. By his speed and my current condition, this wasn't going to take long. We'd either catch him in the next few blocks or not at all.

'This is the police! Stop!' I hear Pollo yell out from behind me, and I'm relieved that he's up and with me.

'He's getting away!' Pollo gasps at me as we run flat out.

My lungs are burning. It's getting hard to think. I see Pollo's right; he's slowly outpacing us. Stealing a step here and there as we sprint, bouncing from streets to pavements, vaulting low fences. Hearts thundering in our ears. How long was that guy in there? How did we miss him?

I'm going as fast as I can, and I know Pollo's faster than me. The fact that he hasn't pulled ahead yet is bad. While Pollo is in his early forties he is still a massive, six-foot-four Samoan ex-rugby player who is mostly muscle and currently angry. Even though I'm almost two decades younger and built a lot slighter, there's no way I can usually keep pace with him. As I glance across at him I see there's more blood on him now, a lot more. So I dig deep and push harder.

I'm not going to say anything. Pollo's a professional, he'll quit when he has to. And I'll need him. Neither of us has our guns. Didn't expect anyone there. No time to radio it in. It's just us.

'Stay on him, I'll go down,' Pollo gasps out, then breaks to the left and goes down the crossing street heading down the steep hill we're running along. It's a gamble, but not a big one.

The city of Dunedin was built on the remains of a massive exploded volcano. The harbour and city lie in a deep bowl surrounded by suburbs clinging to steep hills that run in a broken circle around it. We're on the side of one of them, running along, almost level. The streets crossing this one offer only steep uphill or steep downhill as alternatives. When you chase people on foot, they almost always choose to run downhill at some point if they can. No idea why.

We're both getting slower. Unfortunately, I'm getting slower faster. I'm losing him.

Then, finally, he breaks left and heads downhill as I try to coax more speed out of my searing legs. I hope Pollo's going to make it in time. Because I'm not catching this guy on my own. My muscles are starting to shake and, running downhill, his lithe form eats up the pavement even faster. He's definitely young, late teens maybe.

Out of desperation, I force one last push out of my legs, planning with the seconds of breath I have left to go for a diving tackle at his ankles. I just hope I end up on top once we're down. My head is already swimming. I won't have the energy to fight him from below for long. Where's Pollo?

He must have sensed my dive. He immediately pulls away his back leg and I'm forced to stretch myself out full length as I fly across the tarmac. Reaching. Then, with the fingertips of my right hand, I get just a brief moment of contact on the curve of his ankle.

And it's enough. His legs instantly tangle and he goes down hard. Falling half on the street, half on the raised pavement. His momentum skidding him forward at speed. I hear him grunt. It must have hurt. I'm not as lucky, though. Because when I land, I'm stopped dead by the pavement slamming into my face and shoulder. It knocks the wind out of me and I lose a few seconds as a wave of blurring nausea dulls my vision.

When I come back to myself, it's already too late.

He's up on his feet and turning towards where I'm still sprawled on my side. I know the kick that's coming will be at my head. I'm going to be too slow, I think, as I start pulling away. Throwing an arm across for some protection.

Then, as his boot is still swinging towards me, he's suddenly jarred away as Pollo's massive frame slams into him from the side. They both spill onto the street as I try to stagger up, but I fall over again the moment I try to put weight on my left arm. Something's wrong there.

I hear the car before I see it, and I know it all just got so much worse. By the time I look around, all I see is the car skidding almost sideways as it flashes past only inches from me.

There's a juddering bounce in the car's slide that ends a couple of paces ahead of me. It either hit them or ran over them. As I finally get to my feet I yell out, 'Pollo!' as I round the back of the car. But there's no answer. Dreading what I'll find on the road, I'm momentarily blocked by the driver's door opening.

And then, thank God, there's Pollo and the boy, sprawled together on the street. I see now that it is a boy, no more than seventeen or so. Both of them are still moving and looking alive enough. It's only when I see Pollo's face that I feel something's wrong.

19

I fucked up.

Because Pollo's not looking at me.

He's looking behind me.

And I realise that what's wrong is the silence.

You hit someone with your car and — if you don't speed off — you're going to get out and either say you're sorry or say it wasn't your fault, but you're going to say something. Because it's an accident. You didn't mean to. You're innocent.

Unless you're not.

I'm still turning when the blow from behind lifts me off my feet.

I don't know what he hit me with but the blackness takes me before I even touch the ground.

★　★　★

'Bobby.'

When I was a boy we'd play in the park, and sometimes all the kids would get together and push the merry-go-round as fast as it could go. Then we'd all jump on and lie down, looking up at the clouds spiralling above.

'Bobby.'

If you did it just right, you got the feeling you were falling into that sky. Spinning away into forever. Felt good.

'Bobby.'

It only lasted a few moments. I didn't have the words for it back then. But I knew while it was spinning we were all together. Nothing hurt anymore. I remember being happy.

'Bobby. Don't go into the light, arsehole,' Pollo says.

At which point I finally manage to order my scattered thoughts and remember that I'm not six anymore, and the spinning I feel is probably from the concussion making friends with my head cold. Pollo's been calling my name. So I open my eyes, which makes the headache so much worse. Now coming in only a close second to the nausea.

'Gah. Well, that sucked,' I say as I look around.

We're still on the street where I fell. The car and our two friends are gone. Happy days.

The street is deserted. I'm sure there are people in the houses around us who've seen it all happen but nobody will come out.

It's that kind of neighbourhood.

'In hindsight, we shouldn't have let those uniform guys go get lunch when we got here,' I say.

'No good deed,' Pollo says. 'Well, at least you're still pretty.'

I only notice now that Pollo's still lying in the street next to me as he pokes at the gash on the side of his head.

'How long?' I ask as I turn over, staring down at the smears of blood on the street where my own head was.

'Just a few moments,' Pollo answers. 'But we should probably get up now. Maybe do lunch? Modern policing is about effective time management, you know.'

'Yeah,' I answer as I stagger up, thankful that my arm seems to be kind of working again. 'Maybe Thai food.'

'Or Turkish. I could go for a kebab,' Pollo answers as he gets himself up as well. We slowly head back up the hill.

'Got the plates?' I ask.

'Only the last few numbers, 247 or 241, I think. Red Ford Cortina, older, maybe an '82, with rust along the side and back. I could ID the boy but not the driver. How 'bout you?'

'Nothing on the driver. Same with the boy though, saw his face clear before the other guy knocked me out. There was some kind of flag sticker on the back window. A green horizon under a red sky with a single centred star,' I say.

'Māori?' Pollo asks.

'Maybe,' I answer.

'Fuck sakes. Why's it always got to be Māori?' Pollo says, shaking his head.

But I don't answer. Pollo's Samoan but his wife is Māori. Which to them means their kids are Māori.

'You guys coming over for dinner tonight? Angie's making chop suey,' Pollo asks.

'No, thanks though. It's the new moon so I'm taking Eva and Em to the forest again,' I say as we finally reach Father Mucci's house again.

'Is it helping?' Pollo asks.

'I don't know. I can't just do nothing,' I answer. Pollo gives a grunt in reply.

'Don't be a dick, bro, come by before then. You know I'm sensitive like that,' Pollo answers and I nod, which makes my head hurt again.

When we reach the house, my eye is drawn to Father Mucci's open door. I can just make out the yellow crime scene tape circling his body. It'd be the first thing you see when you open the front door. Who does that?

'At least we have a lead,' I say, fighting down the nausea again as Pollo reaches into the car to call for backup.

But both of us know how little it really amounts to.

Through the blood streaks across his face, I can see Pollo is as angry as I am.

Somebody beat an old man until his body was a puddle of meat while he was still alive, and we just let our only real lead get away.

I hate Mondays.

★ ★ ★

4:10 p.m.

It's late afternoon before we make it back into the station, having had to go first to the hospital, then to an operational oversight meeting, and finally back to Father Mucci's to finish the scene work.

And we're 0 for 3.

The doc gave us stitches and injections, and upgraded our headaches to two mild concussions, plus I was given more pills for my cold. The oversight meeting gave us a procedural violation notice for letting the uniform guys go to lunch while we were there. The preliminary report from the scene gave us a whole lot more nothing in the way of evidence.

'Why do you still keep that?' Pollo asks.

Like he always does when he's in my office.

I see that he's frowning at the old black-and-white picture I keep on my wall of Sister Margaret Pahl.

The first person in the recorded history of the Catholic Church to be murdered and then officially buried by the same priest. She was a nun from her teens into her seventies. Worked alongside Father Robinson until the day he beat, strangled, and then stabbed her thirty-one times. Arranged the wounds in

23

the shape of an inverted cross on her body. The damage was so severe it was impossible to tell if she had also been raped. They only convicted him twenty-six years later. He died in prison, still an ordained priest. Because the Church said crime and sin are not the same thing.

'It reminds me that how you die doesn't really matter,' I answer.

'Seems morbid,' Pollo says, just like always.

Then he turns around and stretches his big frame with a satisfied groan as he takes in the rest of my office, frowning at the stats sheets and printouts pinned everywhere and the scattered piles of textbooks and articles.

'You know, you study too much. The knowing doesn't come from books, it comes from inside you. Maybe you should get a hobby. Regain some fun,' Pollo remarks.

'This is my mentor speaking now?' I reply.

When I made detective at twenty-six, one of the youngest in the force, I was partnered with Pollo as an experienced mentor. We were supposed to rotate after a year but by then we'd become friends, close. So instead, we opted to stay together. Though Pollo still lectures me when the whim takes him.

'And get some colour in here, a calendar or something,' he continues.

Pollo is old-school.

Hunches and instincts and knowing things before he knows why he knows them. He says sometimes he gets what he calls 'a knowing' about things. So he approaches most forensic science and psychological profiling with a kind of bemused curiosity. He gets it all. Just doesn't use it. Doesn't have to.

24

'You got forensics lined up for the Mucci case?' I check, instead of rising to the bait.

Pollo tends to need reminding of the small things when we get stretched.

Statistically, no matter where you are in the world, most deaths — whether natural or criminal — occur between Friday night and early Monday morning.

People tend to die on the weekends, when they have the time.

It means the first half of our week is usually busy.

It's only Monday and we're already behind.

'Maybe something with puppies or nature scenes, you know?' Pollo says.

Pollo's not one to be distracted from the unimportant.

I take the time to check our case roster.

'Hey, Pollo, you know how today was kind of sucky?' I say as I study our next case file on the computer.

'And also — how can a Turkish place run out of kebabs? Without it, they're basically selling salad. I mean, salad,' Pollo answers, shaking his head at the memory of our disastrous lunch.

'You remember Jones Maihi from down south?' I push on.

'Yeah, of the Riverton Maihis. He's one of my favourites,' Pollo answers as he plonks himself down in the chair in front of my desk, then adds, 'Everyone should have someone special.

'He's still up in high security in D-wing, ain't he? Doing a long lag for that thing with the meth,' Pollo says with a frown.

'Turns out not. Got compassionate leave to attend his son's funeral on a twelve-hour pass this past weekend and skipped out. Guess who has to go find him?'

25

I say.

'But we're homicide,' Pollo says, staring at the ceiling as he slowly rotates on the swivel chair.

'Yeah, but he's our collar for that meth thing. We were last to put him away so we have to go get him again,' I answer.

'Dead priests and escaped gangsters. You couldn't make this shit up,' Pollo says.

★ ★ ★

6:03 p.m.

I kill the engine just past six in the garage at home, taking a few deep breaths before I move.

'Eva, Em!' I call out as I close the front door behind me.

'Hey, lover,' Em says as she comes up close and kisses me. For a moment, everything in the world balances in glowing perfection and I taste love.

Emma and I have been together for eleven years.

Actually, since we were both sixteen.

Most teen pregnancies ruin lives.

It completely saved mine.

Emma is my redemption.

It's been over a decade, and I still ache when I see her.

'What's this?' she says, noticing the plaster tape on the back of my head.

'Workplace accident,' I say.

'Let me guess. You ran with scissors again?' Em asks, trying to keep it light. But I can tell she's not happy.

'Barely a scratch,' I answer as I pull her closer to me and kiss her again.

'Liar. How many?' she says, pulling away.

'Only six. And I'm really fine,' I answer.

'That's forty-three now, you know,' she says as she disentangles herself from me.

I look at her but don't reply. I've got no defence.

Em keeps count of the number of stitches I've had since becoming a cop. Like it's an indicator. The higher the number, the more wrong I am for staying in the job.

'And how's that cold?' she asks then.

'Getting better. I think maybe the hit to the head cowed it a bit,' I say.

'Where's Eva?' I ask.

'Up in her room, hasn't been outside once today. I think she stays in on purpose and builds up her strength to go out when it's new moon,' Em answers.

Most eleven-year-olds would regard staying in their room all day as a form of punishment, but with Eva, it's the exact opposite.

Sometimes I still wonder if it's us. Two seventeen-year-olds having a baby. Maybe we did something wrong back then. Should have noticed something sooner. Done something at least.

But the truth is, we thought she was fine.

This happy, cute baby filling up our lives, making all the sacrifices worth it.

It's only when she started going to pre-school that we realised she was different. At first they told us she just needed more time to adapt. Things would get better.

Except they didn't.

More and more it became clear.

Eva didn't want to leave the house. Ever.

Sometimes even going outside into the backyard was too much for her.

27

Being away from the house, especially without me or Em, simply terrified her.

Going to pre-school was a daily trauma. Sometimes she was too scared to even speak.

By the age of six, things got so bad we had to take her out of school.

More tests and specialists followed, and then by age ten the closest they came to a diagnosis was something called 'atypical agoraphobia.' But no one was really sure what it was or what to do about it.

We did what we could. Home schooling and tutors mixed with our ongoing attempts to keep getting her out of the house. Somehow help her become part of the world.

Then, by random fate, we lucked on a break.

One day we took her to a star observatory on one of our day trips. Despite her fear she was immediately, irrevocably, and permanently obsessed.

From that day, everything was about stars and planets and comets.

Strangely, her hunger for knowing more about the universe and faraway stars seemed stronger even than her fear of knowing what's outside the front door.

It wasn't perfect, but it was something.

So now, every new moon, when the night sky is the darkest, we go out stargazing. Steadily building up the time she spends away from the house.

And while she is out there gazing up, Eva is the rare combination of perfectly happy and outside.

'Eva!' I call out.

'Hey, Dad,' Eva says as she comes bouncing down the stairs with a smile.

Even at eleven you could tell that she took after her mother. Would probably look just like her one day.

Big blue eyes against an olive complexion framed with jet-black hair. Em is all curves and grace. Her family were Italian immigrants who came here in the 1800s as part of the gold rush in the South.

I met Em when we were both sixteen. She was the most beautiful thing I'd ever seen.

'You ready for tonight?' I ask.

'Can't wait!' Eva answers.

'Uncle Pollo and Aunt Angie invited us over for dinner on the way. What do you say?' I ask. It pains me to see the fear and uncertainty flash across her face. I know what she fears isn't real, but the fear itself is. I'm reminded of what Bowlby said this morning in class — pain motivates behaviour.

'Chop suey?' she asks.

'You know it,' I answer hopefully. I know she loves spending time with Pollo's family when they visit here, and she especially likes chop suey. I just hope it's enough.

Then I see her take a deep breath and steel herself before answering, 'Okay.'

Small victories.

'Let me get cleaned up. We'll leave in half an hour,' I say, and she bounces off again to go pack her telescope and charts.

'Don't think you're off the hook, copper,' Em says as we watch Eva race up the stairs, but I can tell the relief from another milestone with Eva has already lifted her mood. We both know you can't help but forgive people if you love them beyond a certain point. I think maybe it's not just pain that changes you. Thank God.

★ ★ ★

29

We're on the way out, Em and Eva already piling things by the front door, when the phone rings.

'Bobby Ress,' I say as I pick it up.

'Bobby. Pollo. We're up. They found another one. Same MO,' Pollo says.

'Same as this morning?' I ask, not wanting to say too much in front of Em.

'Yeah, retired priest. Catholic. Lived alone. This one's bad. We can't leave it till tomorrow. Have Em bring Eva over — they can still do dinner and get out to the stargazing. I can drop you after. Pick you up in ten,' Pollo says, then hangs up.

'For the record, I don't want you to go,' Em says the moment I put the phone down.

'Em,' I say, but have nothing to add.

She comes up close to me, puts her hands on my chest, and continues. 'It's okay. I know you need to do this, Bobby. I just wish you didn't.'

I don't have an answer to that so instead I say, 'You guys go ahead. I'll catch up at the stargazing. Pollo can drop me off.'

Then I see her take a deep breath and steel herself before answering, 'Okay.'

In the exact same way Eva did just before.

Small tragedies.

I'm outside waving off Em and Eva just as Pollo pulls up and I get in.

'What have we got?' I ask as Pollo pulls away.

'Problems. You remember nurse lady telling her friend at Channel 3 about finding Father Mucci? Well, reporter lady does her spot for the six p.m. news. It was a build-up to the paedophile priest angle, FYI. Went to the trouble of mentioning that the good Father used to teach mathematics at a Catholic boys' school. But it's done now. Because then reporter lady wants to do a bit more human interest on the story. Speak to family and friends — that kind of thing. So she finds one of his close friends, Father Bern, to interview. Only Father Bern don't say much 'cause when she shows up, he's all kinds of dead.'

'How much of the story got out?' I ask.

'Oh, reporter lady plus camera man called us a good thirty minutes after they found him. Filmed it all, the body, the scene, even potential witnesses living close by. All of it with her reporting on the 'Holy Man Killer' out murdering priests in your neighbourhood.'

'Catchy,' I say. My head is still fuzzy from my cold and the hit I took earlier today.

'This is going to turn into a circus now. We'd better get the report done tonight,' Pollo says.

'You think Spyro will take it away from us?' I ask.

'He'll have to. Too much press attention now. We may still be in it at the bottom. There'll have to be some task force set up with the right kind of front man and that won't be us,' Pollo says.

'Let me guess. Someone from Head Office to smarm the press,' I prompt.

'That'd be about it,' Pollo agrees. 'We'll do what we can.'

'Two priests in the same day. I'm not liking the odds. You thinking what I'm thinking?' I ask with a sinking feeling.

'Yeah. We fucked up. Shouldn't have let that boy get away this morning,' Pollo answers, then reaches across and opens the glove-box in front of me.

'Nobody gets away again,' he says.

I can't help but think back to this morning, looking

31

down at the sick tragedy they turned Father Mucci's body into. And we let them get away.

'Okay,' I say, nodding, as I take my service pistol and holster out of the glovebox and strap it on. Glancing across at Pollo, I now notice the telltale bulge under his jacket as well.

Maybe this morning got to Pollo more than I realised.

I haven't seen him carry since last year.

One dark, wet night, three months into our first rotation, Pollo took a bullet in the shoulder that was meant for my head. He fired back, killing the shooter, who turned out to be a fourteen-year-old girl. We found out later that she was running away from home, her stepdad had been abusing her. She also took his gun. We identified ourselves but she either didn't hear or wasn't listening. We're not even sure she really meant to fire. Either way, we never found out.

They ruled it a clean kill. But after that night, Pollo stopped wearing a gun and I followed suit.

It's not like on TV anyway. We don't really need them.

We only show up once the bad things have already happened and the bad people are long gone.

Until today.

When we reach Father Thomas Bern's house, we actually have to push through a crowd of reporters and onlookers being held back by crime scene tape and uniform officers.

'Who's got site?' I ask.

'Nah. Just uniforms. It's still us,' Pollo answers.

'Semper, which way?' I ask one of the juniors I know who's standing by the front door.

'Didn't you watch the news? Straight through to

the kitchen,' Semper answers.

Then holds out a small tub of VapoRub and I notice he's already got a smear of it under his nose.

'How long?' Pollo asks as we both smear some of the rub under our noses as well.

'Dunno. But a lot of his fluids got mixed together. Messy. You'll see,' Semper says.

It's an old trick. A bit of VapoRub under the nose and you can stand those I'm-horribly-dead-now odours a little better.

'You guys start the witness roster?' Pollo asks him.

'Yup. You want the journalists first?' Semper asks.

'Yeah. Once we're done inside,' Pollo answers.

Where Father Mucci's house was spartan and bare, Father Bern's is cluttered and luxurious, with ornaments and pictures scattered amongst antique furniture.

But it's all just muted background because of Father Bern.

Another old man, naked, looking all wrong.

From the front door, the hall runs straight into the kitchen.

Where Father Bern is hanging suspended about a foot off the floor.

Like some gruesome angel frozen on its way back up to heaven.

He's been impaled on a fence post.

An actual scarecrow.

There's blood and flies everywhere and that warm, invasive smell that clings to you.

You sometimes get it at car accidents if they've been really bad. So bad that people have been torn open and apart enough. It's coming from the floor, where a sick mix of what looks like blood, urine, and stomach bile is congealing with pieces of liver and intestine in it. Nothing smells quite like it. It's a scent you never forget.

'Okay,' I say. Trying and failing to keep calm. Right now, looking at this, I flash back to earlier with Em and I still don't have an answer.

Why do I need to do this?

'Yeah,' Pollo agrees.

'It's definitely they. There's no way one guy did all this,' I say as we move closer.

'And how?' Pollo asks.

Because up close you can see where the thick wooden fence post punches straight into Father Bern's stomach and up into his chest.

It must have taken some doing, because they managed to angle it so that the end of the fence post — which has been crudely sharpened — pierces out again in the front of his neck where his Adam's apple should be. Arching his body and pushing back his head so that it looks like he's staring straight up, mouth agape.

Checking the ceiling height I then answer, 'They did it on the floor. Held him down on his back and pushed that fence post into his stomach, then kept pushing it up through his chest and aimed it so that it went up into his neck. Then they stood him up and mounted the fence post. You can see how they used another fence post cut in half to make a crossed base nailed together and to the floor.'

'There's easier ways to kill people,' Pollo remarks.

'True. At least this would have been quick,' I say.

'That depends on how fast they pushed that fence post in,' Pollo answers. I really wish he hadn't.

'Just how fucked-off do you have to be with

34

somebody to go and do a thing like this?' Pollo says. 'I mean, there's killing and then, way the fuck on the other side of killing, there's this.'

'Same guys?' I ask.

'Definitely planned and controlled again. Two retired priests. Victims knew each other. And of course both scenes have that completely-off-the-fucking-chain feel to it. Yeah, I'm sold,' Pollo says.

Then he watches me as I retreat into the hallway.

'Yeah?' he prompts, sensing I'm on to something.

'This morning. At Father Mucci's. You could see the body from the front door. Same again here. They could have done it anywhere in the house. Why like that?' I ask.

'Staging. Okay, so presentation matters. But who for? Who's supposed to see them like this besides us?' Pollo asks.

'Somebody all this would mean something to,' I answer.

'What's the message then?' Pollo asks.

'Not sure. We still need motive,' I say.

But again, when people take special trouble killing and then staging the bodies in strange and inventive ways, there's usually only two likely messages.

Warnings and monuments.

Mostly, staging a body serves as a warning.

People who see it are meant to think: This could happen to me if I do what this guy did and these people catch me.

These kinds of bodies are good to find. Because you can usually figure out who the warning is to and who it is from by looking at what the victim did to make people angry. Warnings are mostly used by organised groups. The mob, gangs, ethnic groups and

35

religious sects. When it's a group instead of an individual it's always about money or power.

Less often, staging a body serves as a monument.

People who see the body are meant to think: Look at what happened to this person. Whoever did this to them is important and what they think and feel deserves attention.

These are usually tougher to crack. It's almost always an individual, not a group. Which means it could still be money or power, but it's mostly sex. Even then, the reasoning is often unique and personal to the killer. Monuments are most commonly used by serial killers and crime-of-passion perpetrators.

'It took more than one person to do this. For now, let's assume group. So it's a warning, not a monument. If it's a group doing it, then the motive's not sex. That means money or power,' Pollo says.

'I'm with you on the group. That's clear. But look at all this. Think of the effort. The planning. It feels too personal for money or power. A bullet to the head could have done the job of a warning. But this. There's real hate here,' I say.

To which Pollo gives a non-committal grunt, then adds, 'Well, at least you're starting to feel it.'

'What about method? I mean, impaling? These guys went medieval on him,' he says then.

Wait.

'Medieval . . .' I echo, feeling the edge of a thought stirring. If I can only put words around it. Something there.

'I'm Catholic,' I say to Pollo.

'I know. You don't like sex and you feel guilty all the time. Why you telling me this?' Pollo asks.

'Because it also means I know my saints,' I answer.

'They pulled us in to work on this tonight because of the media, right? They need quick results. Think they pulled in the Coroner's Office too?'

'Betcha,' answers Pollo.

'Get them on the line for me,' I say. 'Ask if they've started on the Mucci autopsy yet.'

Pollo walks back towards the front door to make the call in the fresher air.

As my own stomach is starting to turn, I decide to follow him out and catch some of the conversation.

'Hey, is that Mike? It's Pollo. Yeah, us too. Second one's even better. Nah. Hang on,' Pollo says, and hands me the phone.

'Hey, Mike, you doing the Mucci autopsy?' I ask.

'He's on the slab right now,' Mike answers.

'Found any wood splinters?' I ask.

'Nothing yet, but I only just started on him,' Mike answers.

'Look in the soft tissue. Back side of the body, where the skin is thinner. Knees. Arms. Neck. That kind of thing. Call me back if you find anything,' I say, and hang up.

'Spill,' Pollo says.

'I'm not sure yet. But both of these are strange ways to go, yeah? Someone impales and mounts Father Bern back there and they break every bone in Father Mucci's body and leave him arranged like spaghetti,' I say.

'Yeah, special times,' Pollo replies.

'And they're both retired Catholic priests,' I continue.

'Get there faster, Dorothy,' Pollo says.

'I think they killed them this way because they are Catholic priests. Both the methods and the stagings.

You said it yourself — medieval. For centuries, the Church used to torture and execute people in strange ways. They'd stage the bodies to act as warnings for others. Impaling was one popular method and — '

I'm interrupted by the phone ringing.

'Bobby Ress,' I answer.

'Bobby. Mike. Found them. Pattern is consistent with backing impacts from blunt force trauma. How'd you know where they'd be? Scene report says he was found on a tile floor,' Mike says.

'Let me guess. Some kind of hardwood. Maybe hickory?' I ask.

'Hang on, I've just got the wood catalogue out. Yeah. Looks like some kind of hardwood variety. Don't know if it's hickory, we don't have a sample of that one. I need to do some checking. Why hickory?' Mike says.

'Because they used to make wagon wheels from hickory,' I answer, then add, 'look up Catherine wheel.' Then I hang up.

'The firework?' Pollo asks.

'It was a torture method before it was a firework. Saint Catherine of Alexandria. Died a martyr. Patron saint of unmarried women. Was beaten to death with a heavy cudgel wrapped in cloth. It made it easier to break just the bones without causing too much blood loss by also breaking the skin. I should have remembered that this morning,' I say, shaking my head.

'It helped keep the victims alive longer. What they did was lay you on top of a wagon wheel. The gaps between the spokes helped break your bones easier. They beat you, and every now and then would turn the wheel beneath you to get at the parts of the bones

38

that were still unbroken. Kept going till there was nothing left to break. It was used for centuries. They called it a Catherine wheel after her.'

'And you wonder why I'm an atheist,' Pollo says, then walks back inside with me following. For several moments we both stare at the gory scene of Father Bern's death in silence.

What scares me is that people can do stuff like this and then get back to normal things. Driving. Shopping. Watching TV. It shouldn't be like that. People who can do things like this shouldn't be able to be normal as well.

'The Church used to do this? Impale people?' Pollo asks.

'Sometimes. Usually as warnings on the outskirts of big cities,' I answer pensively.

'So someone's killing old Catholic priests in old Catholic ways,' Pollo says, breaking into my thoughts.

'You still think money or power?' I ask him.

'Dunno. This all feels wrong. But the staging is definitely a message — just don't know if it's a warning or a monument. I really hope it's not a monument. There's already two,' Pollo says.

I nod in agreement. Two is bad.

If these stagings were warnings, then we're likely looking at money or power, and you can usually find the group involved by looking at what the victim did that could make them angry. But if these stagings were meant to be monuments, then it's likely the motive is sex. There's only two types of people who tend to leave monuments. Those who do it as part of a crime of passion who, thankfully, usually do it only once. And serial killers.

Who do it more.

Usually until they are caught. With two this close together, things aren't looking good for us.

'Let's go talk to the reporter,' I say as we head out again.

★ ★ ★

The tiny blond woman nursing a coffee against the back of the Channel 3 News van still looks visibly shaken.

She must be new at this.

'Becca Patrick?' I ask.

'That's me,' she answers, looking up at us.

'I'm Detective Bobby Ress. This is Detective Pollo Latu,' I say.

'You mind if we record this?' she asks. Maybe not that new then.

'Come on, you know how this goes,' Pollo says.

Becca nods and settles back.

'Take it from the top,' Pollo prompts as we settle in next to her.

We quickly learn how Becca was first contacted by her friend Kate, the nurse, about Father Mucci, and then after contacting the local Catholic Church, ended up being referred to Father Bern as one of his close friends who used to work with him. They came out here hoping to score an interview and spotted him through the front door window. The door was unlocked. Thanks to their diligent efforts, pretty much everything else worth knowing we could now see on the news along with the rest of the world.

★ ★ ★

40

We're finally on the drive out to meet Em and Eva. Neither of us has much left to say. It's already past 10:00 p.m.

As I look out I see that it's a clear night. An ocean of stars glittering cold above us. Eva must be happy.

Then I think about what we saw today. Father Mucci and Father Bern, and how they died. Maybe Eva's right.

The world is an ugly, scary place. Why am I so intent on trying to get her out there?

'You know, it's been a long-ass night,' Pollo says.

'Yeah,' I say, and there's a heaviness in his voice I recognise.

Pollo drinks. It's not unusual if you've been a cop too long. Only does it once in a while. But when he does, he goes big. Drinks till he falls down. I don't know if it's all bad. He's a good father, a good husband. He tries. Maybe it gives him something he needs.

'You heading out after?' I ask. But I already know.

'Thinking about it,' Pollo answers.

'You still go to Confession?' Pollo asks then.

'No,' I answer. Pollo knows I'm Catholic but we rarely talk about it. I think it makes him uncomfortable. He was raised in the church but left in his early teens. Never went back.

'Takes away the sin, right? You tell the priest all your badness and you have to be sorry and then he takes it away. That's how it works,' Pollo says.

'About,' I say.

'Dunno if I like that,' Pollo says. 'Some shit shouldn't be made to be okay again.'

I can't help feeling that he's right. The things we saw today, you shouldn't be able to walk away from

41

doing things like that.

Then he changes tone and continues.

'I'll do the write-up tonight. You pick me up tomorrow morning at seven. Bring breakfast. Something irresponsible. With cheese. Then we'll go face the music,' Pollo says.

'For letting that kid get away?' I say.

'Nah, doesn't matter about the kid. We'll get blamed for this being so big and so bad. People feel better if they can blame someone. Even if they know it doesn't change anything,' Pollo says.

★ ★ ★

It is 11:00 p.m. by the time I walk up the quiet hill to where I know Em and Eva are camped out on our favourite spot. My head still aches but I can't tell if that's from my cold, my concussion, or from thinking too much. But with every step out here it feels better. This far out into the country there's hardly any lights showing. The dark is almost perfect. It feels like it could be anywhere. Any age. A world without people.

It's only when I look up that the vast glitter above me pulls me out of myself and I pause to stare with, for the first time today, not a single bad thought in my head.

'Coming up here?' Em asks, stirring me from myself.

'Coming!' I call back, and soon find them ensconced on the air mattress in a fluffy island of blankets and cushions. Big red telescope positioned just so.

'Hey, Dad,' Eva says. Her eye to the telescope, a kind of peace to her voice that makes the worries of my day fall away.

'Hey, girl,' I say as I settle in next to Em, who shifts to fit herself into me.

'What are we looking at?' I ask.

'Orion's Belt. It's awesome tonight,' Eva answers happily, then settles back from the telescope and lies staring up with Em and me in silence.

'Still too soon to see Matariki?' Em asks in front of me after a while.

'You mean the Pleiades constellation, Mum. The Māori names aren't the right ones. And yes. Too soon,' Eva answers authoritatively. Then, when the silence stretches out and I think she has fallen asleep, she continues in a quiet voice, 'Dad, tell me one of the Māori legends again.'

'I thought you said the Māori names aren't the right ones,' I tease.

'They're not. I just like them. They'd be true if I could choose,' she answers. I like that.

'Tell the one about Maui,' she says, sounding sleepier now as Em takes my hand.

The Māori say that when the earth was made, the days and nights were too short. The Sun raced across the sky too fast. It was too strong. Nobody had time to do all their work during the day. The nights went by so fast no one could rest. No one could look up at the stars.

So Maui and his brothers waited at the horizon with strong ropes, and when the Sun rose they caught him and pulled him down to the Earth. Then Maui called on the Sun to listen to the people and to slow his course across the sky so that the day and night could be longer.

But the Sun fought, pulling against the ropes to be free until Maui and his brothers could barely hold him down. Then in desperation, Maui grabbed his axe and ran to the Sun, even though it burned him. He beat the Sun with his axe many times. Until finally the Sun cried out for mercy. Hearing the Sun cry out, Maui stopped.

Then the Sun said to Maui, 'Why have you beaten me so? I am weak and broken now.'

And hearing this Maui replied, 'That is what I wanted. Now you will not be able to race across the sky, and the days and nights will be longer.'

But the Sun said, 'But now you will never know whether I am going slowly because of how you hurt me or because of my love for the people.' And when Maui realised what he had done he was sorry, and he let the Sun go. It crept up slowly across the sky. And from then on, the days and nights were longer. And the people were happy. But when Maui looked up at the Sun, he didn't know whether it was going slow because it loved the people or because of what he had done.

TUESDAY . . .

7:00 a.m.

My head still throbs from my cold and yesterday's knocks and it feels like I hardly slept, but I pick up Pollo at his house before dawn. The steaming burger I hand over spills out into the wrapping on all sides and is loaded with inadvisable layers of cheese. It'll help him get past the hangover.

Pollo takes it without a word and starts munching straight away. He plonks the finished report on the dashboard as I pull out into the traffic.

'God I hate mornings. Especially if they contain Spyro,' he says through a mouth full of burger.

'Spyro's good people,' I reply. Spyro is short for Costa Spyronopoulos, our captain.

'It's all that positivity and hopefulness. And he never swears. And he makes eye contact like, all the time. Just doesn't seem right,' Pollo says.

'We could do worse than Spyro,' I counter.

'And sometimes he uses words like 'synergy,'' Pollo continues, still coasting on momentum.

'You have any bright ideas last night?' I ask.

'Nothing new. You?' Pollo replies. I shake my head.

'Fine. It's only Tuesday. Let's keep it simple. Until it all changes, let's go with: It's a group doing the killings. So those stagings of the bodies are warnings. We don't know the perpetrators but we do know the victims. So we start there,' Pollo says.

'You mean until they take it away from us and wrap

45

it up in some task force,' I remind him.

'Nah, I mean to keep at it. They can do the whole task force thing, but me and you, we're gonna make this fit, Bobby. I've seen a lot of killing and I'm okay with that. But that shit we saw yesterday . . . nah, we keep at it,' Pollo says adamantly.

'Yeah, I'm with you,' I answer.

And it's easy enough to do.

It's not like in the movies. Detectives don't have just one case at a time. The clues and reports and leads don't just stack up ready for you to work through them. Everything takes longer than you think. Most of us have several cases open at once. You fill your time doing bits and pieces all over as those pieces become available.

It also means that, even if a case isn't yours, you can still find time to work on it if you want to. And we do.

* * *

8:20 a.m.

'Operation Spear. That's a good name. Kind of testosterone-y, you know?' Pollo says as we head out of the check-in meeting where the new task force to deal with the 'Holy Man Killer' was just announced. Complete, as expected, with a manager from Head Office. They've even announced the schedule of planned press conferences, starting this morning. Regardless of the fact that, as yet, there's no real indication of who the killers are or why they're doing it. Modern policing.

When we're almost at my office door, Pollo pulls

46

me onward to the exit, saying, 'While they're running around preparing for the media, let's get out and talk to some church folk.'

'We've also got a preliminary report due on Jones Maihi's escape. We can drive out to the prison after,' I add.

'Fine. But it's Jones. I reckon he took the gap when he saw it,' Pollo replies.

'At his kid's funeral,' I respond doubtfully.

'Guess he wanted some alone time,' Pollo responds. 'Besides. He's Manga Kahu. He's not going anywhere.'

Manga Kahu is one of the dominant gangs in New Zealand.

And gangs in New Zealand can be different.

Crime is a big part of it, but to them that's not only what it's about. It's often built around families. And being Māori.

Manga Kahu more so than other gangs.

They're also more disciplined than many others. Regimented. With generations joining up. Mostly it's about brotherhood. Belonging. These people usually live together. Work together. Play together. Raise families together.

For many, it's cradle to grave.

Even if those graves sometimes come early.

Jones Maihi is third-generation Manga Kahu, which means he's in it for life.

Pollo's right. Even if we do nothing, eventually we'll catch up to him doing something bad. Because it's his job every day.

For people like Jones, prison every now and again is simply part of the deal, an occupational hazard. Just business.

This makes me think back to what we saw yesterday. Father Mucci and Father Bern and what was done to them. I know we're dealing with a group, and that the staging of the bodies are likely to be warnings. But I can't help feeling that there has to be more to it. Because you can't do things like that every week, it can't be just business to someone.

★ ★ ★

We're back on the road. Heading to St Joseph's Cathedral, seat of the Roman Catholic Diocese in Dunedin, when Pollo says, 'What's big enough to make them kill those priests like that? It's a group, so money or power, okay. But dead is dead. Why all the effort? Why the added scoop of horror? And two at once. They had to know it was going to get a lot of attention. You'd think they'd want to do all this quietly.'

'Maybe that was part of the plan. Make it big and ugly enough to make sure whoever needs to get the warning hears of it. And the media and us, we help get the message to them,' I say, guessing.

'I don't like that. It means whoever's behind this either doesn't care if they get caught or are confident that they won't,' Pollo replies.

★ ★ ★

'I'm Father Corcoran, please come in,' says the grizzled-looking old man who ushers us from the waiting room into his office. His heavy Irish accent curls around the words, softening them in a friendly way. The room he leads us into may as well have come from another age. As does the entire cathedral

48

complex. High stone walls and arching ceilings. Small windows with heavy lead-lined glass, dimpled by centuries. Dark wooden panelling and antique furniture. No computer. Not even a phone in here. Just a scattering of old books and notes on the desk. Things in here feel old. Arcane.

'You sound a long way from home, Father,' I remark.

'True. But you go where you're needed,' Father Corcoran replies with a smile as he sits down behind his desk.

'I've already had all manner of press and police come through here asking questions. Was there something more?' Father Corcoran asks.

'We need to be thorough, Father,' Pollo replies in a more distant tone than his usual. I realise now that Pollo's not really an atheist. That would just mean he didn't believe. That would only create indifference. For his own reasons, Pollo actively hates the church. To feel that strongly, you need some kind of faith. Even if it did work backwards.

'Could you outline for us how Father Mucci and Father Bern knew each other?' I ask.

'As I've told your colleagues, we all know each other. When you become a man of the cloth, the Church becomes your family,' Father Corcoran answers. 'Who do you think we spend Christmas with, or birthdays or holidays? They were both career men. Of the old kind. No wives. No kids. That's a lot of years with the same small group of people. You work together. You pray together. Everyone gets close.'

'Do you know if they stayed close after they had both retired?' I ask.

'To the best of my knowledge, not especially. We kept visiting them, of course. Pastoral. Every week.

49

And they both still made it out to many of the Church calendar's events regularly. I'd say they were friendly, but I can't recall them being overly close. When they came out here they mostly reminisced or talked shop along with the group. Same as everyone,' he says with a shrug.

'They ever work together?' Pollo asks.

'No. And yes, I'm sure. We had the records checked after the first requests. I'm afraid there's not much I can tell you that isn't already known,' Father Corcoran answers.

'Anyone else you know who knew them well? Had some sort of connection to them?' I ask.

'Again, sorry. They were a few years ahead of my time but to the best of my recollection, nothing comes to mind. I'd say I knew them about as well as most. I can't recall anyone close to them. As I said, both of them were of the old sort. Renounced friends and family when they became ordained. They led small lives. Devoted to the Church,' he answers.

'So no link at all that you can think of?' I say.

'Sorry, but no,' Father Corcoran replies.

'How about back before they retired? Anything unusual about them? Anything that stands out?' Pollo asks.

'Father Mucci worked as a teacher at our boys' college here in Dunedin, and Father Bern was a parish priest out near Balclutha. Both were well regarded,' Father Corcoran answers.

'They ever get into any trouble?' Pollo asks bluntly.

I can see Father Corcoran stiffen up before he says, 'As I said. No. These men were committed. Unimpeachable. They gave their lives to the Church. And I don't take kindly to attempts at muckraking their

50

character,' Father Corcoran counters.

'I apologise, Father. Unfortunately, we need to ask these questions,' I say in a placating tone.

'These were good men,' Father Corcoran says firmly.

After a few more questions, we wind things up and head out again.

None the wiser.

'You get the feeling he was stonewalling?' Pollo asks as we get back in the car.

'Difficult to say. I think he was being real. Believed they were clean,' I answer.

'Well, if he's right and there's no special connection between them, then how come reporter lady went from Mucci to Bern after coming here? Who did she talk to?' Pollo says.

'Let's find out. I've still got her number,' I say, then make the call.

'Becca Patrick. Channel 3,' she answers in a sing-song voice.

'Becca. It's Detective Bobby Ress. We interviewed you last night at the scene at Father Bern's house,' I say.

'Oh yeah. How're things progressing with the investigation?' she asks.

'Steadily. A task force has been set up and no effort is being spared,' I say carefully, aware that anything I say may be used against me as a sound bite.

'That's the reason why I'm calling you. We're just making sure we have all the details down right for the report,' I continue, not wanting to alert her to the fact that she knows anything important.

'I'd like to know who told you to go look up Father Bern,' I say.

'Oh. Okay, hang on. Let's see. We went to St Joseph's. We were going to talk to the head honcho there. Father Corcoran. But he was busy. And while we were in the waiting room there was another young priest there who overheard us. He seemed fairly shaken by it all but he didn't want to say anything on camera. He gave us Father Bern's name. Said they were close,' she says.

'Got a name for us?' I ask.

'Can I get an exclusive?' she counters. Reporters.

'Look, I can't promise anything because the task force will have its own press releases and that's not managed by us. But I can make sure you're down on the invite list for any press conferences, and if we crack it, I'll give you first interview,' I say.

'Deal. He said his name was Liam Tull. Said he came from Tegere Servare,' she informs me.

'Where?' I say.

'Tegere Servare. I think it's Latin. Wrote it down. But we didn't look into it. It's just a name to me,' she says.

'Don't worry. Not important. We're just trying to be thorough for the investigation,' I say, hoping to not arouse her journalistic instincts.

'This guy tell you anything else?' I say.

'Not much. He said the two men were friends. That they used to work together at this Tegere place. He said it was a Catholic retreat out in the Catlins,' she answers.

'Yeah, we heard the same about them working together,' I say, lying smoothly. 'Doesn't really help us move things forward. Anything else?' I ask. It's always good to leave reporters thinking they know more than you.

'No. We left after that and got hold of Father Bern's address through our office,' Becca answers.

'Okay, thanks for that.' After I hang up, I look over at Pollo. He's been listening carefully and we share a smile.

'Well fucking finally,' Pollo says happily.

People have been lying to us.

That's good.

Means they've done something wrong.

Means we're doing something right.

'Father Corcoran,' I say.

'You wanna go back in for an uncomfortable chat?' Pollo asks, sounding happy at the prospect.

'Nah. Not yet. No sense in letting on what we know before we know what it is we know. Give Corcoran more rope. Let's find out about this Tegere Servare place. Ever heard of it?' I say. 'No. We need Carol. We'll swing out to the prison and get this Jones thing ticked and then go find her. Let's hope she's not too snowed under,' Pollo says.

* * *

We're back in the car, heading out to Dunedin Prison, with Pollo calling ahead to arrange a meeting with the prison guards who were with Jones Maihi when he escaped. I'm lost in thought when my phone rings.

'Bobby Ress,' I answer automatically.

'Emma Ress,' Em replies in a similar tone before continuing in her normal voice. 'This a bad time?'

'No, just in the car. What's up?' I ask.

'Good things. Eva got up this morning and announced she wanted to join one of the university's

53

astronomy clubs. I don't even know how she found out about them. They meet weekly at the observatory. Yay!' Em says, and I can hear the excitement in her voice.

'That's awesome,' I answer. Feeling so much better that I only now realise how bad I felt before.

'Gets better. She said she wants to go alone. No parents included!' Em adds happily.

'Maybe becoming a teenager and hating your parents is the answer we've been waiting for,' I laugh back.

'I got to go now, lover. You back usual time?' Em asks.

'I'll let you know,' I say before hanging up.

'Good times?' Pollo asks.

'It's Eva. She wants to join an astronomy club and go to their meetings — on her own,' I say.

'That's good. You'll see, she's gonna be fine. I got a knowing about her,' Pollo says. Hope glows in my chest. I know it doesn't make sense, but I need Eva and Em to be happy and healthy and good and fearless. Somehow their goodness makes all the stuff I see at work be okay.

★   ★   ★

Dunedin prison is old.

Unlike many of the modern examples, this looks properly prison-like with its ancient, high brick walls and small windows — barred, of course. Built in 1895, it's seen a lot of life. It's seen a lot of death too, for that matter.

'I always like visiting this place,' Pollo says as we get out of the car. 'Knowing that at least some of the very special people we put away have to stay in shithole prisons like this one makes me feel all warm inside.'

'You're such a romantic,' I remark.

'They used to do it old-style here. Did you know that early on, before things got all humane, this was an end-of-the-line prison?' Pollo says. 'They sentenced you here. And if you were bad, you got life in prison here, which still actually meant life, or, if you were really bad, you got the death sentence. They hung you right here as well. Even buried you out in the back. If you were a bad man, this was your very last stop. End of the line.'

'Maybe that didn't sit too well with Jones Maihi,' I comment.

'He didn't seem to like hearing about it last time I was up here to see him, no,' says Pollo. 'That's the criminal element for you. No appreciation for the symmetry of penal history and whatnot.'

★ ★ ★

It takes a while to get through the scans and searches, but at last we're seated in a deserted cafeteria with two guards who look decidedly pounded upon.

'Jones do this?' Pollo asks, waving a hand to indicate the various bruises and cuts both men in front of us are sporting.

'Yeah. And then there's Carl, too. He's at home with a broken arm,' one answers.

'So how did it happen?' I ask.

'Maihi got compassionate leave through his lawyer. Twelve hours. We took him out for the funeral,' one answers.

'Nice of you,' Pollo comments.

'It's unusual, for sure. But his son, young, only twelve, committed suicide. And you know the Maihis are Manga Kahu. Lots of gang money thrown at the lawyers, and all sorts of threats about going to the media about mistreatment and causing avoidable harm to his family. So the parole board said yes and we got the job.

'It was strange. Everything was going about as you'd expect. Jones is over by the coffin, crying, saying good-bye to the boy. Then he goes stiff and turns and just comes at us. I've never seen anything like it,' he says, shaking his head.

I look at the two guards in front of us, then at the incident report in front of me, and note the details. Three of them, big men, older, experienced at dealing with people like Jones.

'And he took out all three of you? Did he have help?' I ask.

'No, the family stayed out of it. They didn't help him, and they didn't help us. Just backed away and watched. It was weird; nobody even yelled or said anything. They just watched. It was like they knew it was going to go down,' he answers.

'He just went through us. Didn't even seem angry. He was crying the whole time. Once Jones got Carl down he kept coming. Took the hits and kept coming.

'I know it sounds strange — one guy against three — but he just wouldn't stop,' the second guard adds.

'Anyone say anything to him? Something set him off?' Pollo asks.

'Lots of people were talking to him. Maybe. Don't know. It all seemed pretty normal right up until he went off like that,' the guard answers.

'There's no sense to it all anyway,' the other man remarks, shaking his head.

'What do you mean?' I ask.

'Maihi had his parole hearing last week. He was due to be released three months from now anyway. He could have just stayed in his twelve weeks and walked out of here a free man. Now, with this. The escape. Assault and battery times three. He's looking at maybe ten years if he's caught,' he answers.

'When he's caught,' Pollo states.

*   *   *

We're on the way back to the station when I say, 'There's something odd there. Jones is many things, but dumb ain't one of them. Why do this?'

'More importantly, why would Manga Kahu let him?' Pollo says. 'He's a patched lifer. Was a sergeant -at-arms the last time I heard. Men like that don't just get to throw it all away when they feel like it. You belong to them. The gang says what's to be done. And somehow, I don't see Manga Kahu thinking him in prison for another decade is going to help the cause.'

'We'll have to ask him when we run into him again,' I say.

'True. And for now, there's not much more we can do. We'll set up a meeting with his family for the sake of appearances. Finish out the report. It'll come when we've done the waiting,' Pollo says.

That's another Pollo saying. And he's right. Most of what we do is waiting. It works eventually. Mostly.

'But now we need to see Carol about those priests,' Pollo remarks, changing the subject.

57

'Yeah, Carol,' I agree.

Carol is essential. You simply can't do this job without people like her. Carol has a rare and unusual skill. It's not that she knows things. It's that she knows how to find things out. Strange things. Ask Carol the most random thing and she'll have an answer from some obscure expert by the end of the day. You'd think in the age of computers and global databases people who can do that become less important. In fact, it's the exact opposite. There's so much information out there now that you can drown in all the possible options before you find the right one. Unless you have Carol.

★   ★   ★

'You two. You still owe me from last time,' Carol says, but smiles anyway as we come up to her desk. A tall Māori woman in her twenties who could have been a model if it wasn't for her family being cops. That, and the fact that her pretty head also contains a first-rate mind. Officially, Carol works in records. But in truth, people like her are behind more solved cases than street detectives like me and Pollo.

'Ah, Carol. Isn't it better to have the two of us in your debt than not?' Pollo says.

'Only if you actually pay up one day,' Carol retorts.

'Got something for us from yesterday?' I ask.

'Nothing on that partial registration number. Plates are either stolen or you saw wrong. Scene workups are still coming in. So far, nothing. No physical evidence. No signs of forced entry. No witnesses. No criminal links. Nothing. Looks like maybe Bern had a revolver registered to him that's gone missing. We're still checking, but that's about it. It'll be a while before we know anything useful if it's there to be known at all,' Carol concludes.

'We really need a break,' I say to Pollo.

'This it?' Carol says as she takes out and unfolds a big flag in front of her. Green horizon under a red sky with a single centred star. It's exactly what I saw in the back of that car that got away.

'Exactly,' I say. Pollo groans in the background.

'Māori. Ngai Tuhoe tribe, to be specific,' Carol says.

'What do you know about them?' I ask.

'Ngai Tuhoe. People of the Mist. They have ancestral lands up north. Still very traditional. They follow many of the old ways. Trying to protect their culture and safeguard the lands. They're usually involved in trying to save the environment these days. Stopping deep sea drilling and open cast mining. Saving kiwi, that kind of thing. Historically had trouble with the European settlers. There were some killings,' she answers.

'The Māori Wars?' Pollo asks.

'War. Massacre. Depends who you ask. The British took their lands. Things have always been strained. Many of them say they never signed the treaty with the Crown. That they don't recognise the authority of the government over them. That they are the Tuhoe Nation. Separate. They have their own flag,' Carol says.

'How big a tribe?' I ask.

'About 30,000 or so. Mostly up north, but there are some scattered down south here,' Carol answers.

'But traditional, you said. It's all about the people. Bet all the families are close. Keep connected,' Pollo says.

'Yeah, so?' Carol answers.

'So somebody probably knows who drives a red Ford Cortina with a Tuhoe flag in the back window down here in Dunedin,' I say.

'Good luck with that. Ngai Tuhoe are about family. To them, you're a representative of the Crown. No one's going to betray their blood for the likes of you,' Carol says.

'Where do we start?' Pollo asks.

'The Baldwin, maybe. Some of the Tuhoe hang out there sometimes,' Carol says, sounding uncertain, then adds, 'and go easy. You two piss people off too much. And those guys don't play around.'

'We'll take that under advisement,' Pollo says.

'Anything about this Tegere Servare place?' I ask.

'Now that was a challenge,' Carol says. 'And all I've got for you is a maybe. Nothing official. Which in itself is weird. Even this I had to dig for. Closest I can come is the council property register.'

'So what's the maybe?' Pollo asks.

'Turns out the Catholic Diocese of Dunedin is listed as the owner of three hectares of bush way out in the middle of the Catlins. Which isn't that unusual. Somebody has to own the land, I guess. And the Church is old, has assets. It's listed as bare land. Just trees and bush out in the middle of nowhere, but still. It gets interesting when you find out that they've got services laid out all the way there. They've got accounts for water and electricity as well as sewage. Have had them for years,' Carol says.

'And what do three hectares of bush and trees in the middle of nowhere need hot water and lights for?' Pollo says with a smile as he takes the slip with the address from her.

60

'Carol, you're the man. We owe you big time,' I say.

'Seriously, big, brass balls,' Pollo adds, and Carol just laughs as we head out.

'I don't need your thanks. I need red wine!' she calls out.

★ ★ ★

It is several hours later. I'm doing paperwork and Pollo is just back from a court appearance for an old case of his.

'This Tegere Servare place — if that's what's out there — is way out there. I had a look and it's wild country deep in the Catlins. Out in the bush near the coast. I'd say about a three-hour drive. And that's if some of those dirt tracks are still passable. Fancy a road trip?' Pollo asks.

'Let's head by the houses first then,' I say.

'Yeah, get tooled up,' Pollo agrees. 'Don't know what's out there, but if we find another dead priest, nobody gets away this time.'

When we walk in at my house, we find Eva on the couch watching a Channel 3 special on the 'Holy Man Killer' with a bag of cookies on her lap.

'Hey, sunshine,' I say, feeling happy just to see her out of her room, despite her viewing choice.

'Hi, Dad. Hi, Uncle Pollo,' she says, eyes glued to the screen.

'Hey, squirt,' Pollo says as he plonks himself down next to her.

'Are you guys doing this investigation?' Eva asks me as she finally looks up from the screen.

Thankfully Pollo chimes in before I have to decide whether I'm going to lie to my daughter.

61

'Nah. We've done some good parking tickets this week though. Earlier today we got a kitten out of a tree. That was rough,' Pollo says to her, then grabs a cookie from the bag on her lap and munches away.

'Thought I heard voices out here,' Em says as she comes out from her office and we embrace. 'And you're here why?' Em continues as we pull away.

'Dad's going to be working late tonight. He only shows up during the day when he's going to be out all night,' Eva says, watching TV again. I see Em glance at the screen and then frown up at me.

'That's some good detecting right there. Call me about a job when you get bigger,' Pollo says as he reaches for another cookie.

'You two pace yourselves with those cookies!' Em calls out over her shoulder as she follows me into our bedroom and closes the door.

'So, are you?' Em says as she goes to sit on the bed while I start taking off my jacket and shirt.

'Huh?' I say.

'Those retired priests on the TV — is that you and Pollo?' Em asks as I take my bulletproof vest from its hanger and start putting it on.

I turn to her and look her in the eye when I say, 'Yes. We were first on the scene at both killings — '

'And what's the part you're not telling me?' she interrupts, gazing at me steadily. The woman knows me too well.

'A task force has been set up. Me and Pollo, we could walk away from it if we wanted to,' I answer.

'Only you're not going to,' Em finishes for me.

And there it is.

Em and Eva.

I've been given so much more than any man could

hope for and still I'm going to go out there tonight. Not because I have to, but because I choose to. Because I need to.

'I'll be safe,' I say.

'Says my husband while he's strapping on a bullet-proof vest. Bobby, you're wearing a gun again,' Em states.

'It's just a precaution,' I say.

'You mean in case someone tries to beat you to death or impale you like those priests on TV?' Em says.

'Em, this is what I do. Where's this coming from?' I counter, sounding angrier than I mean to.

'Okay. So I'm unreasonable for changing my mind? Bobby. You became a cop straight out of school. We were kids who'd just had a kid. I didn't even think about it back then. But I've started to. We're growing up. You and Pollo. You get older and slower every year, while the next bad guy is always new and young,' Em says.

'I'm twenty-eight, lover. I think I've still got a few good years left,' I say with a wry smile.

When I've finished putting on the vest, I strap on my service pistol again. Then go to the closet safe, take out my backup gun and strap that to my ankle as well. I can feel Em's eyes on me the whole time.

When I'm finished, I go and sit next to Em on the bed and take her hand.

'Tell me why you need this. You don't need to stay street. You could get a desk job. Or do something completely different — we'd be okay money-wise with my design work for a while,' Em says.

'Honestly . . . I just do. I could give you a whole bunch of reasons but I don't really know. It's like loving you. I . . . it feels right, Em. Always has. Even though I can't explain it or really understand it. I just know,' I answer.

'For now . . .' Em says, relenting as she leans in to kiss me. 'Bobby, you've always been like this. You want things to stay the same forever. But that's just not how life works.'

'Only some things,' I reply before leaning in again.

When we're back in the car on the way to Pollo's house, he asks, 'Em okay?'

'She doesn't want me doing street work anymore. It's like the longer I stay in it, the worse it gets,' I answer. 'How did you and Angie deal with this?'

'You're not going to like the answer,' Pollo says.

'Tell me anyway.'

'It's not up to you. Being a cop family. Some people can do it and some can't. Back in our thirties, Angie started having the same fights with me you guys are having now. Everyone does. One of you has got to give. Sometimes it's the guy. Sometimes it's the girl,' Pollo says.

But thinking of how stubborn both Em and I are, I ask, 'What if neither gives?'

'Then eventually you break up,' Pollo says with a shrug.

When I fall silent he adds, 'Told you, you weren't going to like it.'

★　★　★

The sun is setting orange and pink in the rear-view mirror by the time we leave Dunedin behind. Heading for the deep south.

The Catlins are a vast swath of bush crossed with

veins of old forest that stretch from the foothills of the mountains deep inland, all the way out to the sea. No big towns or cities. Just a few people living out there scattered along a network of forgotten dirt tracks. It's old country. Hard to get to. Hard to get through. There are some people living out there who still live off the land. Strange folk who keep to themselves.

It's completely dark by the time we make it out to Tegere Servare.

Or rather, to the start of the last dirt track on our map. The condition of the road forces me to slow down to little above walking pace. Even though it's cold out, Pollo winds down his window to let the night in.

That's when we hear it.

The faint sound of singing coming through the trees.

I stop the car and kill the engine so we can hear it better. When I kill the car's headlights, we see the twinkling streetlamps through the trees.

Tegere Servare.

It's big. Not just a house. Through the trees it looks like a complex. For a few moments we both sit quietly, taking it in. We can still hear the singing rise and fall. The melody seems familiar somehow but through the trees we can only hear strands of it.

'Sounds like open mic night at Tegere Servare,' Pollo says quietly.

'Officially, there's nothing out here but bush. What do you think this place is? Why hide it?' I ask.

'You can be so boy scout sometimes. Look at it. Look at the size of it. You already know,' Pollo says, looking over at me in the gloom.

But when I shrug back at him Pollo continues, 'This

65

is another example of all that book learning messing you up. Your mind is getting in the way of your brain again. Think like a cop, Bobby. The Church isn't the Church — they're just people. What things do people hide?' Pollo prompts.

And of course now that he says it that way, it's simple.

People hide bad things.

And people do bad things for three reasons. The Church has never needed to hide its money or power.

That leaves only one.

'This place. It's gonna be sex, right?' I say.

'Ever wonder where the Catholic Church puts all those paedophile priests you hear about on the news? Because I'm guessing right down there,' Pollo says.

* * *

I start the engine and we slowly make our way down the last steep curve and emerge from between the trees at a manned gatehouse. Complete with guard, fence, spotlights, and cameras.

'See those cameras and spotlights? They're all pointing in,' I say.

'You know what it's like at these relaxing retreats. They spa and facial you without mercy and, after a bit, it just makes you want to run off into the wild. Security measures are needed,' Pollo jokes.

After giving our identification and the reason for our visit as 'enquiries in a murder investigation,' we're made to wait while phone calls are made.

More questions are asked. More phone calls.

We're clearly a bad ending to somebody's day.

That's good.

It's only people with something to hide who don't like us showing up unannounced.

It's when the flustered-looking guard comes back and informs us that visits are by prior appointment only that Pollo gets out of the car and I follow suit.

'Look, we don't want to make things hard for you. You're a guy doing a job. But we're not visitors. We're the police. This is a criminal investigation which is, happy thought, in pursuit of justice. Which unfortunately makes you, right now, an obstruction to justice. You see where we're going with this?' Pollo says as the stricken-looking guard nods uncertainly.

'Maybe it's best if you call back inside and say that we, the police, are refusing to deal with you and are demanding to speak to whoever is in charge here,' I add.

After a final conversation, the guard returns to inform us that Father Black is coming up to see us.

Father Black is another old priest.

With a careworn face, tall, and looking rail-thin in his black suit and stark-white priest's collar as he walks briskly out of the night up to the gate.

We're expecting another argument but instead he smiles tiredly and quietly says, 'You can leave your car here, gentlemen. It's only a short walk. Welcome to Tegere Servare.'

As if on cue, right when he says it, the singing stops. I finally figure out what song it is. 'Amazing Grace.'

★ ★ ★

'Thank you. We appreciate you seeing us without an appointment,' I answer as we fall in beside him after having made our introductions.

'I apologise for the delay. Some of the brothers had

67

still hoped even now to protect the anonymity of this place. You must forgive them their folly. It comes from good intentions,' Father Black says.

Pollo and I share a look at his use of the words 'even now.' Even now what, Father? I think to myself.

'Father Black. What is this place?' Pollo asks as we walk up to what looks like the main building of the complex. A modern, two-storey building with heavy glass doors at the entrance.

'Tegere Servare is Latin. It means 'to shield and to save,"' Father Black says with a calm sadness in his voice. He uses an access card to get into the building and we follow through the deserted halls to his office, which has the title 'Father Black, Sexton' on the door.

Once we're seated, he moves in behind his desk and resumes. 'This is a secure facility built fifteen years ago. It houses up to sixty priests plus fourteen staff. This includes medical, psychiatric, and custodial staff. Everything you see here is fully funded by the Vatican in Rome, and falls under the stewardship of my order, the Gabrialites. And what this place is, Detective Latu, is a rehabilitation centre. To be perfectly blunt, we treat Catholic priests who suffer from sexual deviancy.'

'Paedophiles?' Pollo asks.

'Sometimes. Although there are many kinds of deviancy. Evil has many faces,' Father Black says.

While he says this, I look at a small brass plaque on his desk that has only a chapter and verse printed on its front. Luke 4:19.

When Father Black sees what I'm looking at, he quotes from memory: "He has sent me to proclaim liberty to the captives and recovery of sight to the blind, to set free the oppressed.' It's the mission of my order.'

'This place. The name is unlisted. The title states this is bare land. What you left out of your description is the word secret,' Pollo says.

'A fair comment. Personally, I've always thought it was only a matter of time. Sooner or later, everything has to come into the light,' Father Black says.

'Do you know why we're here, Father?' I ask.

'Of course,' he says, nodding and taking a deep breath. 'You're here because Aldo and Thomas have died.'

'You knew them?' Pollo asks.

'Yes. I knew them well. Good men, both of them. It was the four of us who started this place. Me, Sean, Thomas, Aldo. They both still worked here. I saw them both at Mass this last Sunday,' he answers.

'Sean?' I ask.

'You've already met him. At St Joseph's in Dunedin. Father Sean Corcoran. He lied to you. I asked him not to, but you have to understand. Sean would do anything to protect his brothers. And he loved those men dearly. I think even more than himself,' Father Black says.

'When you say you started this place together . . .' Pollo prompts.

'The Catholic Church can be hard to understand,' Father Black says after hesitating. 'Many of its ways seem strange to outsiders. Sometimes they even seem strange to insiders like me. And, as with many things, you can only reach understanding after acceptance . . .'

As he trails into silence, he looks down at his hands and we linger. Neither Pollo nor I make a sound. Nobody ever wants to talk to cops.

If you've got someone in the rare position where

they are talking openly, it's best just to listen and not push.

Finally, Father Black looks up and says, 'We're here. We started this place because of sin. In the past century, the Catholic Church has faced steadily growing numbers of sexual abuse incidents. It started slowly, but it kept growing. Clergy shamed across virtually all diocese around the world. The problem reached an unprecedented scale. Undermining the sanctity of our calling. Something had to be done. So the previous pope allocated funding and approached my order, and this place was built. Those of us with special skills were brought together. The four of us. To begin this place. To make a difference.

'I was a medical doctor before I became a priest. Aldo was a trained psychiatrist. We all brought qualities and skills that were needed. Our goal was to help these fallen priests.'

'It's the law's job to deal with criminals, Father,' Pollo says.

'True. And it's the Church's to deal with sinners. What kind of Church would we be if we abandoned them? Could we say we believe that Jesus forgave all our sins and then still judge these men for theirs?' Father Black replies, then pauses as there's a knock on the door.

'Yes?' Father Black calls out. A young man with unruly blond hair and a deep tan pokes his head round the door, looking more robust farm boy than priest.

'Beg your pardon, Father. We're ready to begin. They want to know if we should wait for you,' the man says.

'Thank you, Liam. Make my apologies. I'll not be joining tonight,' Father Black says and the young man

70

retreats, closing the door again.

'Would that be Liam Tull we just saw?' Pollo asks.

'Yes. Why do you ask?' Father Black says.

'We have it in our files that he referred the reporter to Father Bern after Father Mucci's body was found. When asked, he said he came from Tegere Servare. That's what eventually brought us here,' I answer.

'Ah. Poor lad. I hope he doesn't take the guilt upon himself. He's a kind soul,' Father Black responds.

'Guilt?' Pollo asks.

'Attempts were made to keep this place a secret. But now, with these murders in the media, I'm afraid our seclusion has come to an end. It's only a matter of time. Many here are uncertain what will become of us,' Father Black says. 'It is human nature, I'm afraid. People always remember the sin much more vividly than what was done to make it right. So it will be with us here.'

★ ★ ★

'Father Black, do you know why Fathers Mucci and Bern have been killed?' I ask, wanting to steer us back to the reason we came here.

'In honesty, no. I don't. But I believe it must be to do with us. With this place. With what we do here. These were good men. Blameless in themselves. They strove to make a difference by working with some of the worst, most broken people. A thankless job. And I'm sure there are others who've come to know that this is more than a spiritual retreat. And the priests we treat . . . many of them unfortunately have long histories of abuse and have caused much suffering with their sickness. Perhaps wrath for what they and others

71

like them have done has been set upon all of us. I know that many in our congregations feel that no punishment is too great for a priest who takes advantage of those who trust him.'

I know he's right. We've seen it many times in our work.

Many people believe sexual abuse to be equal to murder, and often demand the most severe punishment.

When I think of my sweet Eva, if anyone ever hurt her like that, I'd want the same. I know Pollo'd happily hold the gun for me.

'Is there anyone specific who comes to mind? Anyone you can think of who could somehow be involved? Victims? Families of victims?' Pollo asks.

'I'm sorry, no. But I believe there must be a link between the murders and this place. Otherwise, I simply cannot explain to myself why anyone would want to kill those two men. But beyond a general suspicion, I have no idea. We are, as you can plainly see, intentionally secluded out here in the Catlins. The priests we treat are confined here for the length of their treatment. Movement and contact with outsiders are not allowed. We don't receive visitors, and the staff understand the risks and needs of confidentiality. I don't know of anyone outside our order who knows of this place.'

'But it is possible that word has gotten out?' I ask.

'It is. The priests we treat stay anywhere from months to years, depending on their diagnosis and treatment. It is possible that some of them may have been recognised. Or have spoken about this place after they left, although it seems unlikely to me,' Father Black answers.

'Is there anyone else here who was close to them? Anyone else we should be talking to?' Pollo asks.

'There are many. The community here is a close-knit one. The priests we treat, as well as the staff, follow a monastic regimen; everyone lives together. Since we heard the news, everyone has been discussing it. Thus far, nothing of note has come up. But I'd be happy to let you interview whoever you want. I would ask, though, that you keep the identities of our staff and the priests in treatment confidential if you can,' Father Black finishes.

'Well, there's no time like the present,' Pollo says as he gets up from his chair.

★ ★ ★

The first person we meet is Liam Tull.

The last person to see both victims alive.

Liam, at twenty-four, seems too young both to be a priest and to be working at a place like this. It's only after clarification that we find out he has only recently become an ordained priest, and started working here a few months ago. To be close to the fathers. He's a local. Grew up in the Catlins but was orphaned at a young age and taken in by the Church. Raised in the Catholic boys' school in Dunedin, where he was taken under the wing of Father Mucci and then later, by the sound of it, informally adopted and raised by the four priests who started this place.

Aldo Mucci. Thomas Bern. Sean Corcoran. Cedric Black.

Now there's only two of them left.

'They were like parents to me. The only family I can really remember. I was visiting Father Corcoran

73

when I overheard those reporters talking about a priest being murdered,' Liam says, his voice becoming thick with emotion. After taking a few breaths to steady himself, he continues in a more measured tone, 'I don't even know what I said to them. I was so shocked. You have to understand, Father Mucci was such a gentle man. No meanness to him. Good and kind. I couldn't believe it.

'And then we heard about Father Bern. About the things that were done to him. And now I don't feel anything anymore. Father Black says God works in ways we do not always understand, but I . . . I don't know, I . . .' Liam says, and trails into silence.

'Can you think of anything you can tell us that might help us find out who did this? Did either of them say anything to you? Were they acting suspicious or out of sorts beforehand? Anything unusual?' I ask.

'No. We had Sunday Mass, and afterwards Father Mucci and Father Bern sat out in the sacristy talking and I joined them there. It was often so. I didn't think there was anything wrong. They seemed normal. They left together at about 7:00 p.m. to go back to Dunedin. It was their week off, and they had driven out together,' Liam finishes.

After a few more questions, we wrap up the interview.

The second person we meet is a surprise.

Because even from behind, I recognise her immediately.

A tiny old woman in a flowery dress leaning on a cane. It's my lecturer in Forensic Psychology, Ann Bowlby.

'I have to admit, I didn't expect to find you out here at a place like this,' I say to her after I've introduced her to Pollo.

'It shouldn't be that surprising. I don't just teach. And you know my area of speciality. If you really want to learn about pain, then this place is fascinating,' Bowlby says.

'Father Black told us this place is about sin,' I say.

'Well, he would. And I agree with him. Sin and pain. Where you find the one, you usually find the other, although not always in the same person,' Bowlby replies.

'Remember what we were discussing yesterday in class?' she asks me.

With everything that's happened it feels like ages ago, but after a moment I have it and answer, 'Pain can change people. You can use it to make them do what you want, but you also get more. You can get things you didn't expect.'

'That's what this place is about. Dealing with the things enough pain creates,' Bowlby says as she spreads her hands to encompass the place we are in.

'Now I suppose you want to know what I know,' Bowlby continues, and we both nod.

'Unfortunately, very little. I only started working here a few years back. I knew both Aldo and Thomas about as well as the rest. It's hard not to like them. But I wasn't close to them. The four of them — Aldo, Thomas, Sean, Cedric, they really were a family. And parents, in their way, to young Liam. Poor lad. We used to count him lucky that he ended up with four parents instead of just two. But nothing's free. More love comes with more loss as well, in the end,' she finishes.

'Any suggestions about anyone who could be involved in the killings, Mrs Bowlby?' Pollo asks.

'Just Ann, if you're not one of my students, thanks,' Bowlby says. 'And I'm afraid not. I didn't know them outside of Tegere Servare. And as you've likely been informed, this place is kept an intentional secret. But I agree with Cedric. These murders — and especially the methods of killing used — it's highly likely that there is some connection between this place and their deaths. As to who? No idea. What are you using for motive?' Bowlby asks.

Pollo and I share a look and he gives me a brief nod. It's not protocol to discuss an ongoing case with a witness but, given Bowlby's background, I figure it's worth the risk. She knows too much to just ignore the chance.

'Off the record. We're not sure yet. First we're thinking it's a group, mainly because of the practical limitations of the methods of killing used. It's unlikely that one person would have been able to accomplish them. Second, there's the stagings of the bodies, which we think are warnings, not monuments, because we are dealing with a group and not an individual. But as to motive, we're still not sure,' I answer openly.

'Well, it's definitely not sex. So you need to be looking at money or power,' she answers with certainty.

'Why do you say that? This place is all about sex,' Pollo replies.

'Two reasons,' Bowlby answers immediately. 'The first is biological. There's a refractory period after a sexual homicide. Those killings are the culmination of a sexual ritual. Think of it as one massive, very powerful orgasm that the perpetrator has been building up to for hours or days, sometimes even months. Now, just like with normal people after you've had a powerful orgasm, there's what's known as a refractory

76

period. A length of time where you feel good and sated. People call it afterglow. Where you can't and don't want to continue with any sexual behaviour. Like when you don't want to eat any more after having a very good meal.

'The more powerful the orgasm and the longer it took you to get there, the longer that refractory period is going to be. We are, of course, talking of men. No female sexual homicides have ever been proven.

'Now, consider these murders. Think about the methods and timing. In Father Mucci's case, whoever did this had to plan it beforehand, watch the victim, decide when and how to do it, then actually commit to a time and place, get all the required tools together, finally enter the house, subdue the victim, and then proceed to beating him until he was dead. If this was done as a sexual homicide, everything I have just listed would carry for the perpetrator an element of sexual energy. The first things would feel like foreplay and it would slowly build up to the climax. At the least we are talking here of several hours if not days working up to it.

'Given that the victims knew each other, were both priests and both worked here, it's almost certain that the perpetrator didn't accidentally happen to choose both of them. No, he knew them, watched them. Chose them for his own special reasons. That would add that extra element of importance to killing them. If it was a sexual killing, it would make it more intimate.

'All of the above would likely mean a long time building up to a very powerful orgasm. Which in turn would mean an equally long refractory period. Given the close timings of the two killings, I simply can't see how a sexual killer could go from one to the other so quickly. Keeping in mind that the second killing would need to have its own build-up and ritual also. A sexual killer would have needed more time between the two events. Within this time span, it would simply not be stimulating for him,' Bowlby states.

'You said there were two reasons,' Pollo notes.

'The second reason is psychological. Yes, Tegere Servare is about sex. But really it's about sin. About sex the wrong way. It's about lies and threats and coercion and abuse and rape. To put it simply, it's about getting sex by using pain or the threat of pain. If these killings are connected to this place, then it's reasonable to assume that we're dealing with people who feel wrongly victimised. And hence justified in committing these murders. Think of the stagings of the bodies. Think of the cruelty and the brutality of the methods used. The perpetrator or perpetrators believe that this level of violence balances with how they themselves feel,' Bowlby says.

'So you're saying this is about power or money, and you think we're looking at some past victim of abuse taking vengeance?' Pollo asks.

'No. I'm saying this is power or money because it can't be sex. Let's do power first. I don't know if it's necessarily a past victim of abuse. It could be. The self-justification for how horrific the killings are would fit. But ultimately, the perpetrator would feel wronged. It could just as easily have been a sexual predator who didn't want to stop. He would feel that this place, either by his direct experience of it or perhaps by having been stigmatised in other similar treatment facilities or prisons, has done him wrong. Tried to change him when he didn't want to. Because he didn't see anything wrong with what he did, with what he is.

'But it could also be money. If it's a group, it's almost always money or power. Based on what we know now, it's likely that the motive is power. But we may not know everything. It's possible there's some further connection or aspect to all this that we don't know about. So, money or power,' Bowlby finishes.

★ ★ ★

11:15 p.m.

After a few more interviews we leave for the long drive back. We're almost halfway there when Pollo finally hangs up on his last phone call.

'What did Spyro say?' I ask, having caught only parts of the conversation. Lost in driving and my own feelings at seeing Tegere Servare.

'His usual supportive self. I call him after ten thirty at night, at home, to tell him we've been working on a case he didn't assign us, and not even a cross word,' Pollo answers.

'He's filling in the Operation Spear guys now. Significant progress. Stellar work. Above and beyond, yada yada. They'll come out here in the morning and start the official enquiry.'

For a while the tired silence stretches out between us.

From Sunday to now, which is still Tuesday, if only for a few more minutes, we've had some long days. I think we're both feeling flat, all thought out.

It's almost an hour later, after I think Pollo has fallen asleep, when he suddenly says, 'Sin. It's a strange word. It's like love and hate. You wonder who first

79

figured out what names we should give things. Why decide that that word means this thing?'

'I don't know. I do know that initially the word sin meant something else. They taught us that when I was a kid in Sunday school. Back when the Bible was written, the Hebrew and Greek words didn't initially mean to do something wrong. Back then sin meant 'to miss the mark,' like in archery. To sin was to miss the target. It's only centuries later that sin started to mean doing the wrong thing,' I remark.

'To miss the mark,' Pollo says in a sleepy tone. 'That's almost worse than to do the wrong thing.'

'Why do you say that?' I ask.

'Doing the wrong thing is simple. There's an opposite. There's a good and bad. One right for one wrong. But if sin is to miss the mark, then hitting on target is the only right. The only good. And everywhere else is wrong. Everything else is sin,' he concludes.

★ ★ ★

It's well past midnight when I pull up in front of Pollo's house.

'You want me to do the report?' I offer despite my exhaustion, as I know it's my turn.

'Screw it. We did good today. We'll go have a sit-down with the Operation Spear boys sometime tomorrow, and I already gave Spyro the heads-up. Do the report tomorrow. Pick me up at seven. We can head back to St Joseph's and have another chat with Father Corcoran before his day starts,' Pollo says.

'You think there's more to his lying than wanting to protect his friends?' I ask.

'Don't know. But at this stage, those four priests

are the closest thing we've got to targets for whoever is behind this. And there's only two left. It's possible that those stagings were warnings intended for the two still alive. We already know Corcoran is willing to lie. Maybe he lied about something else too,' Pollo says.

'It's possible. And remember what Bowlby said. Maybe the killers feel justified in what they're doing. Okay. So maybe not all four of those priests are dirty. Maybe only one or two. And the killers know them. Know who they're close to. So they go after their friends. Hit them where it hurts,' I say.

Pollo makes a non-committal grunt and slaps the roof of the car before turning and heading inside.

When I get home and finally slide in behind Em, she fits herself to me and I say, 'Hey,' into her neck.

'Long day, lover,' Em says sleepily. 'You okay?'

'Yeah, we had to go out to a place, Tegere Servare, all the way out in the Catlins,' I say.

'Never heard of it,' Em says back.

Before I answer, I think back to the things we've seen in the last two days. In my sleepy brain, something Pollo said fits itself to my thoughts on Tegere Servare, Father Black, and Ann Bowlby.

When something really bad happens, people feel better if they can find someone to blame.

Even if they know it doesn't change anything. Pain. Maybe the hurt is easier to deal with if we know someone did something wrong to cause it. It makes it easier somehow. Maybe we need sin.

'Oh, you will, lover, you will,' I answer Em, before a restless sleep takes me.

WEDNESDAY . . .

5:35 a.m.

'Bobby Ress,' I say drowsily into the phone. I had just grabbed it from where it had started ringing unreasonably loud, jarring me out of sleep.

'Bobby. Pollo. Just got off the phone with Spyro. Corcoran's dead. I'll pick you up in fifteen,' Pollo says, and hangs up before I can even say anything.

I'm now fully awake.

Fuck.

Three priests in three days.

And we're still nowhere close to knowing who's doing this. At this rate, everything will be done and dusted before we can figure out what's happening. Em sits up when I'm almost dressed and looks over at me in the pale promise of morning light.

'They found another body,' I answer her questioning look. 'I have to go. Apologise to Eva for me.' We were going to take her to the university this morning to see about joining an astronomy club. It looks like Em wants to say something more but she just nods as I leave the room.

'How?' I ask Pollo as I get into the car.

'Burned alive. At St Joseph's. Right in his office. Sometime last night or in the early hours of this morning. It was a controlled fire. They disabled the smoke alarms first. Church staff only found him because one of them had come in at five this morning to deliver prayer candles,' Pollo says.

'We're too slow. This is getting away from us,' I remark, feeling more frustrated with this case by the day. A growing sense of anger and desperation burn away my tiredness but add to my headache.

'I know. And we're still missing something. I wasn't too sure about those four being our targets, but with three of them gone in as many fucking days, I'd say the odds are improving,' Pollo says, sounding angry.

'Operation Spear's guys turn up anything?' I ask, without any real hope.

'Nothing new. But then it's only Wednesday,' Pollo remarks, and I can hear the exasperation I'm feeling echoed in his tone.

'We got the pre-lim coroner's reports back for Mucci and Bern. Those splinters were hickory, just like you thought. Still nothing on our young friend who ran away from the scene at Mucci's,' Pollo says.

'If he's even involved. He may only have been there breaking in and we surprised him,' I say. 'I've been thinking about this case pretty much non-stop but I can't get an angle on it.'

'Yeah. But we'd better start having some moments of fucking brilliance, and soon. 'Cause so far, it's been a pretty good week for the multiple murderer community,' Pollo says.

★　★　★

When we get to St Joseph's, it's only just breaking dawn.

From a distance the cathedral tower looks peaceful and serene, the stonework painted pink by the early morning sun. The lawns and trees glittering with dew.

It's only when you get closer that you see the busy

83

human chaos around the main entrance. There's all manner of emergency responders on scene, from cops to firemen to ambulance paramedics, along with a good helping of press stretching the scene tape. Three priests in three days.

'This is going to get crazy,' Pollo says, as if reading my mind. 'It'll go national now. Operation Spear will get beefed up. They'll put everyone on it.'

'Maybe it will help,' I say, but Pollo just grunts.

With unspoken agreement, we both head around the back to a less crowded entrance and get past the uniform guys there.

As soon as we're inside, we can tell it's going to be bad.

It's in how people are behaving.

Along the way to Father Corcoran's office that sense only gets stronger. You can tell by the looks of the little groups of people we pass. When something really bad happens, it spreads quickly. Everyone pairs up. There's those few who have actually seen it. They are usually either crying or just look blank. Mostly you can tell by a certain controlled look of knowing that spreads from face to face among everyone else. It's strange the way people work. When they witness real badness, real tragedy, that's when people start looking each other in the eye again.

In front of Father Corcoran's office door we run into several detectives just exiting, tailed by Spyro, who is looking visibly shaken. A short, heavily muscled man in his early fifties, he looks pale, despite his olive complexion.

'Pollo, Bobby,' he says in a heavy tone as he pauses next to us.

'Spyro,' Pollo greets in return.

84

'What do we do, Captain?' I ask.

'Honestly? Whatever you think is best. Up to yesterday, even though this was high profile, the commissioner thought Operation Spear would be enough. Now, with three murders this close together, everything will get bigger. Most of us will have to get pulled into Operation Spear to appease the press and the mayor. No new cases from now on. Everyone will just work on their existing roster with whatever extra time opening up going into Spear work. I'll shift all the new stuff onto the uniforms until this is over,' Spyro declares.

Even though no one says it, we all know that 'over' in this case may not necessarily mean when we catch them. It's how it goes. It's not publicised because the politicians and the cops want people to feel safe. But in cases like this, where the killer is well planned, dedicated, and knows how cops operate, all the odds are stacked against us.

'But I'm leaving you two out of it. Do it your way. So far you have been responsible for our only real progress. So have at it, but keep me in the loop. Daily reports as of now,' Spyro says.

'Gotcha,' Pollo replies.

'And guys. We need results fast. I can't tell you to pull in big hours, but I'm asking. That . . .' Spyro says in a wavering voice as he points back towards the office door, 'that can't be what happens in this city. These are our people.'

When Spyro moves off, Pollo and I look at each other for a moment and then head for the door.

When we go through into Father Corcoran's office, it's like stepping into another world.

Gone is the gothic-feeling office we visited earlier.

It's been replaced by a whole new space.

For a few moments, both Pollo and I stay by the door as we take in the scene.

'The Church used to do this to witches, didn't they?' Pollo says quietly.

'Witches and heretics. It was meant to purify you,' I say, trying not to breathe through my nose.

Father Corcoran has been burned. Burned at the stake.

The room still feels warm.

Smoke hangs in lazy, twisting snakes above the body, catching the light. The air smells like burnt pork but with a sweet tang to it. Cloying and organic.

'Fence post again,' Pollo says, walking closer. 'Let's hope they've run out of those now.'

When I don't respond, Pollo looks over. 'Bobby. You with me?'

I make an effort to shift into gear. 'Same MO. They stripped him naked. Tied him to that fence post and mounted him. Piled books from those bookshelves around his feet to fuel the fire. Used some kind of accelerant, smells like turpentine. At least this would have been quick,' I say.

'No, it wasn't. Look at the height of the burn marks on his body and the amount of ash. The fire was too small. They kept it hot but they also kept it small. Small enough to kill him slowly. They didn't burn him. They cooked him,' Pollo says as he kneels down in front of the ashes to get a closer look at the body.

People who die in fires seldom actually die from being burned.

It's most commonly smoke inhalation. Or in cases where the person actually gets set alight, organs and veins can burst as the sudden heat causes the fluids in the body to expand too rapidly, sometimes even boiling. When this happens, massive strokes and sudden heart attacks are also common. Even if none of that happens, in most fire deaths, the victims would usually be unconscious and gone in a matter of seconds. It's already bad when that's your best hope for someone.

This is worse.

Father Corcoran is a boundary of horrible opposites.

The bottom half of his body up to the hips is a blackened, cracked-open sculpture of dry, flaking hard edges and foamed red crusts. His genitalia a lurid, burst-open wound of half-cooked meat. His upper body is a sickly, glistening, swollen and deformed thing, his white skin split open in several places, still oozing blood and fat in an oily mix. A scattering of white blisters swarming up his torso to his singed, hairless skull. His face frozen in a rictus of agony. Shrivelled lips cracked back in a grimace of pain. Both eyes burst open across the pupil, congealing blood dripping tear tracks down his cheeks.

'They don't care,' says Pollo.

'What?' I ask.

Not able to look away from the twisted red, black, and white thing that a while ago was still a person.

'To do all this, right here in his office. The chance of people coming and going. And they must have been in here at least once before to know it's possible. These people aren't scared of getting caught,' Pollo explains as he stands up again.

'This can't be just business. Doing things like this. Taking these kinds of risks. Money? Power? Who wants it this much? Groups are rational. Their individual members are careful. This? I don't see it,' I say.

'I've seen enough for now. Let's get some air,' Pollo says as he heads for the door and I fall in behind him.

I pause at the door. Taking one last look back.

'You think there's going to be more?' I ask.

'I think there's already been too much,' Pollo says in an angry tone.

'Sunday. Monday. Tuesday. One a day,' Pollo remarks.

I follow him back out into the main cathedral, where we sit down in the pews.

For a while we just sit and stare at the altar in front of us. There's a fundraising poster tacked to the front titled 'Help us bring hope to the Philippines,' complete with a picture of a smiling Liam Tull, arms around a group of Filipino kids. Below that is a big glass container full of money. Mostly coins. The sign on it reads: 'Only two weeks to go.'

I see Pollo frowning at that money for a long time. He only sees pancake money, I think.

'This isn't about money,' Pollo says in a pensive tone. 'That shit in there. It has to be power. They wanted them to suffer. This is about hate and anger and punishment. It's vengeance.'

'Yeah, I'm with you on that. But who? Past victims of sexual abuse, or past sexual abusers who feel victimised? Or someone angry over something we don't know yet. Or maybe even just a serial killer finding his sexual niche in old priests. It could even be someone who's killing them in these elaborate ways to make it look like this is some crazed killer to hide their real motive,' I say.

'Nah, not that last possibility. With the first two murders maybe. But not now, after this one. This was risky. Done here in the open. They could have easily been caught. You only try and do things to hide your real motive and identity if you're actually worried about getting caught. These guys don't care. The killing matters more to them than themselves,' Pollo says.

'And I don't buy the serial killer option either. Bowlby's right, it's not sex. Especially now, with three in such quick succession. They wouldn't enjoy it. The only way I'd buy the serial killer option is if they'd been at it for a long time. Got desensitised enough from doing it so often that they needed all the hits this fast just to feel good. If that were the case, we would have had dead priests all over the place by now,' Pollo says.

'So victims of sexual abuse or their families or victimised sexual abusers. That's going to be a long list of possibles,' I conclude.

'Until we know better,' Pollo says.

'And we'd better check if Spyro's gonna task some guys to go and guard Father Black. And the entire Tegere Servare, for that matter. We can't be certain that they are the four but, as of now, there's only him left so I'm not risking it. Cover that place in uniforms day and night,' Pollo says.

'What next? I got class this morning, but I can blow it off,' I say.

'Bowlby again?' Pollo asks, and I nod.

'Nah, might as well go. Do some living and see what comes to us,' Pollo says. He says that a lot, too, the 'do some living' thing. Pollo believes your brain should be allowed space to do its own thinking without your interference. That we should all just get on with things and check in occasionally to see if anything's been figured out. He says that's why some people — which usually includes me, in his estimation — can be so

89

smart and so dumb at the same time. Because we constantly try and do our brain's job for it. Which gets in its way.

'For now, let's head back to the station. Get through the paperwork. You go do the class thing, and we can see what everyone else has turned up. Final is due on the Maihi case too, so we'd better go talk to his family. Then, once the day's got some time on it, I say we go to the Baldwin,' Pollo says.

'Three dead and this is beer time?' I say in momentary confusion, not sure why Pollo wants to go to a pub.

'No, dumbass. Finish waking up already. There's still one thread we haven't pulled on yet,' Pollo says. When he says this, I remember. That young guy who ran away from us at the Mucci crime scene. Carol said the flag sticker in the back window of the Ford Cortina they sped off in was Māori, Tuhoe tribe. Some of them like to hang out at the Baldwin Pub.

'Oh yeah. You think it's worth it? Carol didn't think any of them would talk to cops,' I say.

'Nah. She's right. They're gonna stonewall us. But you can't say you're trying everything if you're not. We might get lucky. Maybe. Besides, I'm getting nice and pissed off with all this, good time to go make some new friends,' Pollo says.

★　★　★

'So, picking up where we left off on Monday. Pain,' Bowlby says, her cane clicking the same slow arc of classroom it did then.

'Forensic psychology includes the rules and principles of both the internal world of the psyche and the

90

external, social world of relationships and communities. It does so because it has to. Even though the internal and external world don't always agree,' she says, looking at me.

'Last session we discussed the internal world. The primary motivator of human behaviour is pain. If you want to get people to do what you want — whether it's to start doing something or stop doing something — your fastest, easiest, and most reliable method is pain. If you hurt people long enough and badly enough, you can get them to do whatever you want.

'Unfortunately, people are fragile. There's a price tag. You also get more. Hurt people enough and it can change them. So, in the short term you get the behaviour you want, but in the long term you can also get more. You can get things you didn't expect, things you don't want. Bad things.

'Today we need to talk about why. Why does too much pain cause unintended changes later on? Why doesn't it just change the behaviour you wanted and leave it at that? You can beat your wife until she says and does exactly what you want every time she upsets you — lots of men know this for a fact. It will work fine in the moment, every time you do it. But over the longer term you may get some unintended consequences. Like her leaving you, or killing you with the bread knife in your sleep.

'Let's go back to our previous example. I could get my fat friend slimmed right down by breaking his arm a few times. If I hurt him enough, he's never going to touch that chocolate cake again. But over the long run, there's also going to be some unintended consequences. Most commonly, in the average, healthy psyche, it'll be one of three things: depression, post-traumatic stress, or addiction. Less often, if the mind has the right shape to start with, I may even manage to unintentionally create some form of psychosis as a side effect, but something. Something unintended that is going to be bad. Doesn't seem productive, but that's the psyche for you,' Bowlby says as she finally comes to stand by her chair again.

'Why does this happen?' she asks the class, her question falling straight into our collective, baffled silence.

'Don't worry, I'm not expecting you to know this one,' she says when no one ventures a guess.

'To get to the answer, we need to take the long way round and start with someone who was very smart, for a man. Abraham Maslow. Anyone heard of him?' Bowlby asks.

'Maslow postulated the theory of the hierarchy of needs,' one of the more academic types in the class answers.

'That he did,' Bowlby agrees. 'But big, fancy words aside, we need to talk about what he actually wanted to understand. You see, before he wrote his big, famous theorem, Maslow started out with a laughably simple question: How can we tell things that are alive from things that are dead?

'Sounds silly, right? We just do. But how? Think about it. Why do we know that I'm alive and this chair next to me is dead?' Bowlby asks.

'Okay, you can say things now. How do we know the difference?' she prompts.

'The chair is just an inanimate object but you're moving around,' someone says, sounding uncertain.

'Well, it's good that you're brave enough to be wrong first. Okay, so it's movement. Let's see then,'

Bowlby says as she takes the chair by its back and moves it back and forth across the floor.

'The chair's moving now. Does that mean it's alive? No. What else?' she says.

'The chair is a manmade thing, but you were born,' someone else says.

'And that means I'm not manmade?' Bowlby retorts, drawing some laughter from the room.

'And every person in the world who has died was once also born, but if I dug them all up and piled them here you wouldn't say they were alive just because they were born, would you? No. Next?' she says.

'You've got blood flowing through your veins, your heart is beating, and organs are doing things, working together?' someone says.

'My car has hydraulics with oil, water, and petrol flowing around it when I start it, and a gearbox and a radiator and all kinds of parts doing things together. So does my fridge and my washing machine,' Bowlby states.

'You can think, you've got a personality,' someone else tries.

'Bacteria and microbes don't and they do just fine being alive without them. While our better computers can easily out-think me without being alive,' Bowlby says.

When the silence begins to stretch out, she continues, 'Not as obvious as you first thought, right? Let's make it easier. I'm sitting here and alive, but let's say I died overnight and you came back tomorrow morning. I'm still sitting here. Only now I'm dead. What's changed? How will you know I'm not alive anymore? Aside from the fact that now there's the possibility of all of you actually getting As for this course.'

'You won't be breathing, you won't have a pulse anymore,' someone says.

'We're starting to cover the same ground again. There're plenty of living organisms that don't breathe and don't have a pulse. But you're on the right track. I need the underlying change. The fundamental change. The difference that applies in every single case. The test you can use to ultimately know every living thing from every dead or inanimate thing. Think about Maslow. Think about what he's famous for. Now think of me alive yesterday and dead today. So much is exactly the same. I still look the same. I still have all the same organs and so on. And, yes, the obvious changes would be no more heartbeat, no pulse, no breathing, and no brain activity. But there's something more fundamental,' Bowlby says.

'It is needs,' someone says.

'That is correct,' Bowlby says with a nod. 'Maslow figured out that the difference between being alive and being dead comes down to needs. If something is alive, it has needs. And it will only stay alive as long as those needs are met constantly. Different needs for different living things, but needs all the same. Let's take living me and dead me. Living me needs to breathe. Needs to eat. Needs to drink. Needs it to be not too hot or too cold, and a whole list of other needs as well. As long as those needs are being met, as and when I need them to, I get to stay alive.

'But let's say they don't. Remove all the air from this room and my need for breathing oxygen doesn't get met and I'll start to suffocate. Do it long enough and I die. Keep me in here and don't feed me and eventually my need to eat doesn't get met and I starve.

Do it long enough and again I'm dead. The timings may differ, but the rule is universal. Living things have needs. Being alive means you are, for now, meeting those needs. Dead things don't have needs,' Bowlby says, and goes to the whiteboard where she writes:

Everything that is alive has Needs.
To stay alive you need to meet your Needs.
If you don't meet your Needs you die.

'Now, we've risen to the level of figuring out the plainly obvious. We now understand the difference between living and dead. But why?' Bowlby says.

'How is this useful for our discussion about pain? How does all this meeting your needs stuff fit with pain? Let's jump back to our previous question of the day: Why does too much pain also give you unintended consequences, all the bad things we mentioned? Why when you hurt someone enough can you get them to do what you want but then also get more?' Bowlby says.

Even though everything she says makes sense and seems simple and obvious, it only seems that way after she's said it. Beforehand, I can't see where any of it is going.

Then, thinking back to what I saw early this morning, that look of agony frozen on Father Corcoran's face, it comes to me and I say, 'It's about needs. Needs are where pain comes from. When your needs aren't met it hurts, and the longer they're not met, the more it hurts.'

'Correct. Needs are where pain comes from. Take any of your physical needs — breathing, eating, sleeping, and temperature and so on. The only difference

95

is time. But if you don't meet one of those needs then, given time, it's going to hurt. And the longer you wait, the more it's going to hurt. With breathing, it's seconds. With eating, it's hours to days. But eventually the pain will start, and then just keep building until you either meet the need or die.

'Okay, so we've established that there is a link between your needs and pain. Which again is a universal principle. All living things have needs, and they will all experience some form of pain if those needs are not met. And they will all eventually die if those needs remain unmet. So we're getting closer.

'But we still don't have the answer to our first question: Why does too much pain also create unintended, negative consequences? Why, when I hurt you, can I get you to do what I want in the short term but then also get more? More bad things later?'

'I'll make it a little easier for you,' she continues when no one answers. 'Both this question and this answer get bigger the more complex the organism involved. If we're talking about something as simple as a microbe, the 'more' you get when you hurt them too much is in fact very little. But the more complex the organism, the bigger that 'more' gets. Hurt something more complex too much, say a cat or dog, and that unintended negative consequence can be a lot bigger. I'm sure you've seen how oddly pets who have been abused can behave.

'And then there's us. Humans. People. We are arguably the most complex and developed animals on Earth. Hurt us too much and that 'more' can be a whole big lot. Regularly sexually abuse a young girl for most of her childhood, force her to do exactly what you want by hurting her. It'll work well in the short term. Pain always does. And while she's still young she may seem fine. But by the time she's in her twenties there's going to be more. Like I said before, most commonly with a normal psyche it will be one of the top three — depression, post-traumatic stress, or addiction, or combinations thereof. But with enough pain and the right mind, you can also get other things, worse things.

'Why? Why does too much pain give you more? And why are the changes too much pain creates the biggest in us, the most complex organisms on the planet?'

'Still no one?' she asks.

'Fine. Then let me educate your ignorance. You may have noticed that everything I've mentioned so far as part of the 'more' you get when you hurt people too much are examples of mental illness. Which, you hopefully have realised, all happens in your brain.

'So you hurt people too much and while you get what you want in the short term, you also get more bad things in the long term. And, as we've just said, that 'more' gets bigger the more complex the organism you're dealing with. And we humans, right at the top, our 'more' is the most. You've probably figured out why by now, right? Anyone?' Bowlby asks.

'Our brains are the biggest,' someone answers.

'That's it,' Bowlby says.

'The more complex and developed your brain is, the bigger the negative impacts of too much pain will be. Which means we humans get it the worst of all the living things on the planet. But that fact also helps explain why too much pain gives us any negative impacts in the first place. Which is our question for the day.

97

'You see, the brain, like everything else about you, is — sometimes even despite your own efforts — trying to survive. That's what it's built for. To keep you alive. And, as we've already learned today, staying alive means meeting your needs. And that is actually your brain's job. That's its purpose. To figure out how to best meet your needs. How to live. And, according to Maslow, it does this in a specific order. First, it sorts out the physical needs. Eat, sleep, warmth, and so on. So that at least you're going to survive physically. Then your emotional needs: safety, stimulation, et cetera. Then lastly, your spiritual needs: happiness, belonging, purpose. Done.

'For the most part, the majority of people's brains manage all this well enough. Their brain looks at their unique little world and they learn. They learn how to meet their needs. You do this as you grow up. This process, in fact, is growing up. Again in the right order, as Maslow has pointed out. So when you're born, you first learn about physical needs. You learn how to eat, drink, sleep and so on. Then, once your brain has got the hang of those, from about two years old, you start learning how to meet your emotional needs: safety and stimulation, so you learn how to form relationships with others, how to play. Then finally, and this usually starts somewhere around puberty, you learn how to meet your spiritual needs: purpose and belonging,' Bowlby adds, before ponderously sitting down and pausing before she goes on.

'And as I've said, for most of us it works out well enough. We may all grow up in different worlds, but our needs are always the same. So between the specific brain and the specific external world a person gets born into, you end up figuring out how to live.

'But we don't all live in a simple, perfect world, do we? No. Not all of us,' Bowlby says as she looks over at me.

'Some of us are going to be born into a world where we are going to get hurt. We're going to get born with all the same needs as everybody else. But unlike most people, all our needs aren't going to get met. We're going to get pain. A lot of it. And eventually, it's going to hurt too much. And like anyone would, we're going to try all kinds of things to meet our needs and make the pain stop. But in our case, it's not going to work. Our world just won't let us. I'm not saying it's fair, I'm saying that's how it is. We're not going to be able to meet our needs and it's going to hurt more and more. And despite all of this, our brain will still keep trying to survive, trying to meet those needs; it can't help it. Some of us are going to get hurt so much and for so long that eventually, finally, our brains are going to respond with a last act of desperation. One last attempt to deal with the pain.

'Who knows what that last reaction is?' Bowlby asks.

This time I know what the answer is.

Being a cop. Seeing the bad things people can do. And then, seeing those bad people. People who have real sickness in them. Too often the really bad people come from even worse lives.

'Sickness,' I answer.

'You're right. Mental illness, to be specific. I know it doesn't sound logical but that's what happens. That's the 'more' you get. Hurt people too much for too long and the brain responds with mental illness. But why? Why would your own brain, when faced with too much pain, make you crazy? How does that help anything?' Bowlby asks.

I flash back to those three dead priests and I think again about who could have done such things and why. Why would you want to hurt someone else that much? Why do any of the sick things we've seen? Why murder, why rape, why take drugs?

And the reason is sad but also obvious: Because it makes you feel better.

'Because it makes you feel better,' I say, and everyone looks at me so I explain further. 'The brain, its job is to keep you alive. To figure out how to meet your needs. But then, maybe you're the unlucky one. Maybe you're going to get hurt too much. And you can't find a way out. Only your brain still has the same job, to try and meet your needs and stop the pain. So . . . I think mental illness is an attempt at doing that. If you're in a bad situation and there's no way out, it's how your brain tries to meet your needs and stop the pain when nothing else works.'

'As strange as that sounds, Bobby has got it right. Now, I'm not saying that all mental illness is caused by too much pain. That's a whole different discussion. But what I am saying is that an almost certain consequence of too much pain will be some form of mental illness.

'You may be thinking that doesn't make sense. What about all those mental illnesses that make you feel bad? Depression, post-traumatic stress, all the anxiety disorders, and so many others. Very few sufferers of mental illness will say it makes them happy. Most will say it makes them unhappy. So how does that work? How can your brain's response to too much pain be to then get a mental illness that just gives you more pain?

'To understand this, we need to think about the purpose of mental illness. There's so many different things that can go wrong in the brain. So many kinds of mental illness. But taken as a group, is there one thing that all mental illnesses have in common? A single purpose? A goal, as it were?' Bowlby asks.

'Let's do a little thought experiment. Say we go find about 300 random people. Just everyday, normal people. Now let's say we could give each of them a different mental illness. But we don't just stop there. We then make each individual illness as bad as it can possibly get. Now, with about 300 people having the worst versions of 300 different mental illnesses, you're going to see all kinds of different symptoms. The depressives will be sad. The conduct disorders will be violent. The addicts will all overdose and so on.

'But remember, we're looking for a single purpose, a common goal shared by all mental illnesses. If a mental illness was allowed to get to its worst, to completely have its way with you, what would they all have in common as an effect? What would those mental illnesses achieve?' Bowlby says, looking around the classroom.

'Isolation,' she answers her own question. 'The one, single shared symptom that all mental illnesses share is that they will, if unchallenged, succeed in isolating the person from the world.

'We've all seen it to varying degrees. From the kid in school who everybody knew was not quite right and never had any friends, to that family member who was always so sad and such a drag to be around at Christmas that most people avoided them, to that beggar eating garbage and sleeping on the sidewalk, stinking of alcohol, that everybody acts like they don't

101

see. If the mental illness wins, if it becomes strong enough, it will isolate that person from the world.

'This happens because of pain. In our last session, we said that the primary motivator of human behaviour is pain. Maslow said that unmet needs will continue to motivate behaviour until they are met. This is achieved through pain. And remember that pain-induced mental illness is an attempt by the brain to still somehow meet your needs and deal with the pain in a world where it believes it can't find a way out. It's your brain trying to find a way to still survive. To feel better despite the world it perceives. So even though the mental illness feels bad, and in itself can sometimes be fatal, it has a function for the brain. It isolates you. Cuts you off from the people and world that have hurt you too much, haven't allowed you to meet your needs. You can see it in depression, how quickly those people withdraw from their relationships. In the addict who'd rather be high and hallucinating than face the real world. In agoraphobics who will literally try to never leave the house, never meet people. In anorexics who are starving themselves and ignoring everyone around them while seeing someone in the mirror only they can see. In paedophiles who spend their time living in a fantasy world chasing unrealistic relationships with children rather than deal with their real ones with other adults. To schizophrenics who, in the most severe cases, have completely left almost all of the real world behind,' Bowlby finishes.

Then she gets up again and adds a few more lines to what she has already written on the whiteboard so that it now reads:

Everything that is alive has Needs.

To stay alive you need to meet your Needs.
If you don't meet your Needs you die.
Not meeting your Needs gives you Pain.
Too much Pain will change you.
You will do whatever you can to stop the Pain.

'It's that last point on the board that is the most important for us. In forensic psychology you will at times be faced with the truly grotesque. The darkest side of humanity. People who do the most depraved and disturbing things. What you must remember is that ultimately, those people, no matter how horrific the specifics of the case, are still almost completely just like you,' Bowlby says, looking around at each of us.

'Doesn't sound right, does it? 'But Professor Bowlby, these people — murderers, rapists, paedophiles, and serial killers — they're not like us. We would never do any of those things. We're different.'

'That's what we'd all like to think. That we'd be the exception. If we were put in their shoes, if we had to live their lives, we'd be different. Given their world and their brain, we'd do better. Unfortunately, science tells us not about the exceptions but about the rule. And the rules are those written here on the board. Specifically the last one,' Bowlby says as she points to the last thing she wrote.

You will do whatever you can to stop the Pain.

'Good or evil, strong or weak, sane or insane, right or wrong. These distinctions matter very little. In the end, we're all just people. What matters is pain. We will, all of us, from the best to the worst, obey those

103

six principles written on the board. Don't get caught up in the finer details of the individual situation. The specific shape of the mental illness involved doesn't matter. The pain matters, and trying, rightly or wrongly, to deal with it. People will all do whatever they specifically do, no matter what they say or think or believe or want. They will still do what they do regardless, because in the end — it makes them feel better.'

★ ★ ★

11:15 a.m.

I'm still ruminating on what we discussed in class earlier when I find Pollo at my desk, looking at crime scene photos. Fathers Mucci, Bern, and Corcoran frozen in high-definition colour. Unfortunately, a lot of that colour is red.

Pollo looks up when I come in and says, 'About the only bright side to any of this is at least none of them had families.'

He's right. Dealing with the families is the worst. Because unlike the friends and funeral home people and everyone else grieving people deal with, they look at you with the expectation that you can actually do something about it. And in so many cases, we don't.

'Do you think we're going to lose this one?' I ask.

'These three,' Pollo corrects me. 'Come on, Bobby, it's just us cops here. Set the horror and the tragedy aside and let go of what we really want to happen, and what have we got? Zero physical evidence. No witnesses. And a general motive that could fit hundreds if not thousands of people. Doesn't matter how many

104

cops we put on this, there's nowhere to go with it. These guys are well planned and ruthless, and they know how we work. So far they haven't made a single mistake, and it looks like they're gonna finish it on their terms. Our only hope is that it doesn't include too many more bodies. At this stage, our only chance is if they fuck up somehow,' Pollo says. Pollo's a sore loser. In a cop that's a good thing. Makes you try harder.

'We'll do what we can,' I say, not having anything more to offer. Upon hearing it, Pollo just grunts.

'I gotta get to court. I'll be back at two and we can go out to the coast to do the witness report for the Maihi case, then swing back and head to the Baldwin. And Em called for you,' Pollo says over his shoulder as he heads out.

'There a message?' I ask.

'Nah, didn't want to leave one. Which probably means you're in trouble. When a woman calls to not leave you a message, it means you've done something wrong. You've got till two!' Pollo yells from the hallway.

★ ★ ★

But getting away from the office doesn't mean getting away from work.

Because when I walk in at home, I find Em and Eva in front of the TV watching the latest 'Holy Man Killer' news update. I recognise the sing-song voice of Becca Patrick before the segment ends and Em turns the TV off.

Both turn expectant faces to me.

We've never kept what I do a secret from Eva.

Em and I agreed early on in our quest to get our child out into the world that we wouldn't lie, wouldn't pretend the world is perfect, but instead try to show her that she's strong enough to live in it anyway. But right now, I do wish they'd been watching cartoons.

'You know I can't talk about it,' I say.

'But that means you know things, don't you, Dad?' Eva says.

'I can't talk about that either,' I answer.

'Mum tells me you're joining an astronomy club at the university,' I say to change the subject. I'm soon being bounced from one astronomy concept to another as Eva happily extols the benefits of her new group. Which mostly relates to the size of their telescopes.

While she's talking, Em and I have one of those quiet couple conversations. The kind without any real words. Where everything is looks and body language and the tone you use while you're talking to the people around your partner. I think all couples have them. I think, in those relationships where things go bad, that's how you know. Because you can't lie in the quiet conversations. And you can't stop having them. Once you get close enough to someone to start having these kinds of conversations, even if it later all goes bad, you can't not have them, no matter how hard you try.

I'm staring at Em, lost in pleasant thoughts, when Eva repeats her question to me.

'Dad, I said, what happens to the bad people you catch?' Eva repeats.

'Well, they go to prison, sweet,' I answer.

'I know that, Dad. I mean, how long do they have to stay there?' Eva continues.

'That depends on what they did. Some only stay a

short time, some stay for a long time,' I answer.

'Do some stay forever?' Eva asks.

'Yes, some,' I answer.

Eva is quiet for a moment of thought before she asks, 'But they all did bad things. They are all bad people. How do you know when they're ready to come back out?'

Before I answer, I think of the things I've seen. The things Bowlby was saying earlier today about pain and what it does to people, and I hesitate, because the truth is, we have no real idea, do we?

'I . . .'

'They get let out when they get better, Eva. There's policemen and doctors and judges, and they all get together and decide when people are ready to be let out of prison again,' Em answers for me when the silence stretches too long.

When Em closes the bedroom door behind her she says, 'Bit of a brain fade there?'

'Sorry. It's been a long few days and my head's still fuzzy from that knock I got,' I answer as I sit down on the bed.

'Let's get that dressing off and take a look at the stitches,' she says, and I start fumbling for the edge of the plaster.

'Here. Let me help you with that,' Em says as she comes to stand over me and takes off the dressing.

'It looks good. Nothing wrong. You can probably leave it off now,' she says, having unfortunately built up some experience with these kinds of things over the years.

But having her stand this close to me has made me forget the wound as I slide both hands slowly up her thighs under the back of her dress. Em looks down at me with a faint, assessing smile. Then she pulls her dress up further and finally over her shoulders, dropping it behind her on the floor. Leaving me suddenly staring at a dark triangle of pubic hair as Em pushes her hips out towards my face and repeats, 'Here. Let me help you with that.'

★ ★ ★

The second I get into the car, Pollo immediately looks over and smirks at me, saying, 'Dude, you got laid. Nice.'

'How do you always know?' I ask.

Because he always does, and also never fails to tell me so. Guessing right even if it happened the previous night.

'I just get a knowing of it,' Pollo says happily.

'And this knowing seems to also come with a need for telling, I notice,' I reply.

'Bah. No need to be shy, Bobby. There's not enough love in the world as it is,' Pollo says.

'How'd court go?'

'Looking good. Might actually get this one,' Pollo answers, sounding optimistic. If you work homicide, this is a rare thing.

Most detectives will maybe get enough evidence to arrest roughly one suspect in every four murder cases. But then there's court. Where right and wrong gets replaced by legal and illegal. Which means lawyers. Which means money. Which means sometimes you get justice, and sometimes justice gets left for dead by a really good, soulless legal team. In practice, this works out to maybe one in every three arrests leading to a successful prosecution. So you do the job with the grim knowledge that on average, a killer will get away with it more than nine times out of ten.

No wonder Pollo likes to visit prisons.

'You up to speed on the Maihi file?' Pollo asks.

Jones Maihi's latest arrest may have been Pollo and me as a team, but Jones and Pollo have a history going back about a decade. The file made for interesting reading, as it tracks arrests and warrants for steadily growing crimes, both in frequency and severity, as Jones Maihi worked his way up the gang ranks in Manga Kahu.

'Is that thing about you and Maihi and the slowest ever chase true?' I ask, having heard a few rumours about Jones and Pollo.

'Yeah, happened out near Buller on a riverbed,' Pollo answers, smiling as he reminisces.

'We were out there alone. Jones had rolled his car but got out unhurt and then immediately set off on foot across the valley, hoping to get to the mountains, so of course I gave chase. It looked easy enough, big, open flat terrain. But where there aren't slippery rocks, there's freezing water, or both. Wasn't long before we'd both fallen over a few times, then a few more. He was only a few paces ahead of me most of the time but by now we were both limping heavily. It was just sad, chasing someone at well below walking pace, occasionally yelling threats and insults at each other. Took me almost an hour to finally catch him. I think he finally stopped mostly out of boredom.'

'What about you breaking his arm?' I ask.

Earlier on in their relationship, during one particularly challenging arrest, Jones Maihi cracked Pollo's ribs and Pollo broke Jones's arm. Nothing too unusual, these things happen. It's a physical job. The interesting part of the story was that Jones, who was unconscious at the time of treatment, went straight to prison. But six weeks later, when the cast was cut from his arm, he found a smiling picture of Pollo tucked inside.

'Dunno anything about that,' Pollo says, deadpan.

'You two have some baggage, I think.'

'Yeah, but now he goes walkabout and we have to waste time on this when we know sooner or later he's going to get caught again anyway. It's not like his family is gonna tell on him. We need to be on the priest thing,' Pollo says.

And Pollo's right. This is a waste, really.

Jones Maihi, like most career gangsters, is a known quantity. He can't leave, and he can't change. It's all too late for that. It's only a matter of time before we catch up to him.

'Anything new on the priests?' I ask.

'Nah. Spyro is out at Tegere Servare now. They're going to beef up security and, last I heard, they're considering going public and releasing info about what they do out there,' Pollo answers.

'How's that going to help?' I ask.

'It won't. Just damage control. They reckon it's only a matter of time before the press figure out what's really happening out there and break the story first. And they're not wrong. That reporter lady, Becca Patrick, she called when you were out. Asking about Tegere Servare. Gonna happen,' Pollo concludes.

Then after a pause he adds, 'For the best, really. All those people out there. Keeping a secret like that place for so long.'

That's the thing about secrets.

The ones individuals keep are sometimes good,

sometimes bad. But that's not how it works with groups of people — it's sad but true. The bigger the group, the badder the secret. When's the last time you heard of a big group of people who kept a good secret? That's why nobody ever knows where the mass graves are.

★ ★ ★

I'm still thinking about bad secrets and the people who keep them when we pull up at the dilapidated farmhouse outside of Dunedin. The farm itself is mostly untilled bush straddling a few miles of coast. It's Māori land, owned collectively by the local tribe, the Ngai Tahu people. But inter-marriage between the tribes has always been common, so some Ngai Tuhoe come here too. Various people now live here and come and go as they wish. Mostly the Maihi family, as far as we know. In many ways it's an idyllic existence. Hunting and fishing. Moving from place to place with the rhythm of the seasons, living close to nature.

Aside from the main farmhouse, there are various smaller huts and caravans that all seem occupied, giving the place a gypsy-like feel amongst the overgrown trees and bush.

At first it seems deserted.

Then, as we walk to the front of the car and look around, I hear a faint clicking sound and look up to find a smiling boy taking pictures of us from a nearby tree. The Polaroid camera looks too big in his small hands but he clicks away with it adeptly.

He looks dirty and skinny. Young, maybe ten. He also looks a lot like Jones Maihi.

111

Pollo spots him and says, 'Hey, Little Bird, whatcha doing?'

The boy smiles wider at hearing this and scrambles down the tree.

He runs up to us and throws an arm around Pollo's waist affectionately while Pollo pats his head. Then the boy takes a picture of the two of them with an outstretched arm, which he briefly inspects before handing it over to Pollo.

I'm wondering how Pollo knows the boy when I'm surprised by the kid next turning to me with the same warm embrace, also followed by a photo.

Then the boy looks up at me, his smile fading as it's replaced by a more solemn expression.

'You have to pat his head now,' Pollo prompts me.

So I gently pat the boy on the head and the smile immediately returns to his little face.

'Friend of yours?' I ask Pollo, as the boy abruptly turns and runs off into the trees again, without giving me our picture, then add, 'and shouldn't he be in school?'

'That's Jones Maihi's youngest. He's named Finn but everyone calls him Little Bird. Doesn't talk. Born with something wrong in his brain. Special needs kind of kid. The schooling didn't take,' Pollo says, looking around again.

'How do you know him?' I ask.

'Just from the comings and goings over the years. Nothing says you can't be nice to kids while you're arresting their family, you know?' Pollo answers, smiling.

I soon spot the boy again a little way off, this time in a different tree, camera still pointed at us.

'Well, it's a warmer welcome than I expected,' I say

as we start walking towards the main house.

'Oh, that'll change,' Pollo says, looking ahead at the men who walk out to meet us.

We're not asked inside. They know who we are. What we are. There's four of them who line up in front of us.

Jones Maihi's family.

All of them big, fit-looking men with weathered faces and rough hands, used to spending most of their time outdoors. The group comprises Jones's father, brother, and two cousins. They bear a close resemblance to Jones.

The interview soon takes the expected turn into a Maihi family team rendition of didn't-see-anything-didn't-hear-anything-fuck-you-for-asking.

It's as we're winding up the discussion that I'm looking around and notice the funeral ground on a hillside not too far from us. I think I can just make out the freshly dug grave where the soil is still dark. Jones Maihi's other son. The one who died. Something about the view holds my attention but I can't tell why.

'What happened to the boy? How did he die?' I ask.

There's a slight pause before Jones Maihi's father answers, 'He killed himself. We told the other cops already.'

'But how?' I press, not knowing why I really want to know.

'We found him in his room. Hung himself,' Maihi senior answers, looking at me with a hard face.

'It must have been hard for Jones to hear that,' Pollo comments.

'Hard?' Maihi senior replies scornfully, looking over at Pollo.

'What do you people know about it? About family,

113

about blood. You follow white men's ways. You don't belong to anything. You never fight for anything, never stand for anything. You can't understand this,' he finishes, looking out towards the graves on the hill.

'I've answered your questions. We don't know where Jones is or why he broke out. And even if we did, we wouldn't tell you. Now go. You're not welcome here,' Maihi senior says, then turns and walks away.

I consider saying something more but there's no point. This interview was always going to be useless. Just a requirement for the final report before Jones Maihi gets added to the wanted list again.

'Bye, Little Bird!' Pollo calls into the trees as we pull out, but the boy isn't there anymore.

We're back in the car heading back to Dunedin when Pollo asks, 'Why'd you ask that? About how the boy died. You already read it in the report.'

'I don't know. I just wanted to,' I answer. Not really sure why. Something there that I can't pin down. And something about that kid, Little Bird. Something unsettling. Like when you meet babies or people who are different, who have 'special needs,' like Pollo puts it. Sometimes you meet them and it can be like they look right through you. No politeness, just complete honesty, like when that kid hugged me with such sincerity even though we had never met. Not like normal people. Maybe it's the rest of us who have something wrong.

'Well, you stirred something at least. Up to then they were just lying to us. Maihi senior's anger was the only real thing about the entire conversation,' Pollo concludes.

'So, anything useful?' I ask.

'Silly rabbit,' Pollo replies, 'this wasn't for policing,

114

it was for paperwork.'

'Off to the Baldwin now?'

'Yeah, it's about that time. We've already pissed off some of the Ngāi Tuhoe tribe. We may as well round out the day by offending the rest of the available Ngāi Tahu people as well,' Pollo says.

★ ★ ★

The Baldwin is a pub. It's on Baldwin Street. Understanding Baldwin Street is understanding a lot about Dunedin.

At nineteen degrees, it holds the Guinness World Record for being the steepest urban street in the world. Quite a few cars can't get up it. It is so steep that in fact the argument could be made to not call it a street so much as a slanted wall with tarmac on it. But no local would even think of closing it down. If you were to ask why, why build it in the first place? The most common answer they'd give you — which you'd get about most of the oddities in this city — would be: Because this is Dunedin.

The pub is ancient. As old as the ridiculously steep road it's on. It has a rusting metal sign that reads: The Baldwin. Hard To Get Over.

It's a blustery afternoon when we arrive, and I'm looking up at that sign as we walk in.

This has me bumping into Pollo, who's stopped dead in front of me.

'What?' I ask.

'Look,' Pollo says, staring at the double doors.

'What am I missing?' I say, not seeing anything but the pub.

'Let's call your uncle for a bit,' Pollo then says, and

115

turns away from the pub door, taking out his phone as he walks away from me. 'Calling your uncle' is code between me and Pollo. It's what we say when we need the other guy to play along because something's up and we need to be invisible and there's no time to explain.

So as Pollo sits down on a nearby bench in front of the pub, I head across the road and lean against the side of a parked car. I purposefully face away from him as I also take out my phone.

I answer on the third ring, trying to look bored and blind to the world while surreptitiously scanning around me in the darkening evening.

I still don't know what Pollo's spotted.

'What's up?' I ask.

'Steady, Grasshopper. Car parked next to my bench. Right by the pub entrance. Look familiar?' Pollo says.

And when I casually glance across, I see that it's a Ford Cortina with rust along the back and sides. Except this one isn't red but has a crappy black spray paint job.

'Oh, well done, you,' I say. 'But why'd they even keep it? And then use it now? They had to know we'd be looking. It would have been safer to dump it. Maybe they did already. Maybe there's an innocent guy in the pub without a clue,' I say.

'Gift horse, bro. And people can be sentimental sometimes. Besides, if there's some clueless punter in there, he's not going to run when we ask about the car, is he?' Pollo says as he stretches out and glances over at the car again.

'Definitely it. Different plates already. But you can still see where they scraped that Tuhoe flag sticker off the back window,' Pollo says.

'That kid must know we ID'd him. No way would he be dumb enough to be out and about today,' I say.

'No. But maybe the second guy. Maybe. Besides, it's a chance for something more. So we're likely looking for someone we won't recognise. But he may be able to recognise us,' Pollo says. 'How you wanna do it?'

'I'll go wait at the back door. You go in the front and be yourself for a bit and we see who bolts,' I say.

'What if there's more than one of them in there?'

'But you're so big,' I answer.

'Funny, man. Be ready,' Pollo says, then hangs up.

We don't look at each other as I pass him by.

Two buildings up the steep incline, I find an alley.

It happens as I round the back corner of the building.

Can't say that I hear him or see him, really. I just have a sense of someone waiting in the dark. Instinctively I take the corner wide and fast, bringing my hands up in reflex just in time. The flash of a blade arcs just below my arm and I immediately grab for the person holding it, getting hold of the wrist. He's not big but powerfully built. Much stronger than me. My back is to him now, his knife hand stretched out in front of me. I can't see his face. Already he's able to turn the point of the knife back towards me, despite my grip. So I push it lower, closer to my body, where the leverage works in my favour. I bring my boot heel down on his toes as hard as I can. Hoping the pain will distract him from the knife. He winces, but still stubbornly tries to turn the knife. Confident now that he's stronger than me. The blade is moving up towards me but straining, I slow its progress. With no other options I stomp on his foot again. Then again.

117

Desperation rising. Using all my strength, aiming for the exact same spot. Then again. One last time. This time his entire body flinches. I'm sure I've broken his toes now. With surprising strength he pushes me away ahead of him. Face-first into the opposite wall of the alley. I drop with my head swimming, drunkenly spinning around, arms thrown up to block the next stab. But he's gone. A shadow retreating down the street. The whole fight takes only seconds.

I consider giving chase but then realise that Pollo is still in there. I didn't hear a door. This guy was out here already. No real time has elapsed. Whoever that was, it's not who we are looking for. I wouldn't be the first person to get jumped in a dark alley behind a seedy bar.

So gulping breath, I make it round to the back of the Baldwin Pub. It consists of a small space including one dingy, old service entrance ringed with the time-honoured selections of overflowing garbage bins and crates full of empty beer bottles.

I can feel the adrenaline pumping now.

I briefly consider taking out my gun but decide not to.

Guns escalate things too fast.

Thinking back to those three crime scenes, we already know these guys are killers. They're likely to be armed. If they see guns and draw theirs, we may all end up dead.

Surprise and violence will have to do, which I'm warmed up for now.

It seems like I'm only there a few seconds before I hear raised voices from inside and Pollo yelling out 'Stop! Police!' Immediately the back door flies open in a blur and the first guy out runs straight into my kick to his chest that knocks him down flat and shocks all the way up my hip. I don't have time to check but judging by how much my leg hurts, I'm sure he's not getting up anytime soon. I'm still stepping back when the next guy is on me.

Luckily, he's looking behind him as he comes through the door. He's big. Pollo's size. So I go in low with my shoulder, slamming into his midriff as his own momentum lifts his torso up and over me. I keep low, now bracing myself to take his full weight. The moment his feet leave the ground I twist my shoulders to the side to heave his weight back forward and down, ending with me pile-driving him down on top of the first guy. There's a satisfying meaty thump. We all end up in a groaning pile with me on top.

'Spot of bother?' Pollo says mildly, leaning through the open door, then adds more sternly, 'Stay the fuck down! Don't move. I kid you not, my son! Those hands move and I fucking end you!' Just as the guy beneath me tries to shift out and then suddenly freezes.

'Took your time,' I say as I reach up and he pulls me up off them.

'They had beer nuts,' Pollo says as he grabs the arm of the closest guy and slaps the cuffs on him, then clicks in the other arm I'm still holding onto. We lay him face down. Then we give guy number two the same treatment, but he does little more than moan as the cuffs go on. He's still recovering from the kick to his chest.

'This one's probably going to need some quiet time first,' Pollo says.

Then he turns and says, 'Police business,' in a firm voice to whoever is watching inside the pub's storeroom before closing the door behind him. When we're done searching them, we're both surprised to not find any weapons. Pollo remarks, 'Clean. I would have thought they'd be carrying something.'

Especially since both of them have a selection of prison tattoos and fit the general profile. They have to be gang members or young prospects. One seems young enough, late teens maybe. Even though neither of them are wearing any gang patches; that's often how it's done in public places. You only wear gang tags in big groups. When you want to be seen. When you're out doing business, which is usually with other gangs, then you keep a low profile.

'Let's talk to the more conscious friend first, he was leading the way out,' I say as we each take an arm, picking him up to stand him up on his feet again. He's quick to recover from that kick I gave him. He keeps his balance and doesn't resist as we move him. Doesn't say a word, either. Just breathes deep. Dead giveaway. It tells me it's not his first time in cuffs. An innocent man would be complaining by now.

It's only when we get him up and turned around that I realise we know this guy.

It's the very person we were hoping to meet.

It's the kid who ran away from us at the Mucci crime scene.

Pollo grunts in surprise at recognising him, then pushes him flat against the wall and leans in next to him. I watch as Pollo turns his body into the boy and then folds his arms and rests them on the kid's shoulder and puts his chin down on top.

Right next to his face.

Intimate.

Up close and way too personal.

Pollo has a way with people. Something like the

opposite of charisma.

'Hey there, lad. Looking good. Good to see you out on the town. You and the friend here out for a couple of quiets? Horribly murder any priests this week?' Pollo says in a quiet voice as he pushes some of the boy's hair gently back behind his ear. Now that I have a chance to look at him more closely, I realise there's something familiar about him that I can't place. He's Māori, young, maybe late teens, but he also has a heaviness to his eyes. A kid who's seen things, done things maybe.

'Fuck you, cop,' the boy replies, moving his head away from Pollo's face, heat in his voice.

Then I can see him visibly calming himself. Shutting down. Assumes the carefully blank expression the smarter career criminals learn in prison. They retreat inside themselves and nothing can touch them anymore.

'Touchy,' Pollo says. 'Especially when I'm feeling friendly like this.'

'Am I under arrest, officer?' the boy asks. Trying to see what we know.

'Steady on now, lad. We just got here. Every time we meet it's like you can't wait to run away from us again,' Pollo says.

'Am I under arrest? Am I being charged with anything?' the boy persists. Knows his rights, has to have done this before.

'Yes, you are being placed under arrest. The charges for today include resisting arrest and refusing a lawful request from an identified officer of the law. And then there's this past Monday, for which the charges at this time include trespass, resisting arrest, and assault. And don't worry, we'll read you your rights as soon as

121

we get you back to the car. We wouldn't want to get anything wrong,' Pollo finishes.

'But honestly, resisting arrest and disobeying a lawful request, even assaulting two police officers, is not really your main concern. You need to be worried about the triple homicide of three priests and what's going to happen to you now as the only suspect found fleeing the very first murder scene,' I say.

'I don't know what you are talking about, officer. If I am under arrest I want to see my lawyer,' the boy says in a calm, flat tone. Well trained.

'Come on. Let's get you comfortable first,' Pollo says.

After getting the other guy on his feet, we get the same answers from him. He looks older, early twenties, prison tattoos. We maybe had a chance with the boy but for this one, it's just business as usual. We won't get anything out of him.

So we escort them both back around the alley to the street, and finally down into the backseat of our car. We wait there for the uniform guys to show up and take away the Ford Cortina. While we're doing this, both Pollo and I keep an eye on the pub to see who leaves, but no one shows.

Then, just before going, we both head into the pub again to look around, see if there's anyone we know. Unsurprisingly, we find it almost deserted. That back door must get a lot of use. The barman gives us an unhappy look. Cops are never good for business.

It's almost an hour after we arrived that we drive down the road again without saying a word to the two in the back.

Finally stopping in front of the police station, we both get out of the car. Just leave them in the backseat with the doors locked and the windows up so they can't hear us. We go stand by the headlights and look back at them for a quick round of who-can-look-at-each-other-with-the-most-hate.

'Thumb it,' Pollo says to me without taking his eyes off the two in the back of the car. I thumb the radio I took from the car so we can listen to what they are saying to each other. But as the seconds pass by, we're only greeted by stubborn silence. Neither of them are saying a word.

'Definitely not new at this,' Pollo concludes.

'You thinking gang?' I ask.

'Betcha. Both of them. See how that kid moved with the cuffs on? And asking for a lawyer? Your average teen from the hood doesn't have one of those. You watch, it'll be one of the expensive gang lawyers that shows up. And then there's what I saw in the pub,' Pollo says.

'What?' I ask.

'I spotted him before he noticed me. And that's the thing. I spotted who he was talking to as well. Him and his friend here. Having a sit down with none other than the president of the local chapter of Manga Kahu. Remember Alkaline Ben?' Pollo asks.

Ben Kepu, nicknamed Alkaline Ben, is widely known to be the head of the local Manga Kahu chapter. Often arrested but seldom convicted. That's why the nickname. Alkaline. Because he's as slippery as soap.

'Yeah. A lovely man. Upstanding citizen,' I answer.

'So I looked away and started asking the bartender who owns the Ford Cortina out front. Made sure they could hear me. That's when the boy tried to slip out the back with his friend. Did it slow, calm. Only started

123

running when he saw me coming,' Pollo says.

'You think he did it?' I say.

'Killing priests on his own? Nah. I don't see it. But he's involved in it somehow. There's only bad reasons for him being in that house with that body. And even if the gang tries to protect him, he's our only real lead,' Pollo remarks thoughtfully.

'Could Manga Kahu be killing priests?' I say uncertainly.

'Dunno about that. The gangs have their ways. But they'd not go against the Church. It's common for their kids to be given a Christian baptism and when they die, a Christian burial. Big rituals that everyone attends. They may not fear the law but they respect the Church. To them, killing a priest would bring badness on their souls. It's not something they would do lightly,' Pollo says.

'You think he could though, if they told him to?' I ask, nodding back at the kid in the car.

'Kill those priests? Sure, if he was raised right. Some of these kids grow up all twisted inside. Way wrong, long before they're even grown up. Could easily do it. But not all the drama, the stagings, the pageantry of it. The more important question is why. We're talking about three old priests. What do they have that the gang could want?' Pollo says.

'I don't know,' I say, trying to make the pieces fit in my head.

'We're still too far behind the ball on this. But at least we've got one warm body now. Buggered if I know why though,' Pollo says.

'I know. Three killings in three days. And this kid shows up in the middle of town in broad daylight, driving the same car. It can't be stupidity,' I say.

'And they were clean. Not a weapon on them. When's the last time we arrested two gang guys at a pub who weren't carrying anything?' Pollo says.

'Maybe they didn't get a choice in the matter, were made to. Maybe Manga Kahu told them to come in for a sit-down. The unfriendly kind. Public place. No weapons. That would be how Alkaline Ben would do it,' I suggest.

'Getting the bad boy treatment for killing all the priests? Or for getting themselves ID'd by the cops while doing it?' Pollo comments, shaking his head before continuing. 'That explanation is only plausible if these boys turn out to be Manga Kahu. And then we're still left with why. Why would any of Manga Kahu be involved in this?'

And, as before, we don't have the answer. We don't even really have the right question.

'Come on, let's get them separated and booked. There's going to be no shortage of cops who want to talk to these two,' Pollo says.

'You missed some excitement, too,' I say. 'Someone tried to jump me with a knife in the alley before I got to the back door. We fought but he got away. Not sure if he was with them.'

'You get an ID?' Pollo asks.

'No. Happened too fast. Never saw his face,' I answer.

'The knife?' Pollo prompts. I shake my head no.

'You shoot him? Wound him? Make him bleed?' Pollo presses.

'I broke his toes,' I answer.

'Bah. Can't take you anywhere,' Pollo says, laughing.

'Hey, Carol, how goes?' Pollo says as we walk up to her desk. Even though she looks like she hasn't slept in days, she still manages to look stunning. She's probably one of those people who looks pretty even when they're sick or crying.

'It's been a busy few days,' she says, stretching in her chair. 'Spyro's got all of us pulling extra shifts on Operation Spear. Same as you.'

'Brought you this very large coffee. The good kind from the petrol station across the road with all the girly froth and stuff on,' Pollo says as he hands the tall cup to her.

'God, you do know me,' Carol says after she takes a long pull from the coffee, then continues, 'and you're here why?'

'Just want to catch up on where things are up to,' I answer.

'You mean, get the skinny version from Carol because we can't be arsed reading all the various reports everyone is doing and you know she'll know?' Carol replies.

'See. You know us too,' Pollo says.

She's right. More than half of police work these days is paperwork. With the amount of cops now involved in Operation Spear and the irksome requirement for all of us to write reports almost daily, it would take a lot of time to get up to speed with any developments. That's of course if there actually are any. The smarter option is to talk to someone like Carol.

'Well, it's massive. Teams are working pretty much every angle. We're doing backgrounds on all staff and clients, past and present, of Tegere Servare. So far, a few possibles but nothing likely. Spyro just came in and told us about the possible gang involvement. So there will be more reports on that as well. We've also gone deep on the three victims, plus Father Black. And again the results are not good,' Carol says.

'What do you mean, not good?' I ask.

'I mean, we've found tons on them, spanning back years. And at this stage, the only thing we've been able to prove is that those four priests are pretty close to saints. Not only have they lived the actual and for-real devout life of the Church, it seems all of them have been involved in some other form of charity work as well. Father Mucci even routinely donated huge sums of money to the Red Cross. No convictions. No complaints. Nothing. Saints for real. Even what they did for Liam Tull,' Carol says.

'Who?' Pollo says.

'Liam Tull. Tull. Come on, the name doesn't ring a bell?' Carol says.

Pollo and I look at each other in recognition.

'No,' I say.

'Ah, for fuck's sake,' Pollo says.

How did we not make the connection?

Even though it happened around twenty years ago, the case is still famous. Liam Tull, son of Ian Tull.

Ian Tull, who lived out in the Catlins with his extended family. It was alleged that he had been sexually abusing his children and those of his brother, who lived with them. It all came out when some of the children were old enough to start going to the local school and told.

Alleged.

Never proven.

Because they all died.

Everything was pieced together later from forensic evidence. When the first police team went out there to interview Ian Tull, he started by killing both cops. But that was only the start.

Then, using an old shotgun and a meat cleaver, he set about systematically slaughtering his entire family, and then finally himself. When the first team didn't call in, more cops went down and found them.

In all, it is believed that Ian Tull killed eleven people that day. Nine of them his own family. Wife, brother, kids, then finally himself. Post-mortem examinations on the children showed signs of sexual abuse, and DNA evidence at the house corroborated the allegations. But in the end there were no convictions, no charges. Because everyone involved was dead.

Everyone but one.

Little Liam Tull.

He wasn't found for six days. No one really expected him to be alive. There were bodies scattered all over the place. Some were found in and around the farmhouse. Some a distance away by a stream. Ian Tull's brother was found nearly three kilometres down a sheep track, shot in the back. Everyone thought it was just a matter of time before they tracked down the last body.

But then, almost a week later, they found him alive, still in the house.

He had been there the whole time.

Even at only four years old, Liam was small for his age. Small enough to fit himself into the upstairs heating ducts.

The detectives figured that when the killing started he must have somehow managed to pry open the grate and hide in the duct.

No one knows for sure because Liam couldn't tell them. Had no memory of anything that had occurred. They found him nearly starved and catatonic, drinking from the toilet bowl.

The case received its fair share of publicity and also, for us cops, resulted in a slew of procedural changes to ensure something like that wouldn't happen again. This in itself was controversial in the media because the changes gave cops more powers.

Nobody likes that.

People are always quick to judge trigger-happy cops and police brutality.

But had those first cops who arrived there been able to kill Ian Tull there and then, none of this tragedy would have happened.

'So that was Liam Tull, sole surviving son of Ian Tull,' Pollo says, looking at me.

'How did he end up at Tegere Servare with those four priests?' I ask.

'That's more of the saint stuff. Liam had a lot of problems for a while there. Given what he'd been through, it's hardly surprising. He needed a lot of support, counselling, and special care. He suffered from post-traumatic stress and anxiety. Family services couldn't place him into adoption. Couldn't find a foster family that could deal with it all. So Liam Tull, through no fault of his own, became a ward of the state. He was going to be put in an orphanage when Father Mucci legally adopted him,' Carol says.

'That's unusual, isn't it? An unmarried man being allowed to adopt,' Pollo comments.

'Unusual, yes, but this was decades ago. The Church still had a lot of orphanages and schools. Taking care of orphans was what they did. And I checked the file, it wasn't only Father Mucci. All four of them signed the papers as legal guardians. Liam just started out living with Mucci first, and Family Services agreed. I guess four good priests was a better option than growing up in the orphanage. And by all accounts, Liam Tull came right again under their care. Turned out good,' Carol finishes.

'Yup. Sounds saintly enough. So these four priests do nothing but good with their lives, and then in turn get horribly murdered one by one,' Pollo says.

'I feel bad for Liam Tull. Can you imagine? First losing your entire family like that as a kid, and then getting a new family and growing up and having them die one by one like this,' Carol says.

'Yeah. God can be a real bastard like that,' Pollo replies.

★   ★   ★

5:35 p.m.

'What now?' I ask.

Pollo and I are again sitting in our car in front of the station.

The arrest earlier has given us both a rush of adrenaline, washing away some of the pain and exhaustion of the past few days. But it's adrenaline without a target.

There are so many cops now working on Operation Spear that there isn't anything left for us to do at the station that somebody else isn't doing already. So we both finish up more paperwork to keep ahead of the pile, then head back over to the interview rooms to see how the interrogation is going. It is standing room only behind the one-way glass and they aren't talking anyway.

Eventually, the momentum of being street cops carries us back out here.

'Dunno. Spyro said he'd call us once they ID'd those two gangsters we picked up. We're still flavour of the month with him, by the way. They're running the prints now. Gonna be Manga Kahu, patched or prospects. So let's assume we already know that. If we knew this and we were really smart cops, what would we be doing now?' Pollo says.

'If we were really smart cops . . .' I echo, then pause to think. 'We'd have figured out who's doing the killing and why.'

'True,' Pollo agrees.

'Still nothing?' I ask.

'Nah. Just the general line based on what we know now. It's vengeance, those killings, it has to be. Which makes it power. Method means it's a group, so those staged bodies were warnings. Everything else is a maybe. Maybe the targets are those four priests. Maybe it's Tegere Servare. Maybe the group behind it is Manga Kahu, but I can't see it. I can't get further. You?' Pollo says.

'Same,' I answer.

'Okay, so, if we weren't really smart cops, but instead had to be us, what would we be doing?' Pollo asks.

'Pissing people off?' I venture.

'Already done that today. Twice. Ruined the Maihi family's morning and Manga Kahu's afternoon. You have to pace yourself with things like that,' Pollo answers, then stifles a yawn. 'I'm buggered. It's been a long-ass couple of days interspersed with some real shitty crime scenes. And paperwork. It's all going so fast. A body a day, for fuck's sakes! I know there's no way of proving it but I swear it feels like someone is in a rush to get it all over and done with.'

'Yeah. I know exactly what you mean. There could be ten more killings or twenty. There could be none. What do we know? But somehow it feels too rushed. It feels like there's going to be more, and quickly. And it feels like it's going to end soon. Like it will be too late if we don't catch up,' I reply.

Then, when the silence stretches out, Pollo finally says, 'Fine. If logic can't help us, let's try thinking without it. Let's just go with blind instinct. If we wanted to ruin the day for our priest killers, where would we have to be tonight?'

We turn to each other and, at exactly the same time, say, 'Tegere Servare.'

★   ★   ★

We decide to go home first, and meet up for the trip out to Tegere Servare at seven. Pollo got hold of Father Black to let him know we'd be coming up.

'How'd he sound?' I ask as Pollo finishes the call.

'Philosophical. Three of his close friends murdered in as many days and he's pretty staunch about it. Still there. Still going to work. Doing what needs. It can take some people like that,' Pollo replies.

'Close friends. The term doesn't seem to really cover it. They never had wives or kids, no real families. They had the Church, all of them together, in each other's lives for decades. They raised a child together. There should be a name for it,' I say.

'They must know,' Pollo says. 'Whoever is behind

132

this, whether it's about those four priests only or about all of Tegere Servare and what they're doing there. The killers must know how close those four were. They wanted to hurt them,' Pollo says.

'And then there's Liam Tull. There's a possibility he's on the hit list too,' I reply.

'Spyro's already on it. In case the killers were targeting Tegere Servare staff in general, they've started doing escorts and drive-bys, and all of them are on four-hour call-backs. Plus a ton of background work. It doesn't really matter about Liam, though. He lives out there with Father Black, and there's heaps of cops there now day and night,' Pollo informs me as I get out of the car at my place.

'Seven,' I say by way of greeting.

'Seven,' Pollo echoes as he drives off.

Something feels different the moment I walk in the front door.

'Hey, lover,' Em says as she looks up from the couch.

'Hey,' I answer as I lean down to kiss her, then ask, 'What's up?'

'Can't you tell, detective man?' Em says with a smile.

As I look around, nothing seems out of place.

'We're alone,' Em says. What? I think.

'Eva is not in the house?' I ask, just to be certain.

'I dropped her off at the astronomy club half an hour ago. No fear, nothing. Even told me not to wait outside because 'that doesn't really count," Em says excitedly.

'We're alone in the house?' I say. It feels strange.

For years now this house and Eva have been an inseparable experience. Now it feels strange. We've been trying for so long to get her simply to go out of the house without any real success and now, suddenly, she's out there. Living. In that big, random world. Now part of me wishes she was still safely back up in her room.

'Wishing we hadn't done so well in getting her out of the house?' Em asks, reading my mind.

'Little bit, yeah,' I say as I sink into the couch next to her.

Em shifts herself around and goes to sit wide-legged on my lap, facing me.

'You look bad,' she says after inspecting me up close, then takes a thermometer from her pocket and pushes it into my mouth without asking. Wives.

When she takes it out she adds, 'And you're still running a fever.'

'It's not so bad,' I reply, thinking that one of the few benefits of being this tired is that it means you mostly don't notice being sick, too.

'It's been a week,' I add.

'But it isn't over yet,' Em says.

'Why do you say that?'

'Because you still have that look, lover,' Em says as she leans in to kiss me. 'That, and I spoke to Angie this morning. She's worried about Pollo. Says he's been talking in his sleep. Having nightmares. When he does actually sleep.'

'Pollo can handle himself,' I say, not really wanting to admit anything wrong with what we've been doing. We'll be fine.

But then that horribly honest part of you that knows all your bullshit quietly adds the thought that Pollo's also been drinking more than usual and he seems angrier, more tired. I don't think he's noticed it him-

134

self. Maybe it's the same with me.

'You two aren't bulletproof,' Em says as she gently takes hold of my chin and looks into my eyes.

I know she wants to continue our discussion on me staying a street cop, especially now that all this is going down. I just can't do that now. So I don't reply, just take her hands in mine.

'When are you leaving?' Em says when the silence stretches out. She knows me too well.

'Pollo's picking me up at seven,' I answer.

'Then I'm taking you to bed,' Em answers as she gets up and starts pulling me from the couch. When she sees my smile she adds, 'Don't get your hopes up. You're going to get some sleep. You can at least leave a little more rested.'

That was it, thinking back now, those few moments.

When I was drifting into sleep with Em next to me on Wednesday afternoon, my thoughts slowly strayed to Eva out in the world, imagining her happy and whole out there.

That was the best thing about that entire week.

Or maybe it's all relative in how I remember it. Because despite all the horrific things that had already happened, it was about to get so very, very much worse.

★ ★ ★

10:20 p.m.

The drive out to Tegere Servare feels familiar but still eerie.

A staged retreat of civilisation.

The further out you go, the more alone you feel.

First the houses end, then the power lines, and then finally the tarmac, and last the lights in the distance. Until it's only old, twisted trees, wind-worn bush, the narrow dirt track picked out by our headlights, heavy with time. Maybe part of the feeling is about knowing where the track leads.

I still don't know how to feel about the place.

Professor Bowlby said Tegere Servare is about pain. Father Black said it's about sin. If you think about what the men who are treated there did, about what they are, then I figure it's got to be both. This one hidden-away place to try and heal it all. Make it better. I want to believe in forgiveness. Goodness.

But maybe Pollo's right.

Maybe some things are too bad, too sick.

'Why do you keep fidgeting like that? What's bothering you?' Pollo says some time later, breaking into my troubled thoughts.

'Dunno. Can't put my finger on it. Just a feeling I've been having today. Like there's something I missed. Or something I should be doing. Or that I remember there's something I'm forgetting. You know.'

'Well, trying to remember won't work. Too much stuff in your head already. Leave it. It'll come when you stop looking for it,' Pollo remarks. 'We should talk to Liam Tull again,' Pollo continues after a minute.

'Why him?' I ask.

'Dunno,' Pollo says.

'Is it because we know who he is now? Does that change anything, the stuff that happened to him?' I continue.

'Dunno. I just have a knowing,' Pollo answers.

'Okay,' I say, willing to try anything at this point.

136

'We talk to him again and see, maybe something connects. He seemed pretty broken up last time we spoke. But then, losing your family twice over . . .' I say, shaking my head. I simply can't imagine what that feels like.

'Don't do that,' Pollo says.

'Do what?' I ask.

'Don't put yourself in their shoes until you know what they are. You can't think like them until you really get that they're not like you,' Pollo answers, looking over at me.

'What?' I say, not sure what he means.

'Look. Friends, family, parents, and kids. They're just words on the outside. We like to think that those things carry a lot of weight for people — that they feel almost holy and wrapped up in love and importance. But things aren't really like that. For some — like you — it's true, yeah, but only for some. For too many others it doesn't really mean shit. There's tons of people out there who don't really love their kids. Don't even like them. Same with their partners and families, even husbands and wives. Everybody still plays along at Christmas and birthdays and so on, but I think the people involved, they know. Deep down, it's empty. They're just using each other to make their own lives easier. Doing this because nothing better has come up,' Pollo says.

When I don't reply, Pollo looks over at me and says, 'And there's the problem. People like you, who live on the other side of the coin. You can't imagine not loving your child. Not loving your wife. Comes naturally to you, couldn't stop it if you tried. You look at the world and you can't help assuming it's that way for everyone. You look at little Eva and there's no way you can even fathom that someone can have a child and raise it and not feel what you feel. Live with a woman for decades and feel nothing for her.'

'Yeah. It's true. What's the point?' I ask.

'The point is you look at the world, at the people in it, as if they were like you. As if they think and feel like you. And it's a good thing for you in many ways, because it allows you to believe that everyone has all this love for their families, their partners, and so on. But it can be a problem when you're a cop. You have to look at people and see what's really there. Not just what you want to be there. Even if you can't believe that's how some people live,' Pollo finishes.

'You think I'm not seeing things the right way with Liam Tull?' I ask. Not really sure where this is coming from, or where it is going, for that matter.

'Nah. Not him. I'm not putting anything on you I'm not putting on myself. It's just . . . I've been at this longer than you, Bobby. I've seen some things. I come from a different life,' Pollo says.

'And it's not really about those four priests, either. Maybe. It's more about whoever is doing the killing. Look, I don't know what I'm trying to say. I'm tired and pissed off and we're losing this. Look, some people just come from a very different place. They're not all born good people who've then had a bad life. They're not somehow a worse version of you. They're something completely different inside. They walk, talk, and act like everyone else, but only because it gets them what they want. On the inside, they don't work like you at all,' Pollo finishes, looking away.

'What are you saying, Pollo?' I reply.

'Fuck it. I don't know. You're a good man, Bobby. But try not to let that get in the way, okay? It's not fair to you, but I need you on this. 'Cause I got nothing here. If it's down to me, then we're gonna lose this one. And I'm not okay with that,' Pollo says.

I don't know how to answer Pollo now. Never heard him talk like this before. Take things this personal. I don't have a good answer anyway.

Even though I don't like to admit it, he's right. I can't imagine what it would be like not to love your wife, your child. I can think it, but not really feel it. I'm just not built that way. The people behind all this — the things they've done, Pollo's right there — they can't be people like the rest of us. They can't.

★　★　★

'Bobby,' Pollo says when we finally reach the last turn in the track leading us down to Tegere Servare.

'I hear you, Pollo, I — ' I start to reply when Pollo interrupts me.

'Listen,' Pollo says, suddenly alert, leaning forward. That's when I hear it too.

The staccato rattle of echoes.

Gunshots.

A lot of them.

Looks like Tegere Servare turned out to be the right place to be.

There's a rhythm to gunfights.

It's not all random shooting. People mostly fire and return fire almost as if they're taking turns with the occasional, ongoing volley thrown in before the pattern re-asserts itself.

From the sounds of this one, you can tell it's big and messy.

We can hear a scattering of claps and pops inter-rupted by the ragged bang of a shotgun and urgent shouting.

'Lights,' Pollo says as I kill the engine. I flick them off as he reaches for the radio, clicking through the channels, but this far out in between the hills there's nothing but static.

'Dead spot,' he says, taking out his gun and clicking off the safety.

'No phone reception either,' I say, putting my phone back in my pocket and loosening the clip on my hol-ster as we hear more shots ring out.

'Extra mag,' he says as he hands me more ammo for my Glock from the glove compartment.

'You take the Remington,' I say as we get out of the car and I pass him the rifle I just freed from the gun clamp between us.

'We going in loud?' I ask as we round the car and head down.

'No. I don't hear any Glocks down there. Keep to the edges. Find cover before we open,' Pollo says as we move in step.

It's bad about the Glocks. They are standard issue sidearms for cops, like the one in my hand now. We know there are at least four cops down there. But by the sound, none of them are firing.

We take opposite sides of the track as we move along the edge of the trees, keeping to the shadows.

The road itself drops and turns sharply and there's light ahead, casting stark shadows into the trees. The tempo of gunshots has slowed but is still going.

Most gunfights have that in their pattern too.

There's the initial flurry of near continuous shots of the fuck-you-and-die adrenaline-fuelled variety

140

where everyone just blasts away. Then — if there are enough left alive on both sides — the adrenaline wears off and the fear sets in. Maybe you've seen someone get hit. Or you've had a few near misses. The shots become more tentative as the shooters try to target each other without also becoming a target themselves.

When we round the curve in the road, the forest abruptly opens up into the large clearing before the gates.

The gates, which look to be made of solid metal bars set on a rail, are now bent over and twisted inwards.

A van is still idling with its front wheels suspended up on the bent gate.

They tried to drive the van through the gate and clearly were stopped short.

That's where it started.

Now things have moved on.

I can see two people down just inside the gate by a parked police cruiser. They have that stillness to them that means either unconscious or dead.

There's a good thirty paces of clear, well-lit ground to cross to make it from the cover and shadows of the trees where we are now to the back of that van.

'Anything?' I ask, scanning ahead, but I can't see any movement. Just hear the occasional gunshot echo across the clearing.

'Nothing. I'll go for the back of the van. Cover me,' Pollo says. He's moving before I can argue. There's no other way. But going for that van is a risk if they've left anyone in there as a wheel-man. I hold my breath as long as it takes Pollo to make it over to the back of the van. No one sees him.

Gunshots are still ringing out.

I can even hear the odd shot thud into the trees around me, but nobody seems to be aiming for us.

I see Pollo pop up and check the van's interior, then duck back down and signal for me to move.

When I'm over and ducked down next to him, he says, 'Over there. Don't know if they're friendly.'

From this position I can just make out three figures cowering behind a tree and a low wall, their backs to us as they intermittently pop up to fire at the main building.

The double doors of which are wide open. Broken glass and pieces of debris are lying all across the steps leading up to it.

Then, in reply to their fire, from the darkness inside comes another booming discharge. The bright flaring of a shotgun in the dark. Both barrels.

'Okay, this is point. If it goes bad, that giant oak over there's fallback,' I say.

'Ready?' Pollo asks, and I nod.

Then Pollo yells out: 'This is the police! Cease fire!' and ducks back down just before a hail of bullets comes our way, followed by the bangs of discharge. When people are firing right at you, the bullet travels a lot faster than the sound it makes. They say you'll never hear the shot that kills you.

But you can tell when it's close.

There's a dopplering sound somewhere between a buzz and a hiss.

And as we hunker below the barrage, some pinging into the metalwork of the van, Pollo says, 'That went well. How many, you reckon?'

'More than the three we can see,' I answer. When the predictable lull in firing occurs I shift over, trying to keep myself well behind the cover of the van when

I yell out: 'Police! We have you surrounded! Cease fire! Or you will be fired upon!'

At which point the firing increases again.

'We're fucked here,' Pollo says. 'We shoot at them and we could hit the friendlies behind them. Ideas?'

But right at that moment, the shooting stops and it falls suddenly quiet.

'Eyes on,' Pollo says, and we both scan around. Worried they may be making a rush for us. Or at the people in that main entrance.

'There. Rabbiting,' Pollo says, and I can just make out a small group of men keeping low as they run beyond the far corner of the main building, further into the compound. Maybe four or five, all armed.

'You, in the building! This is the police! Cease fire! You hear me?' Pollo yells out.

Then a voice from the dark entrance yells out 'Please help! We've got wounded in here!'

'We — ' Pollo yells, but his voice is immediately drowned out by another volley of shots, this time from the far side of the building.

All aimed at us.

The new angle of firing has both of us cowering down close to each other. Luckily, the ground slopes upward gently to the buildings so they can't get line of sight to shoot clear under the van. But then it's just a van. Not armoured. Not bulletproof. So instead they settle for trying to shoot us through it.

'Okay, so not running,' I say to Pollo.

'Nah, just went to get more friends,' Pollo answers.

'How many, you think?' I ask.

'More than us,' Pollo replies as he leans quickly out and back in again. Soliciting another few rounds smashing into the van.

'We need to move. They flank us here and we're fucked,' I say, turning back to find Pollo scraping together some of the larger rocks from the dirt.

'I'll take out those spotlights with the rifle. When it's dark, you make a run for those main doors. I'll chuck these rocks the other way. Hopefully the noise will distract them long enough. And they'll have to expose themselves to aim at you. Which means I can aim back,' Pollo says.

'What about the guys in there?' I ask.

Thinking that they might well mistake me for one of the gunmen and use that shotgun on me as I run at the door.

'Well, that's the part where you believing in God comes in,' Pollo answers.

'Fuck it. Okay. You take out the lights. I'll lay down some cover,' I say.

'Ready?' Pollo says.

'Go,' I answer and lean out, repeatedly firing at the far corner. At first a few bullets buzz past in reply but die down under my barrage as the shooters take cover again. My Glock has a seventeen-bullet mag so I keep pulling the trigger. Then the first of three spotlights shatters as Pollo starts up with the Remington. I can't hear him fire over my own noise but I see the lights burst apart one by one. The last one shatters as my gun clicks on empty.

'Now,' Pollo whispers, and I immediately take off in the sudden darkness, sprinting for the doorway. I don't hear the clattering of stones Pollo is throwing as an attempt at distracting them, only the too-loud-too-close gunshots from the far corner. Impossible to know if they are aiming at me or not.

I momentarily consider yelling out to whoever has

144

that shotgun in the doorway that I'm a cop and I'm coming in. But the fear that I'll alert the gunmen at the far corner keeps me silent.

I'm only paces away from the entrance when the shooting seems suddenly louder and the added angry buzzing sounds tells me they're definitely aiming at me now.

It's down to a few seconds.

I've made it this far.

I can make it all the way.

I'm on the last step, tensing for the dive that's going to take me through those doors to safety.

That's when it all goes wrong.

Too late, I make out a shape in the doorway.

Then the sharp jerk of the head in my direction. The shotgun brought up to the shoulder just before I can inhale to shout out.

Too late.

There's absolutely no sound when it happens.

My world becomes a white, blinding flash occurring at the exact same time as I'm stopped dead in mid-air and flung back to land flat on my back.

It doesn't hurt at first.

I just feel dislocated.

It's not me that moved.

I'm still upright and running forward. It's the world that has suddenly spun around to somehow hit me in the chest and back at the same time.

It's when I can't breathe that the burning starts, all across my chest, my neck.

Shotgun.

At point-blank range.

And I know, I don't want to, but I do.

What makes a shotgun special is the fact that it

doesn't fire a single metal slug, but rather the shotgun shell is packed with multiple tiny metal pellets. Usually lead or steel. An average 12-gauge number 8 shell has about 400 pellets in a single shot. They spread out once they leave the barrel. Due to their relatively small size, the speed and weight of each pellet makes them capable of impacting with immense force. I was close, pretty sure I took most of them.

Couple of hundred chest wounds.

This is me dying. Doesn't hurt as much as I thought it would.

Too many holes, I guess. I'll bleed out or drown in my own blood or both, but it won't be long, maybe a few seconds.

The only thing I feel is a wave of regret as I gasp for breath. I'm trying to hold on but I can feel myself slipping. Thoughts swirling down and away into blackness.

Em and Eva.

Everything I have been given in my ridiculously blessed life, and I've sacrificed it all for this.

To die chasing sad, broken people doing ugly things. For what?

Fool.

THURSDAY . . .

12:10 a.m.

'Bobby.' I hear someone calling me, but they're far away.

'Bobby,' the voice repeats. Closer now, more urgent.

'Bobby!' This time it triggers my brain, and it rapidly runs through situations that could fit. It hurts too much for me to be on the merry-go-round and I'm not a boy anymore. Then I think maybe I'm back on the road near Father Mucci's house after that guy knocked me out, but then I remember that's just a memory, too.

It's when Pollo adds, 'You're not dead. It's just a chest wound, you big girl,' that it comes flooding back to me and I open my eyes. I see a ring of faces bending down over me. Pollo. Father Black. Liam Tull.

'Rock salt,' Pollo says as he grins down at me.

'Huh?' I say.

Woozily wondering how it's possible that I'm still alive. 'The shotgun round you took. It's not metal shot. They filled it with rock salt. To scare off animals. Couldn't kill you if they tried. The priests here don't hold to killing,' Pollo says as he helps me into a sitting position.

'And also, dumbass, you're wearing a vest,' Pollo continues in a bright tone. 'You took the blast up close but that burning you feel is just the salt. It broke the skin here and there but that's about it. Give or take a few broken ribs, I'd say.'

147

'Are we good?' I ask, realising exactly where we are and what we're doing.

Just before another few gunshots from outside interrupt us.

'They're still out there. When you got shot they were leaning out to fire at you. I'm pretty sure I got one. But then I had to come over here and take care of you. And I made it across without getting myself shot too,' Pollo finishes.

'I'm really sorry I shot you, Mr Ress,' Liam Tull says in a worried voice.

'It's the thought that counts, lad,' Pollo says to him.

'I know you meant well, son,' Father Black says as he lays a hand on Liam's shoulder.

'That's okay,' I say as I very slowly get to my feet. It feels like someone dropped a fridge on my chest.

'The call's gone out. Armed Offender Squad and three choppers are incoming. ETA ten minutes,' Pollo says as he heads for the wall by the door and starts reloading.

I gingerly move over to the opposite side of the wall and, with shaking hands, load in my last mag; seventeen bullets and then that's it.

'They've got to know it's done now,' I say.

'Oh, they'll know cops are coming. Pulling a stunt like this. Gate crashing, guns blazing. They probably know roughly how much time they've got before they get here,' Pollo answers.

'So the question is, how badly do they want in here?' I say.

'Yup. Pretty soon they're gonna figure it's time to stop shooting at this doorway from over there. They're going to make one last push to get in here or they're going to run,' Pollo says.

148

'And these guys aren't going anywhere. That van is fucked and our car is blocking the only road out,' I say.

'Yeah, but that's pretty wild bush out there. Even with choppers. By the time we get the dogs out here they could be hours ahead. And there's other roads and trails,' Pollo says, then leans quickly out and in again. The lull in shooting seems to have gone on longer than usual.

'No shooting, can't see them,' he says as I also lean out for a quick look. Everything seems quiet.

'There,' Liam says from next to me, pointing off to the right where we can just make out some shapes moving away towards the far fence in the distance.

'Running then,' Pollo says.

'Anything out there, Liam?' I ask.

'There's a goat track that leads down to the old silver mine's railroad. It's not far. I don't know what's beyond that,' Liam answers.

'Go or stay?' Pollo asks, giving me a look.

He shouldn't even be asking.

Standard police procedure is aimed at safety.

Going by the book, we should stay here and secure the area while awaiting reinforcements. Not doing that means trouble later on.

And after getting shot and actually thinking I was dying, I don't want to. Right now I want to go home to Em and Eva.

But I know Pollo. When he starts being bright and humorous in dangerous situations, it means he's angry. He's going to go out there with or without me.

'Go,' I say.

By the time we make it to the fence, using the buildings for cover, the last of them has scrambled through

149

the hole they'd cut. We can just hear the sounds of them moving away up the track.

No flashlights now, as it would both ruin our night vision and make us easy targets. We move together into the growing dark. Pollo stops when we reach the hole in the fence. It's a bad spot. No cover, and we're silhouetted by the light from the compound behind us.

I'm about to whisper a question when Pollo points to the ground in front of us.

In moon and star light, fresh blood looks almost shiny black.

There's a lot of it.

One of them is wounded. Had some time to bleed here in one spot while they cut the fence.

It means they'll be slower.

But they still have the odds in their favour. Because they're running and we're chasing.

It's not fair.

But that's how it is when you're the one chasing.

First off, the runners already have a head start. They also have all the choices. Any path. Any direction. Stay together or split up. They can go fast or slow or both. They can be loud or quiet. Change direction. Stop and hide. Circle back. If they're armed, they can ambush you.

If you're chasing, the only thing you can do is hope to catch up. If you do, hope that you're better or luckier than them.

Once we're through the fence, the first few moments in the bush track are tense and too quiet. But soon we hear them ahead of us again and pick up our pace while trying to keep our own noise to a minimum. Slowly our eyes adjust to the gloom. We've got pretty good visibility among the trees, but while we can hear them ahead, we frustratingly stay too far back to see them.

It's not long before the track curves down and then suddenly opens up where the path crosses an old railway track. With unspoken agreement we pause to look around before going into the open.

They've either followed the track across the railway or followed the railway left or right. There's no sound to guide us now.

But again Pollo points and we can make out the blood splatters leading to the left along the tracks.

We move out and keep close to the edge of the trees, picking up speed now on the even ground.

At least the grassy edge along the railway track means we can move almost soundlessly.

We're about a half a mile or so down the track when it happens.

There.

We finally see them.

So close.

The railway track has straightened out. About thirty paces ahead they're clearly visible. A small group of men moving away from us. One of them being helped along by two others. Slow, vulnerable. Right out in the open. Centre of the track, no cover.

Immediately Pollo and I separate, moving to either side of the railway tracks to not present a single target.

I can't help thinking of the things we've seen.

The things these people have done. Old men killed in sick, horrible ways. And right here, right now, is our chance to end it.

To make this ugly, sad part of the world just that little bit better. I see Pollo is down on one knee already aiming his rifle. At this distance, with a Remington, I know he's lethal. These men will be dead before they have a chance to turn.

I've just taken aim at the person on the far right, knowing Pollo will be aiming at the person on the far left.

Right then.

That's when everything goes wrong.

Because the thing about chasing people is that the odds are always in their favour.

I'm about to yell out for them to stop when my Glock is knocked from my hands. Immediately a gun is shoved into the back of my head as an arm snakes around my neck, pulling me back and to the side.

I see it all happen.

It's up close.

Pollo is only a few paces away from me. Just across the railway track.

He must have sensed the movement because he's swung around and is already aiming the rifle by the time I'm fully pulled in front of the man who's grabbed me.

There's a look on Pollo's face.

Like the one he gets when he's drunk and he tells me about his family and says things he doesn't want to but can't stop, either.

Then Pollo does it.

I was praying for him not to. Praying that he would take the shot. As the gun that was pressed against my head is aimed at him.

Pollo straightens up and lowers the rifle and says, 'Please. Please not him, Jones.'

It's not like in the movies.

Nothing happened in slow motion.

It's just that I can remember every detail clearly. The first shot straight to Pollo's chest. Up high. Above the vest. A kill shot. Me reaching for the gun too slow. The second shot. Low in the abdomen as Pollo falls to his knees. By the third shot I've got hold of his arm and it's off the mark, hitting Pollo in the leg.

Anger now.

With both hands I twist the arm while angling it down and pulling it in towards my chest for strength as I heave myself to the side.

The tension increases the lower I go and when I feel his weight crash against me I step to the side and pull back and up as hard as I can. There's a satisfying pop as that arm is pulled out of the shoulder socket.

Not wanting to give him time to recover, I step in and stamp on the inside of his knee, bringing him down in front of me. I grab his head in both hands, pulling down as I bring my knee up, crunching into his face. One. Two. Three times. Then there's an audible crunch and his head shudders in my hands.

There's no fight in him now. I can already feel his body going limp, but I can't stop myself. I need to kill him.

Then, for the second time that night.

A gunshot hitting me in the chest takes me off my feet.

The wind is knocked out of me but I remain conscious this time. Staring straight up at an inappropriately pretty night sky as a gunfight rages just above me.

It sounds almost like it did before Pollo and I joined in.

Various pistol shots answered from the other side by the ragged blast of a shotgun.

Oh God, I think, Liam Tull followed us out here. On his own. With rock salt shells.

I'm on my side, trying to find my Glock, hoping nobody is aiming at me when finally, finally, there's an almost holy intervention.

Suddenly, a bright-white light stabs down from the sky and with a gushing of wind and the roar of rotor blades the police chopper swoops in. It's when I pull my head to the side to shield myself from all the dust the chopper kicks up that I see Pollo looking at me.

It's strange how quickly everything inside you can change.

Moments ago I was killing a man. So much momentum behind my hate and anger that I would have sworn nothing could stop me. Nothing else existed in the world but killing that man, beating him until nothing recognisable was left.

Now, I'm just done.

There's no more fight left in me. I'm dimly aware of gunshots moving away and figures moving past us as the reinforcements finally arrive, but by then I'm already over by Pollo.

There's blood everywhere but the shot to his lower abdomen looks the worst so I try to put pressure on the wound. But as soon as I try to use any strength, a shocking pain shoots into my chest. Of course. Gunshots on a bulletproof vest. If I didn't manage to break any ribs the first time I got shot, then I'm fairly certain the second time got it done.

So I cradle Pollo's head as best I can while he looks up at me.

'We get him?' he asks quietly.

But as I look over, I see that he's gone.

They must have grabbed him when they shot me.

'Nah. But I've made some significant cosmetic changes to his face,' I say, trying to keep the emotion from my voice.

'Doesn't matter,' Pollo says as his gaze wanders away from my face and up into the night, and I see tears running down his face.

'All of it . . .' Pollo says then, trying to nod and choking on blood, as if he's picking up another thread of conversation we've been having.

'What?' I ask.

And then, as his breathing slows and his body goes still he says into the sky '. . . everything. Them. Us . . . It's all just pancake money.'

★ ★ ★

8:35 a.m.

Pollo is dead.

I realise now that people living doesn't really change things.

It's when that living starts or ends. Someone is born or someone dies, and if you're close enough, your whole world changes.

Everything looks exactly the same and feels completely different.

The hospital was the same. Bandages and stitches and painkillers and a busy chaos of people. The debrief meeting was the same. Cops asking questions, writing things down, bringing me food and coffee.

Everyone acting normal.

But Pollo is dead.

They wanted to keep me for observation as I have some broken ribs and a concussion, but eventually they reluctantly agree to let me go, with Spyro and some uniform guys backing me up.

And it's not like I'm going far.

The morgue is in the hospital basement.

Once I'm dressed, with help from Spyro, the phone call to Em is the first thing I do when I'm again deciding things for myself.

'I'm okay,' is the first thing I say when she answers.

'Bobby . . .' Em says, and I can hear her fighting back the emotion.

'I know,' I answer.

Then I take a breath before I continue.

'I'll be home soon. But I need to do something first,' I say as gently as I can.

There's a heavy silence on the phone and I ache from knowing what I've just done to Em.

'Oh God, no,' Em says, as realisation hits and she breaks down.

Police procedure is clear and simple.

When a cop dies, the first civilians you tell are the family. Not your friends. Not your wife. Not the media. Not even God. The family. Because they deserve it.

But wives have their own procedures.

By now, the media would have reported that there were deaths. So Em would know it's bad. First she would have called me. Then Pollo. Then Angie. Then the station. But no one would tell her anything. Then someone from the station would have contacted her directly to tell her what they could. Which wouldn't have been enough. And now she'd know why. The thing that would be more important than me seeing her and Eva first thing.

'Soon, okay?' I say.

'I love you, Bobby,' Em says.

'I love you, too,' I answer, then click off.

'She's with him now?' I ask, turning to Spyro.

'Morgue viewing room. You want to do it there?' Spyro asks.

I notice now how tired he looks, pale and worn, somehow older and smaller than yesterday morning, less confident.

'Let's go,' I answer.

This part isn't in the procedures. But we do it anyway. If a cop dies and you were there with them at the end, then you go see the family. First thing. Doesn't matter that they already know. Doesn't matter that there's nothing new you can tell them.

This is what you do.

When we get there, Spyro opens the door for me but doesn't come in. Grief already crowds the space beyond.

But when I'm through the door, it all suddenly feels so desolate. In here it's just the three of us. Angie. Me. And Pollo.

Angie has Pollo's hand clasped tightly in both of hers. Doesn't let go when I say her name.

Just looks over and gives me a kind, tear-streaked smile.

'Hi, Bobby,' she says quietly.

It hits me now.

I'm completely unprepared for this.

My thin semblance of calm control is ripped away, leaving only a painful gravity that pulls me to Pollo. Makes me want to rush over and shake him awake.

Pollo running faster than me. Laughing louder, fighting harder. Backing me up no matter what. Pollo smiling at me after saying something horrible and funny at the same time.

Pollo. Big, strong, and unkillable.

'Angie . . . I'm . . .' I start, but nothing more comes and I hesitate by the door.

I feel a shameful anger at myself for not being able to control what I'm feeling. For not being able to be here and now. Be here for Angie. She's got to be hurting so much more than me.

I feel even worse as she takes one of her hands off Pollo's and holds it out to me.

Like we're the only people left in the world.

'Come here, Bobby. It's okay,' Angie says with a calm strength that breaks my heart.

Because I know it's not.

★ ★ ★

10:27 a.m.

The bright morning sun seems out of place on the ride from the hospital.

Spyro drives me home himself.

I know he's got a ton of more urgent things to do, but that's the kind of captain he is. Thankfully, he doesn't say anything to me. Just drives.

On a distant, rational level, I know this is all much bigger than Pollo and me. I just can't feel it.

In total, four cops were killed and one seriously injured. Two offenders were found dead at the scene. Another was found dead in the bush where the rest abandoned him during the ensuing chase that took up most of the night. They're still out there searching, even now, but the dogs have lost the scent.

They're gone.

158

I struggle to gather my own confused, flitting thoughts. My brain seems to jump from one terrible thing to another without being able to focus or make sense. All the bad things that happened flow through my mind of their own accord. Not just last night, but this whole week. A lot of people have died. Good priests and bad gangsters and Pollo.

And I still don't know why.

But there's one thing I do know.

One certainty that anchors my swirling thoughts and focuses me on what I need to do.

Because there's one moment that replays inside me constantly. That I can't stop replaying even though I want to — it's that look in Pollo's eyes. The way his voice breaks just before he's shot. He lowers his gun and looks behind me and says, 'Please. Please not him, Jones.'

Jones.

Jones Maihi.

Who got away.

Who's still out there.

Still alive.

While Pollo lies dead under fluorescent lights in a hospital basement.

And I held his fucking head in my hands.

★ ★ ★

11:04 a.m.

Em doesn't say a word when I open the door, just strides over and hugs me. Too hard for my broken ribs but I don't say anything.

'Dad?' I hear Eva say hesitantly from where she's

159

standing at the foot of the stairs.

'Hey, kid,' I say, trying to put some warmth in my voice.

'Dad, is Uncle Pollo dead?' she asks.

Em lets go of me and we exchange a glance before I turn to Eva and say, 'Come here, Eva.'

But Eva hesitates where she is, looking more and more upset, shifting her weight back and forth from one leg to the other. Her voice grows loud and pleading when she says, 'No, just tell me, Dad.'

As she says it, her hands reach for the rail of the stair and she grips it, as if for safety.

Like she used to do. Back when her fears were worse, she'd only come out of her room upstairs to latch both hands onto the rail. Then only come down as far as the bottom of that rail. Never letting go. Like it was a lifeline that led back up to her room. Away from the world.

'Yes, he is,' I answer. But as I take a step towards her, she takes a step up the stairs. Keeping the distance. Like it hurts to get too close. I think back to how I hesitated at the door, looking at Pollo lying dead on that table until Angie held her hand out to me. I realise Eva has to choose this.

So I hold out my hand to her, hoping as I say, 'It is going to be okay.'

But Eva doesn't come to me.

Instead, tears brim in her eyes. She stifles a sob before fleeing up the stairs, back into her room, slamming the door on the way.

When I move to follow, Em lays a restraining hand on my shoulder and says quietly, 'Don't. She needs to be alone.'

'She needs us,' I answer, feeling frustrated, still

looking up at the closed door.

But as Em moves in front of me, I see her look up at me with a calmness and strength I don't feel.

'She needs us to understand what she needs. Now come on. You look terrible. Let's get you cleaned up,' Em says.

Things start getting hazy then.

With Em's help, I'm washed and shaved. My mind worn down to only being able to cope with these simple, robotic actions.

No thoughts, no feelings.

Grief, fever, pain, and medication stacked on top of several days of violence and almost no sleep has made everything numb and simple.

The last thing I do remember clearly is sitting down on the bed and catching sight of my reflection in the mirror and taking a moment to realise that it's me. Pale, with deep rings under my eyes. Stitches and bandages and a dappling of bruises. I look broken.

I'm sure we were talking but I can't remember what we said.

I don't know when I got in bed or when I fell asleep.

When I wake, it is from such a deep sleep that I have that perfect moment of peaceful disorientation. Where you have no idea where you are or how long you've been out or even what happened. Just right now you feel so warm and comfortable that you're sure everything must be okay and in a moment you're going to remember all the good things making you feel this way.

Then, piece by horrible piece, it all comes back to me. Dead priests. Pollo. Jones. Angie. Eva running to her room.

The clock shows it's 6:35 p.m.

I've been asleep for most of the day.

I'm sure that's due to Em, and probably Spyro, making sure nothing interrupts me.

A part of me really wants to go back to that warm place, but I can't.

Because things need doing.

I have a list.

First, I've got to see Eva.

Find a way to help her understand that the world is still worth it. Even though I don't feel it at the moment myself. I've got to talk to Angie again and also the boys. Be there for them now. Em, take care of her and not just be the patient she tries to put back together, but actually love her back. Then I've got to help Spyro. Four dead cops and three dead priests and the biggest, ugliest killing spree this city has seen and we still don't know why.

And then, once all these things are done, then, finally, I'm going to kill Jones Maihi.

★ ★ ★

7:38 p.m.

Eva's door is still closed but I knock anyway.

No answer, but I know she's in there. Em said she's been in there all day. Refusing to come out. Just like the old, bad days. Like what's happened today has disproved all the good things she's been cautiously hoping about the world beyond her door.

That's part of what makes this so difficult.

Because you can't lie to Eva. Even at age eleven. She fears the world so much that she takes any answers we give her about it with a deep sense of suspicion. Those answers are carefully considered and measured

162

against what she sees, what she fears. If they fail her tests and experience, she takes it very hard. Like she's been betrayed by our love for her. So we stopped trying to act like the world is perfect.

Now, when Eva asks questions — like all kids do — we try to give her honest answers. This is harder than it sounds. But we hope what comes across is our approximation of the truth; our truth, at least. That the world isn't always safe or good or kind but we're here in it together.

I take a breath, then open the door and take a step inside.

Eva is sitting by the window on the floor. Wrapped in a blanket. Telescope positioned up and out into the gloom of early night.

The sight gives me a glimmer of hope. She may have retreated all the way back up here, but at least she's still looking out. Like maybe there's still some good out there worth seeing.

'Hey, girl,' I say.

She pulls away from the telescope, looks over and replies, 'Hey, Dad.'

I make my way over to her and gingerly go to sit down on the bed close to her.

'Dad,' Eva says.

'Hmm?' I reply.

'Uncle Pollo . . . he's dead. But he's a good person. But he's dead anyway,' Eva states, as if she's trying to work through something that doesn't make sense.

'Sometimes good people die, Eva,' I say in a measured tone.

'But the bad guys? They got away?' she continues, already knowing the answer.

It's hard to give her the honest answer but I do.

'Yes, sometimes that happens too.'

'That's not fair!' Eva replies, and I see her eyes well up as she moves towards me.

I take her in my arms. It's some time later, once her tears have slowed and heavy silence clings to us, that she says, 'Good people die and bad people live. That's not okay, Dad.'

For some reason I think back to Pollo's last words to me. About how everything is just pancake money. I've got no immediate reply for Eva. Nothing to say that's hopeful and also real. Something good that I know with absolute certainty is true.

Because my young child is right. Good people die and bad people live. The more you see of the world, especially if you're a cop, the truer it becomes. It's not okay, but that doesn't stop it from happening.

But in this big, ugly world, right now I have my child in my arms and it fills me with a fierce determination as I say, 'I know, girl. You're right. Sometimes, good people live and good people die, bad people live and bad people die. Sometimes things are fair and sometimes they're not. The world isn't good or bad. It's both. It just is. But that's not what makes things okay or not. What makes things okay is us. Me and you and Mum and our friends and everyone. We are here together. It doesn't matter that sometimes bad things happen, because we have each other. That's what makes things okay.'

* * *

I'm downstairs again, filling up on painkillers in our bedroom, when Em comes up behind me. Looks at me in the mirror as she leans in the doorway.

'How is she?' Em asks.

'Okay, I think. We'll see in time,' I answer.

'And you?' she prompts.

'About the same,' I answer, then continue. 'Em. I'm sorry about all this. I'm sorry for bringing this to us. I know this isn't the life you chose, or want anymore. I'm sorry I haven't been willing to talk about it. Being a cop. The risks. This,' I say as I wave my hands around to take in everything around us.

'This isn't your fault. I don't blame you. I do want us to talk about things, but not now. Not this way. Later, okay?' Em says as she comes up behind me and I turn to her.

'Oh God, Pollo,' Em says into my chest, and I put my arms around her. Em and Eva cry in exactly the same way. It's a truly sad privilege to know a thing like that.

★　★　★

9:12 p.m.

I'm in the car, heading over to Pollo's house. Driving slowly.

I must have driven this road a thousand times. Only now the silence in the car aches next to me in Pollo's seat. I called ahead to check that it's okay to come over. Not sure what Angie and the boys need now. Not sure if they're with family. Angie's dad answered. He seemed unsure, but then Angie took the phone and said come. She said I'm family too. Makes it feel worse.

Despite what everyone says, despite the part of me that's a cop, a professional, I still carry the questions.

What if I'd been faster? What if I'd spotted Jones first? Tried for the gun sooner? What if? Something big enough and bad enough happens and I don't think there's a way out of the guilt. It's the price you pay for loving people when they die and you don't.

If I'm brutally honest, part of me unreasonably, irrationally blames Pollo too. For dying, for leaving me. We never said it, too much butch and bravado in our partnership, but he was my best friend. I loved him. If our positions had been reversed, I would have done the same for him.

It still doesn't change things. Because I'm not really heading over to Pollo's house. It's not his anymore.

When I arrive, it's to an unexpected community of people. Many more than I anticipated. There must be around thirty or so people in the house, with some out front, some out back. Like the grieving has become some sort of scattered, shared effort. Angie's Māori, and I remember Pollo joking about it once, saying, 'Births and deaths, Bobby; with the Māoris, they're team sports.'

From what I can tell, relatives from both sides of the family are here. Brothers and sisters and cousins. Every now and then I see an echo of Pollo. Here in a facial expression, there in a pair of hands, there in how someone moves. Like Pollo has been dissolved into all these people. It hurts, but in a good way.

Beyond a swirl of introductions and condolences, I'm suddenly ushered into Pollo's bedroom. As the door clicks closed behind me, Angie looks up from where she's sitting amongst a scattering of things on the bed. Pollo's things.

In here it even smells like him.

166

'Hi, Bobby,' Angie says, still calm, still kind.

'Hey, Angie,' I answer, and move to sit down next to her.

We both look down at the things between us on the bed. Some police gear, some photos, some papers.

'I was getting a few things ready for you,' Angie says. 'I thought maybe you'd be needing them. You know how Pollo gets when he's got a big case on.'

She said 'gets' not 'got,' like Pollo is still around. But then, in here, surrounded by his belongings, his smell, it's an easy thing.

'Thanks. It'll help. I'll take the gear and notes back to the station,' I say. Not wanting to admit that there's nothing useful here. Because we didn't have anything figured out. This case has been beyond us from the start. Too much. Too fast.

'There's also this,' Angie says as she reaches down beside the bed and brings up a shoebox marked 'Bobby.'

I recognise Pollo's handwriting and the world slows down.

When I open it, I see that it's about half-full of random objects. Notes, pictures, some bullet fragments in a little jar, an old key-chain, and so on.

It takes me a moment to realise they're all things from our past. Keepsakes. Mementoes. From our time together. Pollo kept all these things.

'I had no idea,' I say, finding it hard to match the tough cop I knew with this kind of sentimentality.

'We did,' Angie says. 'Pollo was always a big softy. Even though he tried to hide it. Couldn't help caring about people. They were all special to him. And good things that happened; he couldn't let them go. Kept little things to remind him.'

167

I think back now to when Pollo got drunk. The sad memories of his past he spoke about. Maybe he couldn't let the bad things go either.

The shoebox is heavy on my lap now as I turn to Angie again.

'Is there anything, anything you need?' I ask. Knowing how superficial it sounds.

'No, Bobby, it's okay,' Angie says, then hesitates as her calm falters.

'What is it?' I ask.

'You have a right to know,' Angie says slowly, 'but you shouldn't take this the wrong way. He loved you. Wanted what's best for you. That's why I'm telling you this.'

'Tell me,' I say quietly.

'He stayed for you. Because he loved you,' Angie says, taking my hand.

'We were talking about him getting a transfer out. No more street work. No more homicides. Please don't misunderstand me. Pollo was born to be a cop. Loved every minute of it. But the last few years it was getting harder on him. But he stayed on. He said you're not ready yet. That you have the makings to be a good cop but that you still needed time. He said he had a knowing about you,' Angie finishes and smiles at me sadly.

There are things I feel now that I don't know the words for. Different kinds of pain mixing and mingling until they coalesce into a simple need that brings me full circle.

I'm going to find the people behind this. All of it. And then I'm going to end them.

★ ★ ★

11:24 p.m.

It's close to midnight by the time I pull in to the station but I'm not surprised to find the place busy. Four dead cops. Everyone will have been pulled in for this. Whoever's behind this — Jones Maihi or Manga Kahu or whoever else — they should be worried.

Because we're just people.

And now someone has killed four of our own. Partners. Friends. Like the gangs, cops are like family, too.

Yes, we're here to serve and protect. Yes, we wear uniforms and call people sir and ma'am in calm, respectful tones. We have an Internal Affairs Department and cameras in our cars and interview rooms to guard against any possible police brutality. We even have to undergo mandatory rounds of sensitivity training and anger management courses.

But on the inside, we're still just like everyone else.

Now someone has hurt the people we care about. There's 200 of us here. We're trained. Armed. And angry.

Yeah, I'd be worried.

As I pull into my parking space I see a cordon around the main entrance with some uniform guys manning it. Even this late there are still journalists camped out. Trying to get the latest. It has been almost an entire day without anything bad happening. After all, I think ruefully, if you're in the media, this has been a very big week. Stunning drama and tragedy served up every morning. The ratings must be crazy.

To avoid all that, I decide to head for the side entrance instead but am still stopped short. She's not supposed to be in here. This is a restricted area. But that's the press for you. Leaning by the door is Becca

169

Patrick, Channel 3 News.

'Hi, Bobby,' she says as she recognises me and stubs out her cigarette against the wall. 'I need to talk to you.'

'You know you shouldn't be in here,' I say tiredly.

'Yeah, I know. They released the names earlier and, look, I just wanted to say I'm sorry about Detective Latu. He seemed like a good guy,' she says, and sounds sincere, her voice breaking.

It's only now that I notice Becca Patrick looks tired. Her eyes are red, like she's been crying. She doesn't look at all like she's been having the best media week on record. That, despite all the times I've seen her on the news leading exclusives on the 'Holy Man Killer' these past nights. This story could launch her career. Then other parts of my dulled cop brain start working. There are several cigarette butts on the ground by her feet. She's been here a while. How did she get in here? How has she managed to stay without someone escorting her out again immediately? There's cameras all around the station. They know she's here. Then the obvious finally comes to me.

'Who was it?' I ask, guessing.

'Danny. Danny Semper. It wasn't serious,' Becca says, trying to control her voice as she reaches for another cigarette. 'We've only been dating for a few months but . . . you know . . . I had my hopes.'

'Semper,' I echo. I hadn't known. I knew it was four cops. But beyond Pollo, I hadn't yet even thought to find out who the other three were. Semper. Young guy, friendly, easy-going. Maybe twenty-two years old. The last time I saw him was the beginning of the week when he was manning the cordon at Father Bern's house. No. I'm wrong, I realise now.

170

The last time I saw him was last night. He was one of the cops already dead by the gates of Tegere Servare. When we got there too late. Again.

'I'm sorry,' I say.

'Yeah. We all are,' Becca says, taking another deep drag on her cigarette. The silence between us has a certain intimacy now. Unchosen, unwanted, but there nonetheless.

'Look. There's a reason I'm here,' she continues. 'I didn't know what to do with this. So I thought I'd leave it to you to decide.' She looks uncomfortable now.

'Tell me,' I say.

'It's Alkaline Ben, he wants to see you. Out at the Spit at five this morning. Says you guys need to talk. He said he wants a sit-down with you. Only you. Private. Not official. No cops and no gangsters,' Becca says. Not meeting my eyes.

'How is it that you're the one telling me this? How are you connected to Alkaline Ben?' I ask. My suspicions rising.

The gangs have connections everywhere. They have money. And power. Which means they have ways of solving problems for people who have no alternatives. For a price, of course. A price you can't pay back with money. It's not only cops that can be dirty. But I hadn't pegged young Becca Patrick as someone involved with that world. Thought she was too young to owe people yet.

'I'm not, not really. About a year ago I was still only a researcher. I'd just started out with Channel 3 and I needed a break to get ahead. So I tried doing some of my own stories,' Becca says.

'And you thought you'd start by interviewing the

head of Manga Kahu?' I ask, shaking my head.

'It didn't go anywhere. I did meet him — waited for him, then went up to him at the Baldwin Pub and introduced myself. But I couldn't make anything of the answers he gave me. There was no story there,' she said. 'And it was scary. Ben . . . how he is.'

It must have been like when kids fall into the lion's den at the zoo by accident. Sometimes the lions are so surprised they actually don't eat you. Reporters.

'But — ' I say.

'But nothing. Like I said, that was a year ago. Then this morning, it was about eight when I got home. I'd been out most of the night doing camera shots on everything that happened at Tegere Servare . . . I didn't know about Danny yet. Anyway, I get home and he's right there. Waiting by my door. Alone,' Becca says, sounding scared at the memory.

'He knew where I lived. Knew where I'd been. Knew I knew you guys. I don't know how. Told me to come see you right away. Today. Not to call. No messages. Nothing written down. Just me,' Becca finishes.

He wouldn't have threatened her. Not Ben. He wouldn't have needed to. Knew she would have had a year to learn how things work here. Alkaline Ben may be bad down to his evil bones but he's not dumb. Knew she'd do as she's told. Becca hasn't figured it out yet, but he chose her because of Danny. Which means he knew about her and Danny. Knew we'd go easy on her because of Danny dying. Like letting her stay at the station to see me if she said she wanted to. Which means he knew she'd be getting the news today. Which means he knew Danny was dead before she did. That's how Ben works.

'And you did it,' I say, then pause to lean down next

to her tiredly. Thinking that's how it starts. She has no idea what people like Ben are capable of.

'Becca. When this is over, you should leave town. Maybe even the country. I mean it,' I say. But she just looks at me. Maybe Danny dying has taken her like Pollo's death has taken me. Can't think beyond what needs doing right now.

'What happens now?' Becca asks.

I can see the hints of stubborn hope fighting fear in her expression; anger there too. Like maybe she thinks there's something we can do. Somehow the police will keep her safe. Put an end to all this. Go and arrest Ben and put him away, despite the fact that he's broken no laws. Despite the fact that she sought him out first, however innocently.

It happens a lot.

People think about cops that way. Like we should make things better. Stop things getting worse. They don't get it. That's not how it works. We don't stop things. We don't make things better. We show up once the bad things have already happened. Too late. After the fact. Not before. We can't change anything.

But I do have a choice to make.

I could do things by the book. Take Becca Patrick inside. Have Spyro and every cop in Operation Spear know that Alkaline Ben says he wants a sit-down with me only. I could go in with every kind of backup available. The risk is that Ben finds out and doesn't tell me anything. He knew about Danny already. Before the press release even. It's entirely possible that he's got cops passing on information.

My other choice is to not tell anyone.

Take Alkaline Ben at his word. Believe that he used Becca instead of any of his underlings because he

173

really wants to talk unofficially. To me. Without any cops or Manga Kahu's people knowing. The risk here is that I'm wrong and give Manga Kahu the chance to kill another cop. They don't know what we know or what we don't. Maybe they think we've figured more out than we have. Or maybe this is about last night. They lost people too. Alkaline Ben has family in Manga Kahu too.

I really wish Pollo was here.

'I don't know what I'm going to do,' I say at last as I look over at Becca.

'You should get away from this. Leave town. Today. We don't know how bad this is. Or who's behind it. And you're in it now. You're not safe,' I continue. But she doesn't meet my eyes. Doesn't answer. Starts walking away without looking back.

She's like me now, I think. We've already lost too much to let go.

As I watch her leave, I lower myself painfully down to sit with my back against the station. Too tired to go in yet. Too tired to think straight.

Grief is a kind of craziness, I think. It can get you to where things don't make sense anymore. Lose enough things you care about and you reach a point where you don't care if you lose it all. Where the pain from what you've lost outweighs the fear of the pain of what you still have left to lose.

I remember Pollo telling me something like that once.

It was after a bad crime scene. And too much drinking.

He said enough bad things just makes you crazy. Every time. No matter if it's anger or hate or fear or lust or jealousy or grief. Whatever. Eventually enough

174

badness makes you crazy. I remember asking him what he meant by crazy and how he answered:

'This isn't book crazy like in all your classes. It's the real crazy underneath all that shit. It's when you stop believing any kind of goodness can actually be had in this world. You reach that point and there's nothing you wouldn't do anymore. Not a god-fucking-damned thing.'

Maybe that's what this week has been about. Every day. Every new crime scene. Another old man dying in another sick way. Someone out there has truly stopped believing anything good is possible in the world.

And now they are so very horribly free.

When I finally head into the station, I know what I'm going to do.

It's what I was always going to do.

FRIDAY . . .

12:03 a.m.

Things feel different in the station. It's still chaotic, still busy.

Everyone doing what needs. But the cops I see look blank. Efficient and polite, but not too human. There's no banter, no insults flying around, no one yelling at someone. There's a look being passed around from cop to cop though. Four of us in one night.

'Bobby. In here,' Spyro says from his office doorway as I head by.

'Sit,' he commands as I enter.

'You know what I have to say,' Spyro says as he leans back against his desk.

'I know. How much time can you give me?' I answer, looking at him.

He means that I shouldn't be here. That policy dictates I be taken off the case and put on health leave pending assessment. That the regulations state I need to talk to a counsellor now. Not work. Not have a gun. Risk management and health and safety and human resources protocols. Because of too much badness.

I hold his stare for a moment, then he says, 'I'll push out the meetings until Monday, which is the next time I'll officially roster you on. That's the best I can do. We'll say you came in now and asked for the time. Beyond that, it's the rules. Okay?' Spyro says.

'Okay,' I answer. That gives me three days.

'We turn up anything new?' I ask.

I know there'll be tons on file by now. The worse this gets, the more cops are pulled in and the more paperwork is created. The vast majority of which will be completely useless. But like Carol, Spyro has the kind of mind that can burn through all that and retain exactly and only what's actually useful.

'Not much. The pair you picked up at the Baldwin has come back as prospects for Manga Kahu. Forensics are still working out at Tegere Servare. We'll maybe get something more from the DNA workups but it'll take time. Of the three dead we've got positive ID on two so far. Patched Manga Kahu lifers, both. The last will likely be the same, going by the prison tattoos. Weapon traces will be done by tonight but it won't give us much. We're working on ID kits for the rest of the shooters but there's not much to go on beyond the positive ID on Jones Maihi,' Spyro says.

'Anything on motive?' I ask, but I already know Spyro would have mentioned it first if we had anything.

'Nothing. The theories are multiplying by the minute, though. This is a media nightmare. Gangsters killing priests. A secret Catholic retreat for paedophile clergy. Gunfights in the night. And the speed of it all,' Spyro finishes, shaking his head.

'Yeah,' I agree.

'Why did you head out there again?' Spyro asks.

'We wanted to interview Father Black again. Maybe talk to some of the others more,' I answer.

'You had something?' Spyro checks.

'No. But we figured the motive has to be out there. Maybe it's about Tegere Servare. Maybe about those four priests. Either way, we were out of leads, we thought it was the best place to start again,' I answer.

Somehow all that feels like a really long time ago.

'Anything else?' Spyro asks.

'No,' I reply, rubbing my eyes, wondering what I should do next.

'It doesn't get better, you know,' Spyro says then. It's such an unusually negative thing for him to say that it takes me by surprise.

'What?' I ask.

'Life. This. Everything that's happened. It doesn't get any better,' Spyro answers as he looks me in the eye.

'There are times like these, and if you live long enough, what happens is you see them come round again. What gets better is you. You get stronger. You learn to deal with it. This time makes you better for next time,' Spyro says, then after a pause continues in a more official tone, 'Okay. You're off roster as of now. You've got an hour to do what you need to in here, then you need to be out of the station.'

I had thought to see what Carol has come up with but she's off roster too.

Unsurprising, as it's somewhere after midnight and she's likely been here for more than a day. Most of us who weren't already on shift would have been pulled in once word got out, and Spyro would have started sending people home once they've done a double shift. Mandatory after you pull a triple. Which I'm sure a lot of cops will have done after this.

After checking in with the Operation Spear guys and going over it all again, I'm unsure what's next.

So without intending to I end up at my office, which is cold and dark.

I make my way to my chair without turning the light on and just sit there, aching quietly for a moment.

I need to be a cop about this.

This can't be about Jones Maihi for me now.

This can't be about Pollo.

A few days ago, someone started killing people and they haven't stopped.

We know Manga Kahu is involved. But we still don't know the motive. Or who's really behind it all.

There's an old cop saying that goes, 'The Method and The Motive gets you The Man.'

Meaning if you can figure out how it was done and why it was done, it will lead you to who did it.

Thinking of it that way means we may not have the man yet. Maybe Jones Maihi and the rest of Manga Kahu are just the method.

I have a hard time picturing a bunch of gangsters torturing old priests, but that's because I can't see why they would want to. I have no doubt that they are capable of it.

So if Manga Kahu are the method, then maybe Alkaline Ben is the man.

Alkaline Ben who wants to see me.

Out at the Spit at five a.m.

The Spit is a thin strip of coast pushing out from Aramoana Beach between the open ocean and the Dunedin Harbour. It's remote and quiet, no witnesses.

I'm going to need a new vest, I think. And more bullets.

★ ★ ★

3:07 a.m.

I'm walking on a hillside near the coast. It's sunrise, a prism of hues breaking across the sky, glowingly

179

beautifully. I really want to take it all in but I can't. I have to keep watching my step, as there are deep holes everywhere. Someone's been digging. I can't quite place where I am but it feels familiar. Familiar, but not good. Like the place itself doesn't want me here. All the upturned soil is pushing me to leave. Then I wake with a start in my chair.

The jolt hurts my ribs. I hadn't meant to fall asleep in my office. I was planning on going home before my meeting with Alkaline Ben.

I dry swallow some pain pills and look blearily about my office as I turn on the light. Worried that sitting in the dark will make me fall asleep again.

There's a stack of new paperwork on my desk and I see that my answering machine is blinking.

I ignore the paperwork, as I've already spoken to Spyro and the Spear guys, and check my messages instead. Distractedly thinking that I'd better call Em and Eva.

There's only one message and I recognise Professor Bowlby's voice immediately: 'Mr Ress. This is Ann Bowlby. We need to talk. I was wrong. I — '

After the message cuts out, the machine informs me that it was recorded less than an hour ago. The phone hadn't even woken me and I was sitting right next to it.

There's no good reason for Professor Bowlby to be calling me at two in the morning so I dial her back immediately, but the phone gives a busy signal.

I'm about to try a third time when my office door opens and Spyro walks in.

He's got a look on his face.

It's a look I've only ever seen cops get.

Those who have been around for a while.

And with an increasing heaviness pressing on my chest I think, not even for the second or third time, that this has been such a very, very long week.

'A uniform team on protection detail out in Roslyn called this in. House fire. Fire Department is out there checking for cause now. Looks like a gas leak in the kitchen. One fatality. Positive ID on Ann Mary Bowlby. The pre-lim puts TOD at between one and two hours ago. Looks like smoke inhalation. She was on special protection as one of the staff from Tegere Servare. I — ' Spyro stops when he sees my expression and after a short pause looks down at my desk. There's a reason Spyro is a captain, I think, as he immediately puts it all together, sighs, and says, 'Play it.'

So I cue the answering machine on speaker and we listen to Ann Bowlby's message again: 'Mr Ress. This is Ann Bowlby. We need to talk. I was wrong. I — '

It's likely to be one of the very last things she did.

And I was sitting right here, asleep.

After a pause Spyro says, 'I saw your light click on and figured you must have fallen asleep in here. Happens a lot. I have too many good cops working for me.'

'Did they even try and make it look like an accident?' I ask.

'Bobby. No. Stop. You're going to get up and go home. I only came in here to tell you now so that when you heard at home you wouldn't come back in again,' Spyro says.

I'm about to reply when Spyro holds up his hand and cuts me off. 'No, Bobby. You can't be here. You know how this goes.'

And I do.

So I simply nod. Stand up and go, saying, 'I know. Sorry, Captain.'

I leave a note for Carol on her keyboard on the way out.

Before I leave the building I visit the armoury and sign out a new vest and some extra clips of ammo. Judging by all the empty shelves and bare gun racks in here, it's going to be an interesting weekend doing crime in this city.

I figure I have enough time to stop by the house before heading out to Aramoana. Out of habit, I follow my quiet routine. Cops do shift work, so both you and your family devise ways for you to come and go at odd hours without waking everyone up.

I've tiptoed halfway across the kitchen, shoes in one hand, keys closed in my other fist to guard against noise, when the lights flick on.

'Hey, Dad,' Eva says from next to the door. She's wearing pyjamas but she doesn't look like she's been sleeping.

'Hey, girl,' I say, feeling relieved to see her outside her room again. Part of me has been worried that all this has scared her all the way back up there. All her fears justified.

'You two think you can hold out on me?' I hear Em say as she comes up behind Eva. She at least looks like she's just woken up.

'What?' I say.

'Don't try and talk your way out of this one, copper,' Em replies with a tired smile as she comes and kisses me on my still confused cheek.

'Spyro called,' Em adds by way of explanation.

'You're breaking eggs, Dad,' Eva says as she heads over to the kitchen table.

It's only now that I see all the bowls and ingredients laid out.

I realise with a bittersweet pang that we're making pancakes.

Following the old routine.

It used to be a family tradition. Back when I was still a uniform cop and Eva was younger. We were all still getting used to my shift work irregularity and to Eva's challenges. The two didn't mesh. Sameness, routine, familiarity — these were the things Eva wanted to make her feel safe. Change, new things, and the outside world all scared her. My being a part of that world, not following a set, predictable pattern scared her even more. Like I was being taken over by the other side. So Em had come up with the 'Midnight Pancake Plan' as she called it. It worked too. For a few years there we met the unpredictability of my work life with the set, familiar response of making pancakes whenever I got home. No matter what time it was. The three of us together.

For a while, as we go through the old familiar movements and small words, every unhappy thing outside this kitchen ceases to exist.

On purpose or not, no one mentions the world beyond the three of us here. Kind laughter over little things. I feel a sense of peace fill me that's almost searing in my chest, unwelcome there amongst all the badness.

Towards the end, as Eva tastes the first floppy, misshapen pancake, my mind starts working again.

I realise now that there is an impossibility to all this, to me, to people. Something beyond what I can understand. How can we be this way? How can I be here like this with my wife and child? Be filled with nothing but kindness and hope and love so much so that an overwhelming sense of gratitude spills over everything I experience.

How can I have all this?

Feel everything here and not be changed by it?

Be a part of all this goodness, all this love, and still know?

Calmly, rationally, know that soon, somehow, despite all this, I'm going to leave here, walk out into the world, and kill Jones Maihi.

★   ★   ★

The drive to Aramoana Beach is pretty in the promise of the pre-dawn light.

The coast and the mountains still look clean and perfect. Doesn't seem right that it be used for a meeting with Alkaline Ben.

Em helped me fit my new bulletproof vest at home. Too tight against my bruised chest but I didn't mention it. She watched me load my Glock and my backup gun. Didn't say an unkind word. Not even with her eyes. I know I don't deserve her; her or Eva. It makes me wonder if anyone does. Does Alkaline Ben ever think this? Does Jones Maihi?

As I park I look around, but everything seems deserted.

I walk along the beach, keeping to the hard sand. I'm still unused to walking around with guns like this. My standard service Glock is in one hand, inside my coat pocket. The other hand I keep close to my side. Near the holster of my backup, a S&W 500. The largest revolver Smith & Wesson makes. Most cops prefer a smaller handgun for a backup. Something light and compact. Easy to carry and hide. But I follow the Pollo school of thought, which is that if things actually get so bad that you've already emptied your Glock and you still need a gun, then you're probably going to want it to be a big one.

I can spot a few ship lights miles out on the ocean but that's it. Nobody out here. No witnesses. Occasionally I pass a resting sea lion. They chuff threateningly with bared teeth. No sign of Alkaline Ben.

Walking out here armed like this makes me think of the history of this place.

A Māori chief used to live out here, Pollo told me about it. Long ago all of this — the land, the mountains, the sea — it all belonged to the Māori. Or as they put it — it belonged to them and they belonged to it. Then the Europeans came and wanted to have it. The Māori chief agreed. Although his sons said afterwards that what the white people wanted was ownership and what the chief wanted to give them was belonging. But, as Pollo put it, 'In the end that didn't matter, because the white guys had more guns.'

Pollo used to toast to the chief at the pub. Sometimes, when he was really drunk, he'd even play him a tribute song on the jukebox. It was 'The Man Who Sold The World' by Nirvana.

When I reach the end of the Spit I stop and scan around. Nothing more than a teardrop thickening of beach with a few wind-worn trees. I wait. But not for long.

Almost immediately I can hear someone whistling close by and turn to see an old man wrapped in a bright, flower-patterned blanket walking over. For the second time this week it takes me a while to recognise

185

the tune he's whistling. It's creepy when I realise that it is 'Amazing Grace' again.

I see him casually walk within arm's length of a big sea lion but it just looks at him placidly as he passes.

When he sees me looking at the sea lion he smiles and says, 'Don't worry. It's not magic. Just tricks.'

Alkaline Ben is old and thin.

You can tell that he used to be a big man. His frame still has the memory of strength in its shape. He moves easily. Still looks dangerous. Like he's become harder with age, like old wood.

He comes to stand next to me, too close, then stretches and yawns loudly before settling his blanket around him again. He looks comfortable, relaxed. Like this meeting is a friendly happenstance.

'Detective Ress,' he says by way of greeting, then looks out at the ocean before he continues. 'I'm truly sorry to hear about Pollo. We'll sing for him for many nights.'

'You're sorry,' I echo in a flat tone.

Finding it hard to control the flare of anger.

Ben must sense my emotion because he turns to me and I'm surprised to see tears brimming in his eyes. He smiles when he says in a gentle tone, 'I can see you want this to be simple. Good cops. Bad gangsters. But the truth is, I liked Pollo. I like his family. They're good people. He was a good, hard man. I'll miss him, despite the choices he made. Maybe even because of them, if I'm honest.'

'Which are?' I ask.

'You, of course,' Ben answers in that same calm voice. 'Pollo chose the law above his own blood, above his people. That's no small thing to us.'

As the silence between us lingers, I bring myself

186

back under control and remind myself why I'm here.

'You asked to see me, Ben,' I prompt.

'And you came. Alone. No backup. Nothing. Tell me; do you know already what needs to be done? Is that why you came? Or is it just the grief that drove you here unknowing?' Ben asks, looking at me closely.

That's the second thing about Alkaline Ben people never get. He's not what you expect. Even when you know him. Even when you expect him. There's always more to him than you think. Even when you're sure.

You could know that just by remembering he's the leader of Manga Kahu and has been for a very long time. A group of the meanest, toughest, most disciplined criminals in the country. Generations of them, in fact.

He pulls you in with how he is.

There's a humanness to him, a vulnerable kind of charisma.

It can almost make you forget the first thing about Alkaline Ben.

Which is that he is completely, unashamedly, savagely evil.

'I wish I could understand what it all means,' Ben says, sounding contemplative, turning away from me and staring out at the sea. 'You. Pollo. Jones. I can see how love and hate move you. How fiercely it burns you. I was like that once. Long ago. Maybe that's what getting old means. You lose that. Enough love and hate wears you away.'

I have no answer to this so just stare at him until finally Ben sighs and says, 'I know why you are here, Bobby Ress. I've watched you and Pollo over the years. I saw how you were . . . you came because you want to kill Jones Maihi. And I'm going to help you.'

'You, Ben, are going to help me kill Jones Maihi, your own man?' I ask.

Not really sure where any of this is going.

The notoriously careful Alkaline Ben shouldn't be anywhere near this conversation. Given the context of what's happened this week, who he is, plus who he's talking to, this is dangerously close to conspiracy to murder. Second, why would Ben be interested in having Jones killed at all?

If he's trying to draw me in, trying to trick or trap me with the promise of offering me Jones Maihi, then what's the angle? Killing me is easy enough without this. He could have that done without putting himself at risk like he is. Or is it entrapment? Have me try to kill Jones and fail in order to get something incriminating to hold over me? But then what use is another dirty cop to Ben, and again, why risk so much to try and get one? So what then? I wonder. But all I can come up with is maybes.

Maybe Ben does actually want Jones dead. For whatever reason.

Maybe it's tied to everything that's happened. Which I still don't understand. Maybe it's not. The problem for Ben is that Jones Maihi is a patched lifer, gang member, cradle to grave, and so is his family. There's generations of Maihis who have lived and died for Manga Kahu. Not even Ben would survive that. So maybe he finds a cop to do it. After Pollo, I'm the perfect choice. No fingers would point to Ben. There's enough cover there for me to turn it from murder into a justifiable killing. Ben finds a way to put Jones Maihi in front of me. Jones Maihi, presumed armed and dangerous, who this week has had a hand in killing four cops. There wouldn't even be an investigation.

And I know, I don't like to, but I know, if given the chance, I would. If Jones was here right now, nothing would stop me. I wouldn't care if it was called murder. Because part of me is still out there on that railway track watching Pollo's face change as he dies. Like it followed me home.

There's a strange peace in that knowledge. I'm still me. Despite all this. Despite Pollo. I still love my wife, my daughter. I still believe in goodness. In God. I still believe in right and wrong. I believe in the law. I know, in time, things will get better and life will go on after everything is over. But this, this has become something I am now.

But what if there's more?

Maybe Ben has figured all of this out already. Maybe having me kill Jones or try to kill Jones is a way of making sure the rest stays hidden. We still don't know the why of any of this. Or for that matter, who's behind it all. So much of this has become about Pollo for me but it's not where it started or why, and it's not where it will end. It could even be Ben himself behind all this for all I know. Maybe this is him getting all the loose ends to tie each other up.

'Why do you want this, Ben?' I ask tiredly.

'Bah. Come now, Bobby,' Ben replies. 'You know there's nothing I could possibly say that you're going to believe.'

He's right, I think, but persist anyway. The cop in me has to.

'Tell me why we're here. What do you know? What's going on? The murders. Tegere Servare. Us, here and now. Why?' I ask. I ask, because I know that Ben is among the best kind of liars. And the best kind always mix their lies with just enough truth to make them taste right. That's still more than I have now.

Ben is silent for a moment then says, 'Very well, Bobby. I'll tell you what I know. It won't be enough for you. It's just enough to know what needs to be done, but not enough to know why.'

That sums up this whole case, this whole week, I think.

'It happened at the funeral. I'm certain. There was nothing before,' Ben says, and it takes me a moment to realise he's talking about Jones Maihi's son. The funeral Jones went to where he escaped. I'm not surprised. I realise now that I've somehow already figured this out over the past day without consciously recognising it. I didn't know it then. Didn't realise it until it was too late. Too late. Not until that night on the railroad tracks when Jones came up behind me.

That funeral was the beginning.

At least one beginning.

'I've known Jones his whole life. Grew up with his father. Listened to his grandfather tell us stories as kids. I know the Maihis. They don't hide themselves. I don't think they could if they tried. It's not their way. It happened right there. The funeral started it. Jones was there. Only been there a while. We spoke. He was sad, had a lot of hurt, as you'd expect from a father who loses a son that young. Then he's over by the coffin. Looking down at the boy. Nothing strange. I was looking over at him. That's when it happened. I've seen that change come over men a few times. I knew before he turned that it was going to be bad. Told the others to stay out of it. There's no stopping men when they get like that. It has to run its course. And truth be told, I didn't want to stop him either. Jones deserved that. Sometimes a man can be pushed beyond the rage in himself and then he has to fight. It can break a man's spirit if you stop that anger coming out.'

What Ben is saying feels uncomfortably true, and I can't help thinking back to attacking Jones after he shot Pollo. There was something unstoppable in me then. Something beyond reason and right.

'So Jones attacks the guards and escapes. Why?' I ask.

'I honestly don't know. We followed him outside. I tried to get him to stop. Find out what was going on but he just left. He wasn't running either. This wasn't only about escaping from prison. That anger was still on him. Going through those guards like that, that was just the start. Jones had something driving him. You could see he wasn't done. Some of his family went with him. The rest of us stayed and waited. We knew there would be more trouble with the law coming. Then the old women said we had to finish the funeral. They were scared then. Said we needed to lay the boy to rest. Worried about the spirits and the badness we brought to that place. Scared that the spirits would want more death now. So we finished it. Put the boy in the ground without his father there. It felt wrong to me, doing it that way. But people were scared and the old women had the knowing. But still.'

'What then?' I ask. Already thinking, what now?

If what Ben is saying is true — or what he's decided to tell me is true — or has some parts of half-truths mixed in, then there's nothing useful here. Nothing that gets me closer to knowing why.

'Then Jones goes rogue. I know he's pulled in some family and some of his brothers in Manga Kahu, but no one knows why. He's after someone, I'm sure. But I don't know who and don't know why. And all these priests, the way they were killed. Jones could do it, but I don't know if he did. Why? Why in these ways? What I do know is he's not done because he hasn't come back yet. We're his people. He'll come back to us when he's finished this,' Ben says with a calm certainty.

'You're not giving me anything, Ben. If what you're saying is true, then you don't know what's happening or why, and you don't know who's behind it. Why are we here? Why are you offering me Jones Maihi if you know nothing?' I reply, shaking my head.

'Because of Tegere Servare, because . . . of what he did there,' Ben answers, and I'm again surprised to hear the emotion waver his voice to the point of breaking.

No one lies this well, I think.

I decide then that Ben is either a spectacularly good liar or a bit crazed or both. But something. Maybe like truly dangerous leaders, he has the ability to actually believe the lies he tells himself.

It takes him a moment to calm himself before he continues, 'I don't know a lot of things, but I do know the most important thing. The most important thing is our people. Our family. Our blood. Whatever is driving Jones has now cost us the lives of many good men. Even after the earlier killings I could have understood it all if there was justice in it. But after what happened out at that place, Jones has still not come back to us. Many of our people lie dead and Jones doesn't come. Which means he's not done. Which means he believes what he has to do is more important than our people. He went out there and good men followed him. His brothers, his blood. He has sacrificed them for what he wants. He has put himself above the people. In that, I cannot stand behind him,' Ben says.

That answer may have some truth in it, I think to myself.

Maybe he means it. Maybe he doesn't.

If you remove the noble overtones and remember that Alkaline Ben is outright evil, then maybe that translates into him being concerned about a powerful rival in Manga Kahu getting too many of them killed. Regardless of the reasons behind it, or whether Ben actually knows them or not. Manga Kahu can only stand to lose so many men. The amount of attention from the police because of this is going to be bad for them too. Maybe hard enough times will make people reconsider whether Alkaline Ben is still the best choice of leader. Maybe Ben knows this. Maybe, like me, part of him has stopped caring about figuring it all out and just wants Jones Maihi dead.

Or it could be real. Jones may be evil, but he's also Māori. High born, pureblood, son of chief's line. The Māori do follow a different way of life, and family is central to it. I know Alkaline Ben cares nothing for the law and thinks of right and wrong only in terms of what's best for him. But does that mean he thinks that way about his family? Again, he's led Manga Kahu for a long time. A group that exists wholly within the tribes. Would the Māori men and women who follow him have done so for so long if Ben did not believe in family the way they do? Did not put the people first?

This makes me think of what Pollo said to me on that last ride in to Tegere Servare. About how people can think very differently about family and what it means.

Family and blood. They're just words on the outside. We like to think that those things carry a lot of weight for people — that they feel almost holy and wrapped up in love and importance, but things aren't really like that. For some it doesn't really mean shit. There are people out there who don't really love their kids. Don't even like them. Same with their partners and families, even husbands and wives. Everybody still plays along at Christmas and birthdays and so on, but it's not real. The people involved, they know. Deep down, it's empty. They're just using each other to make their own lives easier. Doing this because nothing better has come up.

What if that's Alkaline Ben? Someone who cares nothing at all for family but is smart enough to exploit that love as a weakness in other people? But in the end, I come up empty. No certainties to be had. And I'm here because there is nowhere else to go. No other way to get further.

So I add these questions to the already too-long list. Another small weight piled on top of the aching mix of grief and tiredness swilling around in my head. Every question leading to more questions. But one of them still comes back to the fore of its own accord. I don't know if it's the most important, but it is definitely the most personal.

'So where's Jones Maihi?' I ask.

'I don't know yet, but I will soon,' Ben answers.

'How?' I ask.

'The funerals. Nobody's been willing to tell me what's happening. Or where Jones and the others are. But that was before, when it was the leader of Manga

194

Kahu asking. No one dead yet but one sad boy by his own hands. Now there's many of us dead. And people know it's because of Jones. Some are in the Maihi family and some not. All the families will be coming together for the burials. There will be a lot of pain. The people will want answers then. And I'll know,' Ben answers.

'And then you'll give me Jones?' I ask. Still unconvinced. Again Ben looks over at me and smiles that too-calm, too-kind smile through a spasm of sadness.

'Then we'll finish this, yes,' Ben says, nodding slowly. 'Because we have to. Because people can't live like this. We can all of us do wonderful and horrible things. Sometimes we can even do both at the same time. But then it has to end. It has to be over. Think about it. How do we go on after this? If it turns out that Jones killed those priests that way? And led his brothers to their deaths like that? No, there's no going back for us now. I love Jones Maihi, I honestly do. But he can never be among us again. Can't come back. This kind of badness only ever births more. It has to end. Jones has chosen this and now he can never come back. That's not how life works.'

I see tears shine down Ben's face as he looks out at the ocean, realising that he's right, it's true for all of us now. Not only for the dead. After everything that's happened and because of how bad it was. None of us can go back now.

'When do the funerals start?' I ask, realising what needs to happen next.

'The families have already started gathering. The extended relatives have started arriving. It'll be a few days of that, then the actual rituals start. The funerals as a whole will take a few days,' Ben says, and looks at me expectantly.

'And everyone goes to them, don't they? They all stay together there, eat there and sleep there, right? Until it's all over,' I continue.

'Yes, mostly,' Ben answers evenly.

'Where are these funerals going to be?' I ask. 'You said the men that have been with Jones are close to him, his family. Are any of the funerals going to be out on their lands?'

'No,' Ben answers.

'You're sure?' I ask. But something in the calm way Ben answers my questions makes me realise he's ahead of me, has already worked it out.

'Yes, I'm sure,' Ben answers.

'You already know what I want to do, don't you?' I say then.

'I know because that's what Pollo would have done,' Ben answers, and he looks his old evil self again when he adds, 'The shovel is already in my car.'

Because we're going to dig up the grave of Jones Maihi's son.

* * *

7:48 a.m.

I left Alkaline Ben behind on the beach, sitting in the sand singing some sad gospel song, a sense of complete peace surrounding him. Sane isn't the same as good and insane isn't the same as evil but I'm beginning to get the inkling that Ben may be both.

I was uneasy with turning my back on him, my skin tingling all the way to the car.

We agreed to meet up again at one thirty this afternoon.

To take what Ben called 'the Māori way' onto the lands where the Maihis live.

This means walking out along the coast and then following bush tracks and streams up to the house. No cars, no roads, good cover. The trip should take about three hours and allow us to be there long enough to scout things out before we go out to the family graveyard. If we time it right, we should be ready just after sunset.

Better to dig up a grave in the dark.

We could have gone straight there now and risked it. But I need the time. Things I need to do first. As I head back into the city, exhaustion and the automatic movements of driving idle my thinking into pointless things.

Grave robbing. I wonder whose offence will be bigger. This will be me breaking the law. And it will be Alkaline Ben breaking a taboo in Māori culture. If we're caught I will be branded a criminal. But Ben will be branded 'unclean' by the Māori. I wonder which is worse.

I already know I'm going to do it. And do it illegally; no warrant, no backup. Not as a cop. Because I need to know. If there is something in there that's worth seeing, worth knowing, I have to.

It has to be illegally now too. Because of Alkaline Ben.

His involvement means I can't do this as a cop anymore.

How did Alkaline Ben know which cops were dead out at Tegere Servare so fast?

He got to Becca Patrick before she even knew, only

hours after it happened. The bodies hadn't even been moved yet from the scene. So someone talked. The patients at Tegere Servare don't have contact with the outside world, and the staff would have to know Danny Semper by name and have a contact in Manga Kahu to get word to Alkaline Ben — and actually have a reason. No. Odds are that someone who talked was a cop.

If I go back to Operation Spear with what I want to do now, there will have to be a warrant issued. You can't just dig up a grave on a hunch. A lot of people will have to know. Agreements reached. Based on admissible evidence. What happens if someone along the way talks again?

What happens if Jones Maihi hears of it before we get there? Or someone else? I can't risk losing that lead, however slim it may be.

The cop in me can't help being sceptical though. Jones Maihi's son committed suicide. I read the report. Young, twelve years old, death by hanging. Did it in his room. Locked from the inside. As with all suicide cases, there was a mandated police investigation, which included scene work, full forensics, and an autopsy.

If there was any clue or evidence of foul play it would have been picked up. It seemed nothing other than a tragic death. Unusual for one so young, but simple and clear.

But what if someone did kill the boy? Could that be what's behind all this? Is Jones Maihi taking revenge? And if so, why against all these old priests? Why all the torture? Why against Ann Bowlby? Even if that is what's behind this, what did Jones see in that coffin to set him off? If it wasn't anything about the body, then what?

If Alkaline Ben was honest, at least in that part, then for Jones it started when he looked at his son right there.

How could Jones be the only one to see it? It was an open casket funeral. Plenty of family and friends there looking at the boy one last time. Yet only Jones sees it. It's possible that I won't see it either. But I can't let the chance go.

So it will have to be tonight, and it will have to be with Alkaline Ben. Literally my new partner in crime.

Then there's Ann Bowlby.

Another person I knew who is now dead. Emotionally, I don't feel anything about that yet. I haven't processed it. No time and no mind left for it. Just another fact. She only died a few hours ago. On top of everyone else dying. The captain said it looked like a gas leak led to a house fire, but after this week that's simply unbelievable. But more importantly, why her, why now, and why like this?

Her death changes things.

I didn't realise it when the captain told me a few hours ago but again, somewhere between then and now, my brain has done some thinking on its own while I was busy with other things. And what it has figured out is slowly seeping into my conscious thoughts.

If these killings have been about Tegere Servare, then it's conceivable that Ann could be a target too. She worked there along with the other victims, but that's where the similarities end.

Ann Bowlby wasn't a priest. She didn't found the place like the others and her murder doesn't fit. No torture and no archaic method of execution related to obscure Church history.

I remember the words of her message exactly. 'I was wrong. I — '

So Ann Bowlby figured something out. Something that she initially considered and then reconsidered later. Because something changed.

What she realised was important enough to call me in the middle of the night. Which makes it likely that this was when she did the figuring. Ann Bowlby was a very smart woman. Understood things about the sickness and insanity of humanity that goes well beyond the norm. So what did she find?

Was that why she was worth killing now?

If she was always part of the killer's plan, always on the list of people who had to die, then why spare her the gruesome torture and ritual murder the others got?

Or did she force the killer's hand somehow? Did she see or hear something incriminating? Something that the killer knew she could or would figure out. Maybe killing her wasn't part of the original plan but became necessary now? No time to do anything more elaborate. Maybe the killer made a mistake?

Conjecture and thin reasoning. Must be something there though. I need to know what Ann figured out, but I can't see a way to get there. It's a very slim hope. Another one to go with digging up a grave.

I'm almost in the city, still lost in thought, when I register a 1210 code repeated as an all-units call from dispatch. I have my police radio on out of habit but mostly don't even hear the chatter anymore. I don't even know how long it's been repeating that code.

All-units calls, which go out to everyone on duty, are unusual. And always bad.

A 1210 is a kidnapping.

As I reach for the radio I already know it's going to be worse and it's going to be about this case.

'Dispatch, this is Car 22. Detail all-units 1210 code. Over,' I say, hoping that with Dispatch being a busy place, no one notices me calling in when I'm supposed to be on leave.

'That you, Bobby?' I hear a familiar voice reply. Damn.

'Hey, Carol, why're you on dispatch?' I say.

'Spelling people on double shifts,' Carol replies, 'and you're not supposed to be working at all. Yeah?'

'Yeah,' I answer, but say nothing else.

Then after a pause, Carol must have come to a decision and tells me, 'The 1210 is for Liam Tull. He's gone. Happened about an hour ago. He was at Father Corcoran's office here in the city. Making arrangements for the funerals. Two uniforms with him at the church from Operation Spear as protection detail. One was out at the squad car when the other one got knocked unconscious in the church. He came to and Liam Tull was missing. Signs of a struggle, some blood. We have a witness in the street who says she saw a masked man running away with a heavy limp. Not sure if it's connected. No serious injuries to ours but nothing to go on.'

'What's Spyro doing?' I ask.

'The full scene is already up. Dog teams. Perimeter out at 50. Grid search. The works,' Carol answers, and even though that's very fast work for only an hour, I can hear the doubt in Carol's voice.

It's doubt that I echo.

This whole week we have been irrelevant.

The murderers have done exactly what they wanted

when they wanted. No matter about the police. We haven't stopped or even slowed them. No impact.

'What are you going to do?' Carol asks when the silence stretches.

'I don't know yet. Talk to you later,' I answer as I hook the mic back on the radio.

I wonder now if the man they saw limping away was the same one I encountered behind the Baldwin Pub. The one whose toes I broke, giving him that limp. Seems more likely now. He'd be Manga Kahu or Jones Maihi's family or both. Maybe the lookout again. Still too many unknowns.

Aldo Mucci.

Thomas Bern.

Sean Corcoran.

Ann Bowlby.

Now Liam Tull is missing.

What do we tell ourselves when we find him?

I can feel the anger building in me, because odds are we'll be finding him too late again. Dead after some horrible torture.

Liam Tull, whose father killed his entire family, who grew up only to have his new family killed off one by one all over again before facing the same fate himself.

How's it fair that one person has to live with that much pain?

What measure of justice can we actually give him?

Even if we do catch whoever is behind this, could we ever do enough to make it better? To make it right again?

And Cedric Black, alone now, truly, out at Tegere Servare. What does he say when he prays now?

I had intended, out of instinct more than any clear decision, to head out to Ann Bowlby's house. Or rather, her crime scene. It's unlikely that there'd be anything useful there after a fire, but I can't think of anything better to do. I need to do something. But now with the news of Liam Tull's kidnapping, I don't know where to go. There'll be plenty of good cops working both scenes, working all the scenes from this week, I correct myself, but somehow that's not enough. Not this time.

In most cases our job is after the fact. We show up to figure out who did what and if we're lucky, why. But here that doesn't matter, because we need to figure out what they are going to do next before they do it. I don't know where to go to do that.

So instead, on exhausted auto-pilot, I find myself pulling up outside my house. Too tired to get out of the car. I sit there in the clear morning sun. I miss Pollo. I hadn't realised how much of being a cop was actually about being a cop with Pollo next to me. I realise it now.

I wonder what he'd say about me teaming up with Alkaline Ben?

★ ★ ★

12:07 p.m.

Stop . . . Start.

As I jerk awake, I realise I'm still sitting in the car, having fallen asleep again. No dreams. Nothing. No sense even of time passing. Like I had just blinked. As I check my watch, I see I've been here more than four hours. The various aches and pains start checking in one by one so I head inside for more pain pills.

I'm still so out of it that I only realise something's

wrong by the time I'm swallowing pills in front of the bathroom mirror.

The house is empty. No Em. No Eva.

With an irrational, growing panic, I call out their names as I search through the house. My hand going to my gun without meaning to.

Certain that something bad has happened, that somehow all the evil I've seen this week has followed me home.

On my second track through the living room, I finally notice the blinking light on the answering machine and immediately press it.

'Hey lover, we're off to a breakfast meet with Eva's new astronomy group. There's leftover pancakes in the fridge, and don't forget to have your pills,' Em's voice sounds through the speaker.

As relief floods through me I realise Em had told me about it, I'd just forgotten and then assumed the worst.

It's actually a milestone for Eva, for all of us.

I'm relieved to know that she's still going ahead with it, despite losing Pollo this week.

But I also feel a pang of regret for not being there with them.

I'd be lying if I pretended it wasn't my choice, my choice alone.

No one is making me do this. I could put down my guns and walk away from this right now. What's worse is, I really want to. I want to be a good father. A good husband. Yet I can't stop. I can't really be those things if I walk away from all this badness now. Maybe that's another thing loving people enough teaches you — that good and bad aren't the same as right and wrong.

Before I leave the house I decide to leave two messages for Em.

One on the fridge, telling her not to worry and that I'll be back tomorrow.

And a second one in case things go wrong.

It's a letter telling her what I'm going to do and who with and why. Seeing it on paper makes it seem even more foolhardy, more desperate, but I don't have any other options I can think of.

Before I leave I lock the letter in my gun safe, hoping that Em will never have to read it. Then I drive out to meet Alkaline Ben. I take all the bullets I have.

★ ★ ★

1:34 p.m.

The lone figure I find on the windswept sand of a nameless beach is again Alkaline Ben. Although it started out clear, the day has already turned cold and a wispy fog is rolling in from the ocean as I get out of the car. Ben is dressed in an old, tattered-looking hunting jacket and faded army fatigues and, as promised, he has a shovel in one hand. It's the rifle slung over his shoulder that captures my stare though.

'It's deer season. If anyone finds us I'll say I came across you lost in the bush while I was out hunting,' Ben says by way of explanation when he sees me eyeing the rifle.

'Which way?' I ask.

'This way,' Ben replies, nodding behind him. 'We'll have to hike along for about an hour before we can start heading in. I know the place.'

As that hour passes, the fog slowly thickens until it hangs all around us. Dulling the light and muffling sound to the point where it feels like we could be any-where in the world. Ben, at least, has the sense to walk without talking, leading the way without comment or looking back at me once.

'We need to find a tree,' Ben says as he suddenly comes to a standstill in front of me. After the long silence between us in the thick fog, his voice startles me.

'What?' I ask.

'There's a tree. It marks the start of the trail we need. It's an unhappy-looking tree. Scary. They tried to chop it down once but it just keeps growing again,' Ben replies as he scans inland through the fog.

'Keep a lookout. You'll know it when you see it,' Ben continues, then starts walking more slowly.

'That it?' I ask as I spot a tree that clearly has had an interesting life.

Trunk bent and gnarled, with branches growing off at odd angles. Old, grey, splintered wounds where limbs have been broken away. In the fog it looks like something you'd find in a fairy tale, the bad kind.

'Yes, that's it,' Ben answers, nodding.

'From now on you have to move quietly. People hunt in this bush and you'll be a white man on Māori land without their permission. If they see you they may decide to accidentally mistake you for a deer and have a tragic hunting accident,' Ben warns.

It occurs to me, not for the first time, that if this is a trap then I'm walking straight in.

'I thought you said everyone will be at the funerals,' I say.

'Most, yes, for sure, but you can never be certain. And many of the people out here still live off the land. Hunting isn't like going to the mall. Sometimes you come back with food and sometimes you don't. If things have been hard, someone may have come out regardless. Even the boys will be sent out if it gets bad enough. Nothing teaches a young boy to be a good hunter like hunger. This is where I learned to hunt,' Ben says.

'Something tells me you haven't gone to bed hungry too many nights in your life, Ben,' I say.

'Maybe I wasn't always the criminal mastermind you detectives seem to think I am,' Ben counters, then sighs. 'And even if I was, I still would have been out here. The Māori are always hungry. We've had a tough couple of centuries, what with the invasion, losing our lands, and all those killings.'

Even though this isn't why I'm here, and I don't actually want to talk to Alkaline Ben at all, I can't help rising to the bait. 'And your way to help your people is to lead a criminal gang involved in drugs, gun running, money laundering, and murder?'

'You judge things so easily,' Ben replies in a calm, gentle tone. 'Yet is it that simple? Can you show me a people anywhere in the world who are happy that white men came to colonise their country? You can't talk of the law without talking about the right and wrong underneath it. What justice is left for the Māori in this land? How do we keep our children safe? Why do you think so many Māori choose life in the gangs for themselves and their families? Are they all just bad men? Crime for crime's sake? I know you're not that naïve, Bobby.'

That's something Pollo would have said to me, I realise to my annoyance.

'I'm not saying the world is fair. But that kind of reasoning won't work on me. I've seen the things the gangs do to people, Ben. Nothing you say will redeem them,' I answer.

'Could Jones be hiding out here somewhere?' I ask then, changing the subject to bring things back to why we are out here.

'I doubt it. The bush is too open this far north. Besides, all those police dogs were through here after he escaped, and then again after the gunfight at Tegere Servare. So no, it would have to be further south,' Ben replies.

'Why?' I ask.

'Better bush. More old forest as the Catlins start giving over to the lands before Fiordland. It's colder the further south you go but there's more food and more shelter. You're not hemmed in by the coast either. The land gets nearly impassable; even horses have a hard time. A man like Jones could disappear down there if he wanted to. But I don't think he's hiding. I think he's waiting,' Ben replies.

Waiting to murder more people, I think. Or is he already busy doing that to Liam Tull?

'You said before that you think he's not finished because he hasn't come back to his family yet. You still think he'll come?'

'I didn't say family, I said to his people. And yes, I know he will. Jones may have lost his eldest son but he still has Little Bird, the rest of his family and all of us. We're the centre of him,' Ben replies. You can sense the closeness between these two men. Which again makes me doubt why Ben is doing this.

'And you're out here helping me dig up his son's grave?' I ask.

'Yes. Because it's inevitable. Either you or Pollo. It was only ever a matter of time before someone realised they had to see what Jones saw. This way, if we're lucky, no one in the family ever has to know. I can spare them that at least. I don't want to be here. I have to be here,' Ben answers.

'You are here. With me. To find him and kill him before he comes back,' I persist.

I'm needing to spell it out. Partly to chase off my own recriminations. Put words to why we are here. But also because my suspicions are coming out. I don't trust Alkaline Ben's motives in all this. I don't really believe that he'll find and hand Jones over to me. Can't make myself fully believe it. I know Ben is a killer, but I don't know if I can trust him to be this killer. But he's right about it being inevitable. I do. I need to see inside that coffin and, right now, he still seems the only one to help me do this.

'No, I don't want to, but it's what's going to happen. There's only us now left for each other and there's only this,' Ben answers, shaking his head.

It's an odd way to express it, but I have to admit that he is right. Not liking to agree with anything that Ben says, or that it's happening more often. He really is very good.

It's some time later when Ben suddenly says, 'Did you know that in the Bible, in the original text, the root of the Hebrew word for 'wisdom' is the same as for 'taste'?'

'No, Ben, I did not,' I answer.

'Seems strange to us now, doesn't it? But to people back then there was no difference between the two. Not like now. We think of wisdom as something you have to learn over time. Something that comes from careful thought and intelligence, from age and experience and skill. But taste is something immediate, unconscious and involuntary, you're born with it. It's a sense, not a craft. Doesn't matter if you're a hundred or just a child. No thinking involved. Tasting is knowing. Simple.

'Now taste itself is interesting. Of the five senses we're born with, it's the only one that works right from birth all the way to death. Everything else develops later. Everything else comes and goes. Get old enough and you'll lose your sight, your hearing, even touch. But your taste will stay with you forever,' Ben finishes.

'Your point being?' I ask.

'Not sure I have one. Just the ramblings of an old man, Bobby,' Ben says, frowning to himself before he moves on.

After that exchange, we move in silence.

Slowly following the climb of the land. The fog has outpaced us inland, masking our journey, sheening the trees in coats of silvered droplets. The sun is setting by the time Ben finally slows in front of me.

'We're not far now. The main house will be in sight just beyond this rise,' Ben whispers to me.

Looking around, I'm surprised to see how rough and untainted the bush still looks even though we're close to the houses. Still no real signs of people.

'Police are watching this place from the main road, parked a few miles down. But they can only really see who's coming and going. The Maihis threatened them with a trespass order through one of the Manga Kahu lawyers so they won't be coming too close. They won't know we're here. That only leaves the house. I'll go and check it. I know the way in the dark. Then I'll come for you,' Ben whispers as he hands me the shovel.

I nod to him, then hunker down behind an old

fallen log. Ben slips away into the fog.

I wait. Forced to finally sit still and do nothing. Alone with my first thoughts. None of which I want. I miss Em and Eva, but I consciously try not to think of them now. I have to be here. What Ben said earlier comes back to me then. About the law and how it's not the same as the actual right and wrong underneath it. And about wisdom and taste. I'm breaking the law right now, but I'm also sure I'm doing the right thing. When I come face to face with Jones Maihi, I'm going to kill him. My only regret is that I didn't do it before. I have no doubts. It's the right thing to do. But then my second thoughts are, maybe that's what every killer tells himself.

And beyond that, beyond Jones Maihi, is still the question of this whole week. The why of all of this. I don't know if I'll find it in this boy's coffin.

★ ★ ★

6:12 p.m.

It's fully dark by the time Ben returns.

Materialising as suddenly and silently as he left.

'No one there. No lights either. Horses are in the stables too, so no one is out hunting. It's this way,' he whispers as he turns away.

My eyes have adjusted to the dark by now and with what moonlight there is above the fog, there's enough ambient light to see things clearly when you're up close.

Anything beyond a few metres is nearly invisible though.

The graveyard is on a hillside opposite the main

211

house.

I remember looking out at it when Pollo and I visited the Maihis earlier this week.

When we reach it, I realise it's bigger than it seemed then, older too. Maybe a hundred graves scattered in an irregular pattern. Some with simple wooden crosses, white paint still fresh, others with moss-laden headstones that look ancient. The Maihis have been out here since before the European settlers arrived.

'It's this one,' Ben whispers as he kneels down beside a fresh mound of soil. No marker, no stone. I see him press his hands into the soft earth and bend his head for a moment before he straightens up and hands me the shovel.

Digging up a grave is hard work.

Six feet is further down than you realise. The hole is small though. A child's coffin. Jones Maihi's son was still a young, small boy. The file said he was twelve, but in the autopsy picture you could tell he was still much more boy than teenager.

After a while I hand Ben the shovel and he wordlessly starts where I left off.

As the hole gets deeper, the work gets harder and more macabre.

The practicalities of digging up a grave also mean that the deeper down you go, the more obvious it feels that you're standing on someone's grave.

Somewhere during our toil the fog starts to lift, becomes patchy, the odd clear shaft of night light shining down on us. Colouring everything in crisp hues of blue, white, and black.

Despite the soil being soft, we're both sweating before too long. Handing the shovel back and forth in silence now.

Ben is digging when the shovel hits wood the first time. The hollow thunk louder than I thought it would be.

He takes care then, works slower. Scoops the last dirt away with his bare hands. The night finally clears completely as we look down at the exposed coffin.

The coffin lid is white, tinged blue in the moonlight. It has a split halfway so the top part can be hinged open like they did at the funeral.

Ben kneels down and stares at it for a moment before reaching down.

'Stop. Wait,' I say then, surprising myself. 'The boy. What was his name?'

In all this time I hadn't even thought of him as someone real.

Someone's child.

I realise it now.

'He was named Jones too, but he was such a gentle spirit. We always called him Aroha. Means 'love' in Māori,' Ben answers as he looks up at me.

'Okay,' I say and nod.

Ben nods back and then hinges open the lid.

The smell is bad, but a lot better than I expected. More chemical than putrid. But then the boy has only been dead and buried a few days.

Like the other dead people I've seen, Aroha doesn't look real. A doll wrapped in a Māori shroud.

His face looks odd, painted.

'It's makeup,' Ben says as he follows my gaze. 'I was told about it before the funeral. The morticians paint the faces to make them look more normal. More alive. It's not usually done, but we wanted him to look more like he used to. Before . . .'

Getting down into the hole next to Ben is a tight fit

but I manage it. Then, with Ben kneeling and me standing over him, we finally look down at what Jones saw.

There's nothing unexpected about the body.

Even through the makeup you can still make out the marks around the neck. Bruising and torn skin from the hanging in a regular pattern from the rope.

The shroud hides the rest of his body.

He looks too small.

Too young.

What needs to happen to a child this young that they would kill themselves?

What would he have thought about as he strung the rope around his neck?

Adults committing suicide I can understand.

You can do so much wrong, make mistakes so big and so many and with so much regret piling up around you, that eventually there's no way forward. No way out. Nothing left to hope for.

But a child this young. How much guilt could they have had? How could all the hope built into youth have been stripped away so soon?

As I lean in further beyond Ben, I notice several objects piled in next to the body.

Another common custom. Especially with kids, I'd imagine. Keepsakes and letters and things. Tragically absurd and sad really — like most things about funerals — we do it more to ease our living than their dying.

In this coffin there's a similarly poignant collection:

A small art set, complete with paint brushes and palette.

A man's old, worn-looking gold watch.

A bar of chocolate.

A few photographs.

'This is what Jones saw?' I ask quietly.

'Yes. This is what we all saw,' Ben answers in a hushed tone.

'Did he take anything out? Put anything in?' I ask, my eyes tracing every object, unwilling yet to reach out.

'The gold watch. It belonged to Jones's grandfather, then his father, then him. It's been passed on in their family for generations. He asked me to bring it to the funeral service. I gave it to him there and he went to put it in with his son. I was right behind him the whole time. He kissed his boy, like he used to. Touched his face. Nothing else. He talked to a few of the family, then came back to look at the boy again. That's when it happened. I don't know if he took anything out. If he did, then it wasn't in there before. I think this is what he saw when this started,' Ben answers.

So not the watch.

'The boy painted?' I ask, inspecting the art set.

'All the time. The Maihis have always been gifted. Part gift, part obsession really. Every generation it was something new. Jones Senior, the one I grew up with, he has the Sight. He doesn't talk about it much anymore but we all know. With Jones himself, it's music. Even Little Bird has his pictures. I don't think I've ever seen him without his Polaroid camera. And for Aroha it was painting. Done it as long as I can remember. He was getting real good too,' Ben replies.

'That his favourite chocolate?' I ask.

'His mother put that in for him. Little Bird put in the pictures,' Ben answers.

As I reach down for the pictures, Ben stops me by grabbing my wrist. Not harshly, but fast and firm.

215

'No. I'll do it,' he says, then slowly takes out the three pictures.

'Little Bird has a thing about odd angles. He's either taking pictures while lying on the floor or from half-way up a tree. Sometimes they're good,' Ben says as he hands me the pictures.

I risk taking out my flashlight. We're still in the grave. Unlikely the light will show up. I angle all the photos in the light so we can both see them clearly.

The first picture, true to Ben's description, is a selection of feet grouped together under a table. It's a well-lit area. Like a dinner party from the floor up to the ankles only. The feet are all bare, different sizes. Adults and kids. Twelve feet in total. Six people. An old, scuffed wooden floor. White painted chairs and table legs. Nothing much visible in the background.

I stare at it for a long time but can't make anything of it.

The second looks like a family barbeque seen from above. He must have been fairly high up a tree for this one. No faces visible, just the crowns of heads on shoulders. Several people arranged in a loose circle around a fire. This one was taken at night and the shadows play out from the central source of light. A wild pig is being readied to go on a spit. I think maybe I can recognise Jones Maihi himself by his size and the set of the shoulders but I can't be sure. There's a lot of big men in the Maihi family. It could be a gathering anywhere, of any group of people. Nothing here I can make anything of.

The last picture is harder to make out.

There's no immediate way to tell what's up or what's down, left or right. Then I realise it's a picture from above again. Taken from a high point downwards. From the outside down through an open window, capturing the view inside a room. The majority of the picture shows the interior of the room framed at the edges by the open window itself. Due to the extreme angle, what's visible is mostly the carpet area directly below the windowsill. There's a selection of paint pots and tubes randomly scattered on the carpet. Also an oval-shaped painter's palette that looks well used. Smatterings of various colours covering it completely.

But there's also something more.

The moment I see it, I feel my instincts jolt. I'm sure, with complete, irrational certainty, without reason or logic. No idea how. I'm sure this is what Jones Maihi saw. This picture. Here, finally, even if only in part, only in a picture, is a fraction of the truth. I know I'm right. There's something here, something significant. I can feel it.

At the very edge of the picture, the furthest into the room the camera angle allows, there's a pair of hands.

They are clearly those of a man, square and masculine. Fingers spread out, they are placed side by side, close together. Palms down, pressed onto the carpet. There's a slight curve to the fingers as if the man is digging into the carpet for a better grip. From their position you could guess that the man was either lying or kneeling head down on the carpet. At face value it's just another picture. After all, what can you tell from an anonymous pair of hands digging into a carpet? But no. Something about the image feels wrong. Sinister. This is what Jones Maihi saw. I know it.

I'm still staring at it when Ben whispers, 'What do you see?'

'I . . . I don't know,' I reply. Hesitating now. Not sure how to express the clear sense that there's something in this picture. Pollo would be proud of me. This has got to be what he calls getting a 'knowing' about something.

'Do you recognise this room?' I ask.

Ben silently takes the picture from me and studies it closely.

'No. But it's not here. The main house only has wooden floors. I know that painter's palette though, it belonged to Aroha. I gave it to him as a birthday present,' Ben answers.

'You think it's this, don't you?' Ben whispers. 'You think this is what Jones saw that made him do it.'

'I don't know,' I answer.

I'm trying to muster some rational doubts against my own intuitive certainty. I know, I know something now. I just don't know what. Or how.

Despite the horror and exhaustion and grief of this week, despite the pain medication, the cracked ribs and everything else, I'm certain.

'We take these with us,' I say to Ben as I take back the pictures. Ben only nods quietly, his eyes back on the boy.

'It never sat right with any of us. I know it happens. Kids kill themselves. By accident maybe. Or if they had problems. Even at twelve. But not Aroha. This boy was loved. He had real happiness. Saw beauty in everything. So much life in him,' Ben says, shaking his head.

When I climb out of the grave, I scan around to see that the fog has completely lifted. A crisp sliver of moon adds a silver tinge to the unforgiving light of hard, white stars.

As I turn back I hear Ben whispering, still in the grave, kneeling down close to the boy. I look away when I realise he's leaning in to kiss him.

The intimacy of it is not meant for me.

My gaze wanders to the farmhouse as I hear Ben climb out of the grave behind me. Then back down to the picture. Something here. My thoughts stray back to the day Pollo and I came visiting. Little Bird was in a tree with a camera then too. Clicking away.

A thought strikes me and I turn with the question on my tongue.

Too late.

I only have time to register movement before the bright gunshot flare.

Too close.

Too loud.

★ ★ ★

8:05 p.m.

The bullet strikes Alkaline Ben with terrific force.

It hits him high in the shoulder, picking him up and spinning him over in the air like the hand of some invisible giant as the momentum flings him past me.

The world becomes a stuttering of flashes.

The shots echoing so rapidly they become a continuous roar.

I'm diving for cover. Three fast shots tracking across, following me. Catching up.

No time to draw my gun.

I'm still airborne, aiming for the cover of a nearby gravestone, when I feel something slam into my ankle hard enough to rotate me partially in mid-air.

I land hard.

Knocking the wind out of me.

I've got my Glock in my hand now, scrabbling up behind the gravestone before I take my first gasping breath.

Heart pounding.

Ears ringing.

Everything shaking.

No sound. No movement. He could be anywhere. I need to move. Now. The shooter could be flanking me. Or already aiming. No time for thought.

Pumping with adrenaline, I burst out to my left. Diving behind a bigger gravestone. This time the shot splinters stone next to my head, shards of granite slicing open my cheek.

But it's enough.

Because my brain has finally had enough time to use that last desperate breath to do some thinking, and what it comes up with is that it's five shots he's fired now.

And the muzzle flash I saw before the first shot was wide and messy.

Not a pistol or rifle.

Something with a short barrel.

And the way Alkaline Ben flew away like that.

He had to have taken most of the force that bullet had in it.

A high-velocity round at that range would have sped straight through him. Punching a hole but taking most of its energy along with it. Too fast. So a low-velocity round. With a soft-nosed bullet that flattened on impact, delivering all its momentum to the target.

Short barrel.

Low-velocity rounds.

Soft-nose bullets.

Five shots.

Has to be a revolver.

And most revolvers only have six.

And after that last shot, I know where you're hiding.

I'm moving the moment I realise all this. Can't give him time to think. Time to reload. My own revolver in my left hand and my Glock in my right, I duck out the far side of the gravestone, firing wide before I'm fully exposed, tracking across to my target. Guns coming around the corner firing before my head follows.

The barrage of shots works as he ducks down to avoid my fire rather than take another shot. He's hunkering behind a gravestone about ten paces from me. I can clearly make out his shadow but I've got no clear shot. I keep my guns trained on the edges of the gravestone, my nerves thrumming.

I've got him, I realise. He's got nowhere to go now. No way out from there.

The sudden shock and fear start solidifying into anger.

I'm about to step out further to get a better angle when a sudden light shines directly into my eyes. Momentarily blinding me. I'm forced to duck back down for cover.

Immediately another shot rings out, but this time it's not close.

He's running, I realise. I can hear the footfalls retreating fast.

The light is still bright in my eyes, shining from directly above the gravestone he was hiding behind.

As I come up again, my first shot takes out the light. It's a moment before my eyes adjust, then I spot him already drawing away, down the hill, running full tilt.

It's only when I take the first step of the chase that I realise my ankle is busted.

The gunshot.

In stubborn desperation I try to limp after him regardless, but my ankle can't take the weight. At the edge of the graveyard I stop and take aim once more. He's already too far away. I see him limping along at speed, favouring his right leg; maybe I did hit him?

I still empty my clip in black hope.

He never stops running.

Away into the trees.

I'm still shaking, warily checking all around, but the graveyard is deserted again. Only the gun smoke moves in the air.

When I pause to check myself I see that I'm not shot. The heel of my boot is missing though. The bullet must have taken it clean off and the impact twisted my ankle.

Alkaline Ben is not so lucky. He is lying very still. Face down.

A dark, glistening patch high on his left shoulder blade.

He's heavy to turn over but surprises me by groaning when I do.

It's hard to say how bad it is.

There's no exit wound, so the slug is lodged somewhere in him.

The wound is too high and too far out to have hit any major organs. Not a lot of bleeding either. It could be lodged in his scapula and only be a few inches in.

Or it could be bad.

There's a major artery that runs near the armpit. If that got nicked he could be bleeding internally. Or the bone itself could have shattered. The shards spearing into the rest of him like shrapnel. Sometimes a bullet will even bounce inside a person. Ricocheting off your skeleton, tearing up flesh in crazy paths until it runs out of energy.

'You get him?' Ben asks quietly, eyes still closed as I kneel down by him.

'No. He got away,' I answer, thinking I'm going to have to leave him here to go get help. I don't know if I should move him with this wound, and I wouldn't be able to carry him with my ankle in any case.

Then Ben surprises me by turning himself over, something halfway between a growl and a groan issuing from him.

'Did you recognise him?' Ben asks as he holds up his hand.

'No,' I say, hesitating before taking his hand and helping him to his feet. He's cradling his arm and he looks disoriented, swaying alarmingly before finding his equilibrium and looking around.

'Unusual gun. Snub-nose revolver. Sounded like a .38 cop's gun,' Ben says in a measured, neutral tone. When I don't respond Ben continues, 'He was either here for us, or for the same thing as us.'

'Could anyone have tracked us coming in?' I ask.

'It's possible but I don't think so. If he followed us here it means he would have seen us dig the hole. If he wanted to stop us doing that he would have had plenty of opportunity. It took long enough. If he wanted only to kill us he could have easily done so when we were down there in it. Why wait until we're above ground again where we can escape and fire back? No. He came upon us here by accident because this is where he was going all along,' Ben answers.

'Innocent people don't visit a graveyard at night,'

he adds.

Present company included, I think.

Ben suddenly staggers and grabs hold of my arm to stay upright.

'We need to go,' I say.

'I need to make a phone call,' Ben says, nodding. 'But first this. We can't leave things like this.'

Looking around, I realise the scene looks chaotic. Ben's blood is spattered across several gravestones. Aroha's casket is still visible. The pile of freshly dug dirt next to it has our footprints. Our would-be killer's flashlight I shot out is lying in pieces not far from us. Next to another shovel.

After leaning Ben against a gravestone, I start gathering things together. I've been to many crime scenes as a cop, so it feels odd to be hiding evidence instead of investigating it.

I check that I still have the pictures in my pocket before taking up the shovel and turning to the open grave. I can clean the blood off the gravestone by rubbing the spots with dirt. It won't remove all traces, but should be enough to fool the naked eye. Once the hole is filled up and everything else removed, it will hopefully look about right, I think.

'Just take my rifle, my shovel. Leave everything else,' Ben says as I'm busy levering up the first shovel full of dirt.

'That's blood. Our prints at the scene,' I protest.

'It's not a scene, Bobby. It never will be,' Ben answers calmly. 'This is Māori land. The Maihis won't call the cops. This will help the family. When they find the grave open like that, people will know Aroha didn't just suddenly kill himself. That there's more happening here. It will give them something to be angry about. Anger is useful.'

I'm uncomfortable with the idea of not doing everything we can to hide what happened here. But I realise this isn't my jurisdiction, isn't my world. I know Ben is right. No police will ever be involved. It's not how people out here do things.

'Do the Maihis have a phone?' I ask as I start gathering up the things we're taking with us.

'No, but the neighbours do,' Ben replies. That'll be an interesting visit to have out here in the night, a limping cop and a wounded gang leader.

'Who are the neighbours?' I ask.

'Me,' Ben answers.

★ ★ ★

9:46 p.m.

Getting down to the main house takes longer than I expected with Ben moving slow, cradling his arm, and me limping along nursing my ankle.

'That one. You drive,' Ben says, pointing to an old station wagon parked near the house.

As I round the car, I'm momentarily surprised to find the door unlocked, keys hanging in the ignition. Ben catches my stare and says, 'No one would dare to steal a car here, Bobby.'

With Ben giving directions I drive slowly, heading further south. Luckily away from where the police would be stationed on the road to the Maihi lands.

'Where are we going?' I ask.

Knowing from his file that Alkaline Ben has no residence listed out here. Lives out near Blueskin Bay on the other side of Dunedin.

225

'I don't own it on paper. It's a place we sometimes use,' Ben answers. We. That means gang house, I think. One we don't know about. There'll be some random person or trust listed as the owner in the registry but it will have been bought and paid for by Manga Kahu.

It's about a forty-minute drive along a dirt track. I crank up the car's heater as Ben is looking pale and sweaty. I'm worried he might be going into shock.

When we get there, the scale of the place takes me aback.

It's a mansion.

A two-storey villa, heavily decorated with wrought iron and woodwork in the Victorian style. It looks original. Both in the sense that it was probably built more than a hundred years ago, and that nothing whatsoever seems to have been done to maintain the place since then.

Wild bush grows all the way flush up to the ancient walls of the house, where thick creeper vines compete with flaking paint and patches of grey, aged, bare wood. Some lead-lined windows are cracked. Others missing. There are plants growing on the moss and lichen-covered roof.

The only thing that seems well maintained is the driveway.

'Honey! I'm home!' Ben calls out loudly as I help him out of the car, then stifles a laugh. Most of his back is now sticky with blood. He needs a doctor.

We both stagger up the steps to the front door, leaning on each other.

The interior of the house is as decrepit and broken-down as the exterior. A grand design brought low by neglect.

Once inside, Ben points to the left and off the foyer.

We enter what must have once been a grand, long reception hall with high, vaulted ceilings, twin fireplaces, and doors leading off into the house.

It is now furnished by a large, loosely arranged ring of couches, chairs, and recliners of varying colour, condition, age, and design. Enough seating for about thirty people.

A Round Table for the Knights of Crime.

Ben takes the lead across the open space in the circle and collapses more than sits down on an old, orange La-Z-Boy recliner on the far side. I realise now that it's the only chair in the room that backs onto a solid wall. That would be Alkaline Ben's chair, wouldn't it?

'There's a phone by the fireplace,' Ben says, breathing heavily as he shifts himself so the wound on his shoulder blade doesn't touch the chair.

'Call Asian Dave and tell him Ben says we've got a runner. Only that. His card is there by the phone,' he adds.

The phone is on the floor next to the fireplace, along with a little pile of cards and phone numbers on scraps of paper. As I sort through them I find a business card actually titled 'Asian Dave.' Studying the details on the card I learn that 'Asian Dave' is in fact a horse doctor. Good with all breeds.

As I look back over at Ben, he meets my gaze and says, 'Fast would be better than slow.'

Asian Dave answers on the second ring and hangs up without a word after I give him the message.

'It'll be about an hour,' Ben says tiredly. 'There's alcohol in the kitchen. I'd be obliged if you'd bring me a large amount.'

In the kitchen I also find a first aid kit and some

bottled water so take those back also. Ben refuses the water, swallowing the pain pills with whisky instead.

Without anything else urgent to do, I lower myself down in the chair next to Ben and take the time to reload my gun. My backup revolver is empty now. I spent all that ammo missing the man who got away. That leaves me two full clips for my Glock.

I hope it's enough.

Enough to finish this.

I realise I've become a part of this case now.

Have been ever since Pollo looked up at the night like that.

Whatever feverish desperation is driving the people behind all this is driving me too now. No stopping till we're done. Till it's finished. No going home.

I'm suddenly very tired, feeling the pain from various injuries this week start to clamour for attention. Running on adrenaline too long will do that to you. One moment you feel fine and the next you're one big, exhausted bruise.

Before I close my eyes I go for the painkillers and whisky option too.

★　★　★

I wake with a start. Something roused me but I don't know what.

From that perfect, black sleep that takes you a few moments to realise where you are and what you're doing. The second knock on the front door brings it all back and I loosen my grip on the gun. Alkaline Ben is snoring loudly next to me, feet up in his recliner chair.

Asian Dave turns out to be Asian — a small skinny

228

man, somewhere over sixty. He's carrying a big wooden crate in his arms that has him bending backwards to keep his balance. Small, round wire-frame glasses peer at me from just over the lid of the crate.

'This one's a cop. He one of yours?' Asian Dave says in heavily accented English, looking past me.

'No. He's one of his own,' Ben answers from where he's standing right behind me. I didn't even register that he had woken up.

'You take this,' Dave says as he pushes the heavy crate into my arms, then looks Ben up and down before adding, 'You sit down.'

Once we're back in the reception hall, Dave motions for me to put down the crate next to where Ben is sitting, then impatiently shoos me away with his hands before popping it open.

Asian Dave reaches in and puts on a hard hat with a mounted headlight. It's only when he flicks it on that I realise we had been sitting here in the dark.

Dave cuts away Ben's shirt back and frowns down at the bloody mess around the wound as he massages the flesh around it.

'Usual favour for this?' Dave asks.

'The same,' Ben answers, and Dave nods in reply.

'Can you move the arm? Make a circle,' Dave instructs. Ben manages to do so, although slowly, and with sweat breaking out on his face.

'Okay. I can do it right or fast. Which you want?' Dave asks, feeling around in Ben's armpit.

'Fast. Things to do still,' Ben answers, then takes off his own leather belt and puts it down in his lap.

Fast turns out to be very much so.

He's immediately got me holding a bag of clear fluid that he hooks up to a needle in Ben's arm. Dave then uses a big syringe to make a few rapid injections around the wound, then takes up what looks like the kind of sharp-nosed pliers you could buy in any hardware store.

I'm relieved to see him pause momentarily to messily dunk and swirl the tool in a jar of clear fluid, which by its smell I believe is alcohol. Then he unceremoniously jams it into the wound.

Ben grunts but otherwise does not move.

Dave is definitely not gentle as he searches around with the pliers for a few moments.

'Horse doctors are among the best physicians in the world,' Ben says to me as he stifles a wince, then takes a large swig of whisky straight from the bottle.

'When you think about it, they have to be,' Ben continues in a calmer tone. 'Their patients are often worth millions and their treatment has to get, quite literally, winning results. Asian Dave is among the best horse doctors in the profession today,' Ben says to me in a conversational tone that seems completely removed from the fact that someone is currently digging around inside him.

'Like with most people, you can tell his worth not by what he gets paid, but more importantly by how he earns it. Asian Dave only works on commission of winnings,' Ben finishes.

As if on cue, Asian Dave makes a self-satisfied noise and pauses when he finds what he's looking for. Then says, 'Okay. Time to bite now.'

Ben takes up the leather belt from his lap and loops it in his mouth, then takes a deep breath before giving a single nod.

In response, Dave takes hold of the pliers in both hands and gives it a firm twist before suddenly yanking it out. I see Ben visibly sag down in his chair.

Dave holds up a bloody, flattened, coin-shape of dull grey metal that he inspects closely before declaring, 'Lucky. Whole bullet. Don't have to go in again.'

The entire operation, which includes stitches, takes only a few minutes.

'You'll need hospital in about a day. No more,' Dave says as he starts packing his tools back in the crate, pausing to unhook the now empty bag of fluid I'm still holding.

'These are for pain. Only one every three hours. No more alcohol,' he says, handing me a bottle of pills.

'These are for if he needs to move fast. Only one per day, okay. Only one.' He hands me another bottle of pills.

And with that, Asian Dave is gone, slamming the front door behind him.

'Now what?' I ask, looking over at Ben.

'Now we find Jones Maihi,' Ben answers.

SATURDAY ...

12:10 a.m.

Ben dresses himself in an old coat he finds in the kitchen, then heads over to the phone as I check my watch. Past midnight. It's Saturday, I realise. The first killing was seven days ago. Long week. Short week too, somehow. How many of us are there, I wonder. Living like this now. How many of us are still in the chase? Both the good and the bad. Can I even tell the difference anymore?

'Tell me,' Ben says immediately when someone answers his call.

He is silent for a moment then says, 'Thank you,' and hangs up. Ben was confident earlier on the beach that someone would talk at the funerals. He believed that enough grief would finally break down the last loyalties close family had to Jones. That too many of that family would now be dead, too many of those left behind needing answers.

Ben is quiet as he looks over at me. I can't read his expression.

'I know where Jones is going. Not far from here,' he says, looking unhappy as he sighs and finally shakes his head before he finishes. 'It is south of here, in the Catlins. His family helped him slip past a police blockade earlier tonight. Since Tegere Servare, he's been hiding down beyond Riverton.'

'You have an exact location?' I ask. Starting to think like a cop again. Neither I nor Ben are in any shape

232

for another fight but I could get word to Spyro, and with the resources Operation Spear has they could easily take him.

'It won't work like that, Bobby. No reinforcements. No cops. Jones sees cops and this is over. All we'll have is more killing, more death. He sees me and maybe we still have a chance. We had a deal remember?' he says, as if he can read my thoughts.

Alkaline Ben suddenly looks a lot more dangerous than he did a moment ago.

'Now ask me where Jones is going,' Ben prompts calmly.

'Where?' I say.

'The family farm of Ian Tull,' Ben replies.

Makes an evil kind of sense, I think. Of course it would be there.

Mucci and Bern were both killed in their homes. Corcoran at the church, which pretty much was his home. Then Liam Tull is kidnapped. If you wanted to horribly torture and murder another priest, then where do you go? Tegere Servare is Liam's home, but you've failed getting in there once before. It's doubly covered in cops now, so where else? Where would you take Liam Tull that would allow you to take your time with him? Somewhere that could add just that little bit extra to his suffering?

'We may still have time. It's a long way from Fiordland. Not risking the main roads. We have a much shorter trip,' Ben says, interrupting my thoughts. Then he takes up his rifle, wincing with the motion before continuing, 'We should go.'

I realise, reluctantly, that Ben is right. If Liam Tull is still alive, we're the only slim hope he has. Jones Maihi has already killed a lot of people this week.

There's no way it ends well if cops show up. There will be no negotiations.

'Why is Jones doing this?' I ask as I start to gather my things.

'Has to be about his son,' Ben answers as we head outside again. 'Jones saw more in that picture than we do. At first I thought this was revenge. My people understand revenge. Sometimes it's needed. The only way to heal. If it's clean. If it's personal. Yet I do not understand this. So many killings, and how. I do not see why all these men should have to die in these ways.'

At hearing this I involuntarily flash back to the rooms I've walked into this week.

Rooms you can never really walk out of again.

The only thing I can imagine being worse than finding the murders already completed like we did, would be to actually witness it all being done. The slow, caring intricacy of it. The obscenity of doing something like that, meticulously and calmly, taking your time to measure out the cruelty, not to waste a life too soon. It must be the work of the deranged, the truly insane, which again leaves me without understanding. A father seeking vengeance for the death of a son I can understand, there's logic to it. Maybe Jones believed someone drove his son to suicide. Or maybe even that the boy was murdered and the killing made to look like a suicide. Either way, responding with vengeance still makes sense. But to go from that starting point to everything I've seen this week still feels wrong.

Maybe that's the mistake we're making, I think. Sane people can't reason in insane ways. Maybe Jones Maihi has truly gone beyond the end of himself.

As we get back in the station wagon a tired, selfishly raw part of me fears what we'll find out there if we arrive too late. It fears arriving during it even more.

★ ★ ★

1:01 a.m.

Alkaline Ben knows the way to the Tull farm. I'm too tired to ask how. My mind flits from one unfinished thought to the next. Too tired to hold a line.

I don't know where we are anymore.

Somewhere in the Catlins.

Deep South. Deeper than I've gone before.

'They tried to raise me Catholic, you know. This was years ago, when the government could still take Māori kids off their parents for no reason,' Ben says after some time. His tone pensive, eyes on the road.

'It didn't really take,' Ben continues. 'The nuns said I was too Māori for it. But I remember the stories. The old ones. Good stories. There's one about Saint Paulinus. I forget the point of it now, but there's one part I remember: A king sits in a vast hall in winter surrounded by his flags and vestments and all that. All his advisors and people with him feasting around a big fire as a storm blows outside. Then a sparrow flies in one window and immediately out the other. The sparrow is only in the room for a split second. In that time, its world turns from something cold and dark into a brief flash of light and warmth, full of music and colours and smells. A world of things far beyond its small ability to comprehend. Just a flash, and then it's all gone again,' Ben narrates.

'Sometimes that's people, I think. We're all of us

235

that bird,' Ben says, then winces painfully and takes some of the pills Asian Dave left him.

I don't respond.

'Then other times, times like tonight, I think no. Some people are like that bird, and then people like us kill it.'

★ ★ ★

Soon the network of dirt tracks all flow into each other in the headlights. My mind goes numb, buried in exhaustion and questions. The drive seems time-less. Like there's only this one endless road out here. Looping in on itself without ever showing you a way out. No fences here, no gates. Just old-growth forest and stands of bush crowding the road. Scraping the sides of the car in an unwelcome embrace.

I don't know what we're going to do when the road ends.

I still don't really understand why all of this hap-pened. Why it started. Who did what? And why? It matters, but it doesn't change things. I have to do what I can. The things I've seen this week. And Pollo.

If we can find Jones Maihi, then I can at least end one part of this. Understanding or no.

Jones and I are the same now, I realise. Revenge is the only certain thing left.

★ ★ ★

1:18 a.m.

Ben cuts the engine and the lights at the same time. Coasting us to a standstill in the dark.

'We walk in from here,' he says, then pauses to dry swallow a pill from each bottle the horse doctor left him. Too many already. Offers them to me.

'What's in these?' I ask, not taking the bottles from him. But hesitating, so tired and aching now that the exhaustion feels like something close to physical nausea. I can barely think straight anymore.

'You really don't want to know,' Ben says, then offers them to me again.

I take one from each bottle too.

'We'll come in on one of the side tracks. Enough cover to not be visible from the house. Once we get close we can work our way around to the house. You stay in the trees. I'll go to Jones, call out to him. If he spots you early it's over. You have to be patient. Wait for the right time,' Ben says, then starts moving down the track slowly.

Now, here, feeling like we're finally at the end of things, I still don't trust Ben. Will he actually go through with this and deliver Jones into my hands? Keep an unlikely promise? Dare I believe it — an incredible offer from an untrustworthy man? Will he turn on Jones, his friend, his family? Or will he turn on me? And if so, will it be before? Or after?

At least he's out in front of me where I can see him.

The moon and stars are all out, a still, clear night down here. The quiet would make it hard to creep up on someone. I've got one full clip left in my Glock, my cramping fingers holding it in a too-tight grip. Hard to relax now. Before long I can make out the house by the lights through the trees.

Someone's home. And awake.

The closer we come to the light, the more alive I feel again. Maybe it's the pills, or maybe it's something

237

inside me that senses that this is finally going to be over.

As we come to a curve in the track, Ben moves into the trees and I follow, drawing my gun. Giving him more distance.

It's hard to move quietly among the trees so we slowly work our way around to the side of the house. My nerves buzzing. Ben finally unslings his rifle and quietly chambers a round as we silently study the house. Up close, with the lights on, the place is not what I expected.

I had imagined another ruin.

An abandoned, overgrown house lost in the bush. A forgotten monument to the insanity of Ian Tull. Instead we find a large house freshly painted in bright white. Lights are shining from every window. Looks like every light in the house is on. I can make out neat garden paths and a manicured lawn. Strangely, I notice there's a selection of flowers and birds painted low along the sides of the house, wrapping around the building in happy colours. Simple designs, like the work of children. The front door is open.

This is all wrong.

Then.

Finally.

Realisation begins.

A burning epiphany rising through my mind.

I can feel it happening. Slowly, the mass of tangled questions collapses under the weight of experience and a cascade of answers open themselves, one by one.

As Ben moves clear of the tree line, I figure out my first mistake.

As Ben moves towards the door, hands held high,

calling out, 'Jones. It's me!' I realise my second.

When there's sounds of movement in the house, I realise my third mistake.

As gunfire erupts, I realise my last mistake.

As I race out from the trees, now, finally, I know it all. I understand.

★ ★ ★

Ben reaches the door first. Doesn't hesitate and runs straight in, still calling out to Jones. I follow close behind. The gunfire sounds like a conversation. A pistol asks and a revolver answers.

Everything comes in flashes now.

A broken bookshelf in the entrance hall.

A kaleidoscope of toppled paint tins scarring the carpet in a puddle of bright, wet colours.

Footsteps in paint leading away.

Blood splattered on the walls.

Bullet holes leading up.

A figure limping up the stairs.

Another catching up.

One last flurry of gunshots echo from above.

Then yelling.

The sounds of a struggle.

Movement right above us.

In front of me, Ben flies up the stairs in huge, leaping strides.

Then just as he reaches the top he's suddenly knocked violently backwards.

I slip to the side just in time.

Ben flies back past me, grasping air. He falls a long way. Hits hard behind me. Far below.

As I reach the top of the stairs, it's over. I've finally

reached the end.

Because here on the floor lies Jones Maihi, defeated at last. A helpless rage in his eyes, hands held up, empty now. His pistol lies out of reach. He's looking up at Liam Tull, who is standing over him with a revolver pointed at Jones's face. The barrel shaking.

Both are breathing heavily, blood everywhere. The anger of the fight still a tangible momentum between them.

In the moment my first step lands, split-second realisation turns to instant conviction.

Enough.

I know what happened and why.

I understand it all.

And I know what I have to do.

Pollo would be proud of me.

I shoot Liam Tull.

In the head.

★   ★   ★

From this close the bullet punches a neat, small hole in Liam Tull's temple upon entry but explodes hugely out the other side, violently flinging a chunky red salad of blood, brain, and skull messily down the hall. A cloud of warm red mist settling all around.

Liam Tull is gone in an instant.

His body spasms with the impact. Remains standing for a second. A breath catches in his throat. His spine not yet aware that his brain is gone.

Then his body slowly topples over.

Collapsing with a dull, wet thud next to Jones.

Jones already has the gun aimed and our eyes meet.

It's too late for me now.

I can see straight down the barrel.

Then Jones Maihi's head jerks back, a red explosion spraying back beyond him, splashing down over Liam Tull's body, their gore mingling together on the floor beyond.

As I turn, Alkaline Ben is aiming his rifle at me. His hands steady. Smoke still curling from the barrel.

'Why?' Ben asks, his voice calm but cold.

'Because it's always true. You always get more,' I say as I sag down to the floor. Lowering my gun. Suddenly exhausted.

'If you hurt people badly enough for long enough, you can get them to do anything, absolutely anything you want. But there's a price. Always. You also get more. In the short term you get what you want, but in the long term you get more. And that more is always bad. You get sickness. But with the right kind of mind, and the right kind of pain, you can do so much worse. You can even turn a good person into something like Liam Tull,' I say.

'Look around you. What do you see?' I ask. Ben's a smart man, would have made a very good detective I think, as almost immediately he spots it.

'The carpet. The walls. This is the place. This is the house from the picture we found in Aroha's grave,' he answers as realisation dawns.

'It'll be the upstairs bedroom. The tree outside the window will be the one that Little Bird climbed. Like you said, he has a thing about extreme angles when he takes his pictures. And he's always clicking away. Doesn't just take one. But you don't need to take my word for it,' I say, as I reach over to Jones Maihi's body.

The two pictures are in the second pocket I check.

I knew Jones would carry them with him. How could he not? Those pictures carry the horrible truth he could never let go of. I would be no different if it was my little Eva. Looking at them would have fuelled his rage. He would have wanted to confront Liam Tull with them before he killed him. Vengeance turns us all into the same person.

'It bothered me that Jones left that picture in the coffin. That was my first mistake. If, as you said, this all started with what Jones saw in that coffin, then why leave it behind? That's not vengeance, that's not how it works. And what, after all, could he really see in that picture we found? An anonymous pair of hands clawing at a carpet? How could there be enough there to infuriate him so? No. There had to be more. And there was. It was the other pictures. The ones that show the rest of that room. The ones that showed Liam Tull and what he did to Aroha. Those are the ones he took with him,' I finish, as I turn the two pictures face up.

A sad sense of confirmation settles in me then. I don't want to know the things I know anymore.

The angle is almost the same as the picture we found in Aroha's grave. Same room, same objects. But you can see more than just hands. Liam Tull is naked. Aroha is too. Sweat gleams on their skin. The photograph is undeniably sensual. Two figures frozen mid-movement. Limbs entwined. Passion etched in every curve.

It's the proportions that signal the evil of it.

The wrongness.

One body is large, manly, and mature.

One is small.

Too young.

Too small.

It's hard to look at.

Ben manages to stare at the pictures longer than I can.

He swallows before he whispers, 'Aroha looks happy. That would be why Little Bird took the pictures. He likes seeing people happy. A sweet child. It would have been why he put them in the coffin with his brother too.'

'That was my second mistake. As soon as we found out that Manga Kahu was somehow involved with the killings of those priests, we should have gone back to Jones Maihi's escape. Focused on why. None of it made sense. Why would Jones Maihi break out like that when he had only twelve weeks left before release anyway? No. Jones knew he was running out of time. He realised it right there at the funeral. He had these pictures of Liam Tull in the coffin. And when he looked up, he would have seen exactly what we saw when we were at the church too. He would have seen that same man in the pictures with his son smiling down from the fundraising posters for the Church's missionary work in the Philippines. He would have known that Liam Tull was leaving the country in two weeks. If we had dug up that grave earlier, we would have known exactly what Jones wanted and why,' I say.

'I understand this perfectly. Jones needing to kill Liam Tull. And needing to do it himself. It's a right I would deny no parent,' Ben says. 'But why did he kill these priests?'

'Jones didn't do it. Liam Tull did,' I answer. 'That was my last mistake. Remember what I said before: If you hurt people badly enough for long enough, you can get them to do anything, absolutely anything you want. But there's a price. Ann Bowlby told me that. I should have remembered. You didn't know her, but I think the two of you would have gotten on well,' I say.

'She died last night. Murdered. She worked at Tegere Servare with Liam Tull and the other priests who were killed. I was so tired it just didn't register. Earlier when you made that phone call and found out where Jones was, you said he'd been hiding out down near Riverton since the night they attacked Tegere Servare. That's more than four hours from Dunedin. So there's no way Jones Maihi was up there last night killing Ann Bowlby,' I conclude.

'You're wrong,' Ben says, looking shaken. 'I did know Ann Bowlby . . . from here. Amazing woman. The Church bought this place. Turned it into a youth centre. She did counselling here. Confidential and anonymous. It was a good spot. People would think the kids came for the art or dance classes or to learn Māori. They could talk to her without being forced to tell the police or school or their families. I even saw Liam Tull here a few times. He gave art classes. Two years ago, when Jones was out on parole, he brought Aroha out here. Signed him up for painting. I dropped him and Little Bird off here a few times myself,' Ben says, sounding sad.

'But that still doesn't prove anything,' Ben adds, his tone sobering.

'But we know it wasn't Jones at least. The timings and locations wouldn't work. It had to be someone who knew her movements. Knew when she'd be coming home. The murder was made to look like a gas explosion, but those are tricky to time. You can't just cut the gas and hope the victim comes home in time.

No. The killer had to know when she'd be there. Knock her out and then cut the gas and set a fire. It's the only way to be certain. Her murder was also different than the other killings. No elaborate staging of the body. No long torture. And she called me just before it happened. She never had time to tell me, but I think she figured out it was Liam Tull. I don't know how. But then she was a very smart woman and understood psychopathology better than anyone I know. She knew Liam for a long time. Maybe she saw through him somehow. Maybe he made a mistake in his responses, didn't quite act the traumatised innocent well enough to fool her. We'll never know. I think she started figuring it out at Tegere Servare when she saw him last, at least grew suspicious, and I think Liam Tull realised it when she did. That's why her murder was quick and simple. Because Liam was desperate for her not to get word out to anyone. And he didn't have time in any case,' I say.

'What proof do you have?' Ben replies.

'That Liam Tull killed Ann Bowlby? In isolation, none,' I answer.

'But her killing was part of a spree of murders. Things change when you take them into account. Aldo Mucci. Thomas Bern. Sean Corcoran. From the start the extreme cruelty, the brutality of those murders, were almost overpowering, making it hard to focus on much else. But in the end, when you set aside the horror and sickness of it all, there still had to be means, method, and motive.

'The killer had knowledge of fairly obscure Church history. It was essential to his methods of execution and torture. Being a priest raised as an orphan by priests, it's reasonable to assume that Liam would have had access to that knowledge. But still, he wouldn't have been the only one.

'The killer would also have had to be physically strong. First, he would have at least needed to be able to overpower the victims themselves. But much more than that. Both Sean Corcoran and Thomas Bern were found suspended in the air by fence posts. Whether they were dead or alive, the killer had to be strong enough to lift their bodies off the ground and then mount them carefully upright. Liam Tull, as you can see, is a solidly built young man. And I know for a fact that he is very strong indeed, although we'll get to that. But still, there are other men who would also be strong enough.

'The killer also had to know the movements of all the victims. Where they would be at what time. That they would be alone. And that no one would miss their absence for some time. Liam Tull not only worked and lived with these men, he was their adopted son. It's reasonable to assume that he would have been able to learn the whereabouts of all three men. But still, there are others who may have known these things too.

'But this killer had to also be sick. Those crime scenes. No one could do those things and manage to be a happy, normal person at the same time. The killer didn't just kill that way on a whim. Think of the planning. The tools and preparation required. No. So not a random choice of method. Not all that. And not three times. No. That kind of sickness doesn't just suddenly materialise one day. It has history. And Liam Tull comes from a very dark past. It's a matter of record that he was sexually, physically, and emotionally abused for several years before becoming the sole

246

survivor of a family murder. But still, sadly, there are many people with dark pasts that have changed them.

'Then there's entry. Three different crime scenes. No signs of forced entry. Two private homes and one public building. Even if the locks were picked, forensics would have shown up the markings. So either the killer had the appropriate keys and alarm codes for all of them or he knew the victims and they let him in. Now here, again, even though Liam Tull isn't the only possible candidate, he's one of the very few on a shrinking list of suspects,' I conclude.

'So we're looking for a disturbed, unusually strong man with a traumatic past who has knowledge of obscure Church history and knows the whereabouts of all three victims in advance and has the means to gain entry,' Ben summarises. 'You're right, it could be Liam Tull. But it still doesn't prove it beyond a doubt that he killed these men. And Bobby, setting your recent lapse aside, you're still a cop. A cop Pollo gave his life for. I saw you. You shot him the very moment you saw him. You knew already, you were sure,' Ben prompts me.

'I was. Because of two things,' I say. 'Firstly, the gun. Father Bern had a gun registered to him. Kept it in his bedroom safe. Went missing the day of his death. His nurse mentioned it in her statement. We know because he also kept his medication in the safe. The nurse comes by every day. Confirmed that she saw him put the syringes in the safe and that the gun was there same as every other day. Then he gets killed and the gun is missing. Nothing else taken.

'That was the only thing taken from all the crime scenes, as a matter of fact. But why? The killer is clearly able to murder people without needing a gun.

And if this is Manga Kahu, they have more than enough of their own. But what if the killer didn't want to obtain one legally, with paperwork and proof? What if he had wanted the gun not to help him murder, but for the same reason most people have one. Protection. From Jones Maihi.

'I hadn't given it much more thought until someone started shooting at us at the grave. A snub-nose revolver, six-shot. The same as the one that went missing from Father Bern's house. It's possible that the gun was stolen by someone else, but then it turns up at the gravesite of a suicided boy and then again here. That is conclusive. It links all the murders together,' I state, pointing at the gun lying next to me.

'Then secondly, there's the limp. At Aroha's grave I saw that the man who shot at us was limping as he ran away. I didn't hit him. So that injury came from before. And a witness to Liam Tull's abduction reported seeing a masked man limping away from the scene. Earlier this week I broke a man's toes outside the Baldwin Pub. I didn't get to see his face. This was when we were there catching that kid who came to see you. I assumed at the time that I had just come across a lookout for Manga Kahu, or maybe someone who recognised a cop and had warrants out for arrest who was scared I had recognised him. But I was wrong. That person was there for the same reason we were. To find Jones Maihi. He really couldn't afford to be recognised, and especially not there.

'I didn't realise it then, but they were all Liam Tull. He had abused the boy probably for a while. Those pictures. I don't think that was the first time. Or the last. I don't think it was suicide either. I think Liam killed him. Maybe because he was leaving the country soon on his trip to the Philippines and was worried the boy wouldn't keep the secret. Maybe because Liam Tull is sick and he was always working up to it. Either way, I think he did it. And I think he liked it. Too much. Somewhere in that sick mind, killing the people you love started making sense to him. After all, it's how he was raised.

'I think, like the truly insane, it gave him something. It had meaning. Purpose. And once he got started, he couldn't stop. Like all serial killers. Because it felt too good. So he started with the other people he loved. To get the same feeling out of it again. He killed his family. The priests who adopted him. And there was no real risk to him.

'At first he must have thought he was getting away with everything. The boy's death was ruled a suicide. And it felt so good. And Liam had an exit ready. He was due to leave the country within days to go do missionary work in the Philippines. Why not do more? Feel more? And if he did it fast enough he'd be long gone before the cops could really figure anything out. Liam was intelligent. Careful and controlled. Clearly knew how to plan well. Confident he could do this.

'But almost immediately, Jones Maihi's name starts coming up. It's in the news, in police questioning. The sudden escape from custody at the funeral. The father of his victim. A known Manga Kahu gangster. So he gets suspicious. Worried the father may have noticed something. But where to start? So he does the same as us and goes to the Baldwin Pub. He knows what Aroha's close family look like by now, so he intends to either find Jones or follow his family, hoping they will lead him to him. That's where we meet when I find him in the alley. I'm not big but I'm pretty strong, and when we fought I also had the benefit of position and leverage, and still that person was much stronger than me. The strength needed to commit those tortures. In the struggle I broke his toes. It would have hurt pretty badly but it's the kind of injury you can conceal if you walk slowly. But not if you're running. The limp would definitely show then. And it did.

'Now, even though things start going wrong for Liam, at the same time it's helping him. The police are thrown off track by gang associates at the first crime scene. What we didn't know was that they were there looking for Liam Tull, and only happened onto a crime scene by accident. Liam had no listed address but sometimes stayed at his adoptive father's house when he wasn't out at Tegere Servare. Then Liam's suspicions are confirmed when Jones attacks Tegere Servare itself. Almost succeeding. Jones was there for him and Liam knew it. He had to kill Jones and destroy whatever evidence, if any, Jones had.

'Liam will have worked out now that it's likely physical evidence. Something Jones found or saw at the funeral. If it was just the boy telling his father, having word passed on to him in prison, then why would Jones wait until the funeral to act? Why didn't any of the rest of the family or the gang come after Liam sooner? Or tell the police? And Liam is a priest. He will have been familiar with the custom of putting gifts in the coffin. What if it was still there? Confident the only possible link between him and the death of the priests is what he did to the boy and his father's proof of it, Liam comes to the same conclusion as us. He needs to be sure. He needs to check the coffin. Just in case Jones left it there. And Ann Bowlby needs to be dealt with also. Once the evidence is destroyed she's the last remaining person who can link him to the boy. The records here can easily be destroyed but she needed to die before she made the connection. But by now there was no way of doing these things.

'He was getting more desperate as time passed. By now he had a twenty-four-hour police escort for his safety and he had no way of knowing when the farm would be deserted. But the attack on Tegere Servare gave him his chance. One last big play. He knows how Māori rituals work during funerals. Knows the family will all attend. That Aroha's grave will finally be unattended. So he stages his own abduction. The perfect solution. If he can find Jones he can kill him, and Ann Bowlby, and destroy whatever evidence he finds. Then stage another crime scene. Blame the death of Ann Bowlby on Jones and say that he killed Jones in self-defence before escaping. After all, Jones had already killed cops this week. Already openly attacked Tegere Servare; no one would ever doubt him. The man limping away from the scene at Liam's abduction wasn't a lookout as I originally thought. It was Liam Tull himself.

'I know Ann figured something out based on the message she left me. Maybe Liam knew that she did, or maybe this was just him silencing anyone who could link him to Aroha. But he used his fake disappearance to kill her, knowing the cops, as we'd done all along, would only attribute this to Manga Kahu too. Ever since that boy ran away from us at the first crime scene.

'So Liam waited for dark and then made his next move. But he found the grave freshly robbed. And he found us. He tried to kill us but failed. I clearly saw the man running away from us limping. By now

251

everything had gone so very wrong for Liam. He couldn't go back to Tegere Servare. Couldn't go to the Church or any of the priests' houses, which he knew were all being watched by police. He knew he was a missing person, that the cops were searching for him. He couldn't go anywhere on the main roads, so where does he go from the Maihi farm at the edge of the Catlins?' I ask.

'The only place he can,' Ben answers. 'He goes home.'

'Yes, this home. His first home,' I agree.

'By now he's realised that the only way to salvage things is if he can find Jones Maihi, and fast. He's failed to find the evidence he had been hoping to destroy. Knows it's not just Jones who is now looking at Aroha's death. Doesn't even know if the evidence was left behind in the coffin for us to find or not. But if he can find Jones he can find out. There's still a chance to get away with it. Kill Jones and destroy the evidence, or at least find out what it was. With luck, his ploy can still work. Besides, he's already staged his own kidnapping now. If he has to, he can try to disappear if he finds out that something incriminating has fallen into our hands. But to decide, he needs to know. Despairing now, sitting here, he comes up with his last plan. He calls Jones Maihi's family from here. Tells them exactly where he can find Liam Tull. Tells them to tell Jones. It's a risk, but Liam has no choices left. He needs Jones. Knows Jones will come. He wasn't out here hiding. He was out here waiting. That's why all the lights are turned on. That's how the family knew where Jones was heading. Right?' I ask.

'Yes. They said someone called them not long before. They got word to Jones. They thought it was a

252

trap but Jones couldn't be stopped. Revenge has its own momentum,' Ben answers.

Finally he lowers the rifle. Slowly he sits down next to me on the stairs.

'Why did you do it? Why kill Jones then? You could have just let him blow my head off and the two of you could have slipped away in the night. You already know I'm out here without backup,' I say.

'I've already told you. The most important thing is our people. Our family. Our blood. Jones sacrificed his own brothers for the sake of his vengeance. He put his hate for a stranger above his love of us. Some things are so big, so bad, they can never be undone. No. There's no going back now. I don't judge him for wanting to kill Liam Tull. But his brothers. And Pollo. And Danny. Now even you. How many more children must grow up fatherless because Jones lost a son? And after all this killing, how can he ever come back to us? No. It was always going to end this way. You don't know this yet, Bobby, but one day, one day if you get old enough, you will: Love and hate. That's all people really are,' Ben says, looking away from me.

Then Alkaline Ben slowly gets up.

I watch him as he makes his way down the stairs.

At the bottom he stops and turns, looking up at me.

There's a look on his face, in his eyes.

When he asks, he looks younger somehow, like Pollo did that last night, that last time:

'Would you have done it, in the end? Knowing it all. If I hadn't? If Jones was there without the gun. If it was your choice to kill him or spare him. Would you have done it?'

One Last Kill

by
Finn Bell

WANT MORE?

Get Emails about my: New Releases, Free Books
and Special Offers (I won't ever spam you or share
your info with anyone).

To sign up for free visit:

www.finnbellbooks.com/subscribelink

SLIGHTLY BIASED MOSTLY TRUE THINGS . . .

Baldwin Street

At nineteen degrees (along its worst/best part, depending on your needs), Baldwin Street in Dunedin, New Zealand, is in fact the steepest residential street in the world.

Tourists walk up it, their selfie-backgrounds peppered by frowning locals in 4x4s. As with most things you probably shouldn't have done, it holds an almost magical attraction for people. Various races and events are held there annually. Those who are fit and sound-minded race up it. Those who are less so race down it. Usually on things with wheels. Over the years these events, both sanctioned and not, have included bicycles, skateboards, luges, shopping trolleys, wheeled garbage bins and once, a motorcycle with only one wheel. Gains of bragging rights and dubious personal epiphanies have been offset with various injuries ranging from the slight up to actual death.

For those with more family-friendly interests, it also hosts the annual 'Jaffa Race' or as it is locally known, 'The Running of the Balls.' A Jaffa is a tiny chocolate ball covered in an orange-flavoured shell. Increasingly large numbers are released every year (the last was 75,000 Jaffas at once), with spectators offering opinions on which exact Jaffa will get to the bottom first. Go there. Eat some. Take a selfie.

In reality there is no pub on Baldwin Street, which, given the above, is probably for the best. The pub I had in mind when writing this story is real and is in fact in Dunedin, but shall remain unnamed. Because if you don't know it already you really, really shouldn't go there.

Bobby Ress

Bobby Ress has become someone I'm curious about, despite the fact that I probably made very nearly half of him up (I think). I sometimes think it would have been really cool if both he and Pollo could somehow magically become a part of Captain Ahab's crew in Moby Dick (if we could somehow set all that inside a cascading zombie apocalypse, that would be even better).

His character first appeared in one of my previous books, *The Killing Ground*, where we encounter him much later in life than the events of *One Last Kill*. In *The Killing Ground* he has become a middle-aged priest with a complicated past as a criminal profiler and detective, who now finds meaning in organising elaborate bake sales.

Back then his name had a point, which I reproduce here from that book's section of 'Slightly Biased Mostly True Things':

Father Ress, or Bobby Ress, is in name and function a homage to the great Robert K. Ressler, often credited with first coining the term 'Serial Killer.' Robert Ressler started his career in the US Army and later joined the FBI, where he worked in the Behavioural Science Unit. He went on to write several books and treatises on psychological profiling and criminology. He taught across the world, and was also involved in several high-profile criminal investigations. If you ever get the chance, read his works. He is certainly a man who saw more horrible things than most, and what's more, had the capacity to understand it with a sense of mercy. I had tried to contact him as part of the research for this book but sadly, he died May 5, 2013. Too soon. Like all the best people.

Bowlby

The character of Ann Bowlby is named in honour of the late Edward John Mostyn Bowlby. Known as one of the founding fathers of attachment theory. He was a British psychologist, psychiatrist, and psychoanalyst.

He was particularly interested in early childhood development and how the incidents and occurrences of our very early years can have a lasting impact on our lives. For better or for worse.

What I found interesting was that he had put forward the idea of what a perfect, ideal childhood would look like. And in turn how a healthy, balanced, functional adult would result from this halcyon upbringing. A real-life, shiny, happy person.

Then I thought (as you do) how so very few of us can rely on that perfect start with perfect parents.

The world is, after all, a bell curve of truths, equally amazing and appalling. The sanctity of Mummy and Daddy are not exempt.

This made me wonder what someone would be as an adult (and had to have gone through as a child) to be on the other extreme end of Bowlby's thinking. What if you had the worst possible start in life, with the worst parents that led to the worst possible adult? Who would that look like?

So after some tinkering I came up with an approximation of Liam Tull, although I didn't know what to do with him at the time. It was only several years later, after I learned about the case of Margaret Pahl (see the section on her below) that I thought to include him in this book.

Catherine Wheel

Catherine wheels were real. It is one of an unfortunately very large menu of experiences the Catholic Church was able, and at times overly willing, to subject people to. All the methods of torture and execution described in this book are real and were employed to varying degrees of severity during the past two millennia.

Sometimes they were used only a little bit. Other times they were used until they killed you (which only rarely included the small mercy of allowing you to die quickly). What they told you before was usually a sign. When old white men started talking about comfortably vague goals like 'purification' or (when you must have known you're really in trouble) 'in order to save your immortal soul' was when you should have already started running.

Killing (whether you hold to the concept of it being justifiable or not) is one thing. Of necessity, it happens in nature. What sets people apart from other living things, however, is our reasons for doing so, coupled with the innovation and creativity we incorporate into doing it really well. Sadly, this trend is not limited to Catholicism but spans various religions and attached cultures. I sincerely hope this isn't because of the involved god's influence.

Catlins, The

The problem with people is that there are altogether way too many of them.

They're just everywhere. It can annoy me to no end.

This is one reason I like the Catlins. It remains one of the most remote and least known areas of New Zealand, although I have no idea why. Because the solitude is chock-full of awesome things almost nobody enjoys.

This includes such a passel of stunning natural landforms and coastal features that many of them don't even have names yet and aren't shown on maps.

To name a few (so you at least know where to head) this includes Cathedral Caves, Nugget Point, the

Purakaunui Falls, Frances Pillars, Cannibal Bay, Curio Beach, and the proverbial 'much more.'

Go there (but keep your distance, please).

Colonisation

Several times this book touches on the reality and tensions of colonisation.

I come from a colonised country, and not a happy one (if there is such a thing). I was lucky enough to be born on the right colour of it (and by right, I don't mean morally, just that we had more power and the inclination to abuse it to our benefit).

I clearly remember the slow, two-fold realisation of it all as I grew up.

First realisation, that people must be crazy.

That there's no good reason for people to treat other people like this. That there must be something wrong with most people in order to honestly believe doing these things to people from the other side of town was okay. For the longest time I couldn't connect the reality of good, normal people who love their families with the reality of those same people callously being party to the oppression of other families. The only explanation that worked for me was that most people must be a little crazy.

Second realisation, that it's actually worse.

People weren't crazy. They were just like me. They didn't really see things differently. Most of them didn't believe in the various 'isms' they supported. The truth wasn't that people were classist or racist or fascist. It was worse. The majority were normal. They didn't really believe these things that then made them do these horrible things. No. They did the horrible things anyway, while they knew full well it was wrong. What's worse, they mostly did it for money (a stronger currency, a nicer house, and easier job prospects).

This country was not New Zealand.

Although New Zealand is also a colonised country. My line of work (prior to writing) allowed me to talk to a lot of interesting people around New Zealand about what this means to them. Much from those conversations informs the tensions touched on in this book.

And I do believe people are more or less the same no matter where you go in the world. (If you actually want to understand why people are the way they are, then I'm probably not the best person to ask).

I will however (unasked), say that the New Zealand of the present is by far the best possible version of a post-colonial country I have come across (which is part of why I've never left).

As incontrovertible proof, I offer the following:

A dildo.

Very recently, a sitting minister and member of the New Zealand parliament was speaking at a national memorial day. Mid-speech, he was confronted by a political protester who, with unerring accuracy, threw a large sex toy at his face. Cameras of the world watching.

Let's pause right there. (The clip is out there on the Internet if you have to).

Now then, the moment phallus hits unprepared face is significant (as in most cases). Because from here on, things could go in very different directions depending on where in the world you are. Let's say this was any of a number of more conservative regimes, be they communist, democratic, or other. The consequences could range from a criminal charge to that protester simply disappearing in the night, or much worse.

It is, in fact, a very good litmus test for the health and authenticity of a given nation's political rhetoric. Can a country put its dildo where its mouth is (so to speak)?

New Zealand passed this test with flying colours. The (clearly misguided) protester is alive and well. And uncharged, although people did ask her to please go away. And the (probably equally misguided) minister is still employed and giving speeches (although with slightly more sudden, random head movements).

The point is that New Zealand, for all its (trust me, really very minor) failings, is a country where the people with power don't abuse it. When they easily could. Even to the point of taking a sex toy to the face.

How many countries (post-colonial or not) can say that?

Dunedin

Dunedin is awesome. It's the heart of Otago (which, even without this cool city, would be worth the trip many times over). The city combines a raft of natural, cultural, and historic features in a quirky way that makes it hard not to have a very good time. Do come.

Māori Culture

In 1931, one hundred people were annoyed.

(This is not unusual.) What made them special was that they were all annoyed together at the same person. (Which must have been nice.)

That person was Albert Einstein. The unhappy people got so very worked up that they actually stopped life to get together and write things down (always a bad sign).

What they came up with was a book titled *One Hundred Authors Against Einstein*. The book was a collection of essays criticising Einstein's theory of relativity from every angle they could think of. Einstein, they agreed, was so very clearly wrong about everything in every way (including the fact that Jewish people couldn't do real science anyway).

When Einstein was asked about the book he retorted by saying, 'Why 100 authors? If I were wrong, then one would have been enough.'

This book involves several aspects of Māori culture, both good and bad. I'm not Māori. Serious people will be annoyed. In the spirit of Einstein, I shall attempt to measure my impact by number of respondents (setting aside my lack of comparable brilliance).

But for those willing to take this story in the spirit it is given, I will say that I find the Māori and Pacific Island peoples endlessly fascinating. In many ways, the people I've met span the extremes of humanity. Some are so clearly, authentically themselves that having met them makes me wish I was more like them (and that it would have been a far better world if they colonised us instead of the other way around.) But on the other end of the spectrum, I've also met those who fall well beyond redemption, whose cultural identity is but another handy tool to exploit the people around them. But then that's people everywhere, isn't it?

Manga Kahu

Manga Kahu is real. They make up one part of a vast network of gangs and criminal groups that exist within New Zealand. I've spent a lot of time talking to them. (Both the good and the very, very bad.) While criminal activity forms part of the life and times of gangs, it is often not why people choose the path.

For many it gives them much more important things, like family, brotherhood, belonging, and purpose. It keeps their children safe, values them, gives them pride, feeds them, and ultimately helps them understand the world and their place in it.

It's not a happy thought, but the gangs' existence is perhaps less a judgment on the people inside of them than the surrounding society.

New Zealand

By now you'll realise that I'm an unashamed fan of this country. It really is the best one. I'd soon run out of adjectives if I had to list all the goodness. The more you do and see here, the more you'll want to. Do so. It'll probably make you a better person too.

Otago

The text below is taken from the Otago Tourism website (www.otago.co.nz). I'll only add that, unlike many things in life, it will entirely live up to expectations. It's not marketing, it's actually true. Come see for yourself:

Otago is the second most southerly region of the country, and one of the most diverse. It is 32,000 square kilometres encompassing mountainous regions and vast open plains, glacier-fed rivers and deserted sandy beaches.

Nestled near the bottom of the South Island, Otago has a traditional farming heritage plus many little-known natural and historic treasures. Where else can you walk among wild seals, visit a life-sized but miniature castle, kayak through semi-submersed caves, or jet boat down rock-strewn rivers? Otago has it all — accessible wildlife, adventure tourism, world-class vineyards and restaurants, historic sites, deserted white sandy beaches and vistas of staggering beauty.

Otago is a region of contrasts. Its unique character is defined by a magnificent landscape and diverse climate. Queenstown winters bring snow while Alexandra summers are among the hottest in the country. Snow-covered mountains, native forests and stunning southern lakes populate the west of the region while dry, tussock-covered mountains and valleys of rock complement this wild and beautiful land.

Pahl, Margaret

I've always found priests interesting by association. Because sin is interesting (both the various practices thereof and the concept), and priests always seem to show up where enough of it happens. It's a big job description: Celebrant, Orator, Advisor, Therapist, Community Calendar Organiser, Sin-forgiver, etc. It must be a very odd window into human beings and doings.

Then I attended a funeral where the priest involved mentioned that he had been this young woman's priest her entire life. He had baptised her as a baby. Officiated at her wedding, and now he was conducting her funeral. He explained further that he had of course heard most of her sins in between as well. He jokingly said he'd heard much worse.

There's a rare breed of intimacy there. Intimacy is a kind of power.

Matters of faith and religion aside — how wonderful it must be to share all of this with one good person. Conversely, how toxic to share it with the opposite.

And so, having reached this point of reasoning (and having run out of useful things to do one dark and rainy night), I decided to try and find that opposite.

The closest I came was the compellingly tragic case of Margaret Pahl. The only recorded person in history to be murdered and buried by the same priest.

You couldn't imagine the story if you tried:

On April 9, 1980, in Ohio, USA, there's a funeral Mass. It's the week after Easter.
Four days ago, on Holy Saturday, Margaret Ann Pahl was still 71.
She was one day away from her 72nd birthday when she died.
It happens.
From her teens to the day she died, Margaret was a nun.
She lived for the Church.
And she died in one.

On that Saturday, at the Toledo Mercy Hospital Chapel, she was strangled and stabbed 31 times. The extent of the damage made it difficult to know whether she was also raped. Or in which order they were done to her. Some of the wounds were arranged in the shape of an inverted cross. It happens.

The priest leading her funeral service, Gerald Robinson, knew her well and had been working closely with her at Mercy Hospital up to the day of her killing.

He prayed for her, he sang for her, he blessed her. He buried her.

Twenty-six years later, on May 11, 2006, he was also convicted of her murder.

Gerald died in prison on July 4, 2014. At the time, he was still an ordained priest of the Catholic Church. Because crime and sin are not the same thing.

I remember when I first heard of the case. Then years later, learning how it ended. It made me wonder if God ever feels like swearing.

And if he does, who to?

Self-Determination and Morality Meets Crime and Punishment

This book touches on these concepts (or tries to at least), hence their inclusion here. That line 'Self-Determination and Morality Meets Crime and Punishment' can more accurately be read as 'Something-that-doesn't-exist and Something-we-can't-define meets Something-we-don't-understand and Something-that-doesn't-work.'

When I think of it, it always makes me smile and helps me take life just that little bit less seriously. Because it reminds me that the human brain is clearly unsuited for the job of thinking, and it's probably best if we build more machines to do our reasoning for us.

As oxymorons go, this one has layers.

Self-determination, or the simple notion that there's a 'conscious you' thinking and making decisions; that 'you' that's basically in charge of you, is becoming harder and harder to believe, let alone prove. To appropriately creepify this concept, try to realise that the 'you' choosing to read this sentence really isn't choosing at all. In actuality, there are various sneaky parts of you that get together to make the calls and then trick the 'real conscious you' into believing that you made that decision after the fact. Simply put: You are not in control. You are not really you. (Not a safe, warm feeling, huh?)

Various branches of science, ranging from neuropsychology to quantum physics, are steadily disproving our sense of self, agency, and free will. If you want to read more (assuming that the rest of you will allow you to think that you had the ability and inclination to choose it) you can start with these authors: Benjamin Libet, Itzhak Fried, Marcel Brass, Simone Kuhn, Amir Javadi, Angeliki Beyko, and Vincent Walsh.

It gets even worse when we try to define what morality is.

A couple of thousand years ago, the ideas of right and wrong and good and bad were mostly underpinned by religions — basically morality translated as 'God tells us what to do.' Most religions, of course, were led by old men of various cultures.

In time, religions made room for philosophy (in some places) and this changed morality from the basic 'God tells us what to do' approach to the more crafty 'God told us what to do but if we don't like the answer then we can get really smart people to tell us what God actually means instead.' (Which should make you wonder what the pope is really up to these days.)

Over the past millennia, the fields of philosophy have, again, overwhelmingly been led by old men.

In the last few centuries, both religions and their attached philosophies have also had to make increasing room for the average person. Enter politics. Whether it be by democracy or socialism, people have decided that they, too, should have a say in defining what's right and wrong and good and bad.

Finally, all this has helped develop the general operational concept of morality into the honest (but probably stupid) 'We mostly tell ourselves what to do but act like we don't really.' Plausible deniability for us from us. You will, of course, notice that most politicians and lawmakers are still old men.

Now imagine morality as it exists within a given person.

That one brain (which may or may not be entirely sane — but don't get me started on that) will have to contend with the competing and often shifting internal and external pressures of their personal experiences and understandings of religion, philosophy, and politics, and somehow make day-to-day decisions that are still 'good' and 'right.' (Without actually having self-determination to do it with anyway.)

Now consider crime. Or rather, let's complicate the sometimes conflicting forces of right and wrong and good and bad by adding legal and illegal to the mix. Now the brain has to do what it thinks/ feels/senses to be 'right' and 'good,' but also factor in whether it's 'legal.' If this still sounds easy to you it means you have money. Enter basic economics.

Before you protest, let me change that to 'have enough money' not to have to face the really hard moral choices on a daily basis.

Go to parts of Africa, Asia, the Americas, and various bits in between, and put yourself in far too many people's shoes (if they're rich enough to have them): Would you kill someone to feed your starving child or watch her die? How about just hurt them then? And it's not a watershed test. It's a lifestyle. So keep in mind that you're likely going to have to make the same decision in a few days' time. Still sure you're going to find the 'right,' 'good,' and 'legal' way forward every day? Every time?

(Don't knock it till you've tried it.)

And then, finally, there's punishment.

Within the context of crime, this usually translates into some kind of consequence of hardship ranging from fines and restrictions all the way up to corporal punishment, prison, and death.

They are intended, once all the lofty rhetoric and pretentious jargon is removed, to hurt you (and scare everyone else).

The origin of the word punish in Latin literally means 'to inflict pain upon.'

The pain is meant to impress upon you the simple message, 'Don't do that!'

The problem with pain is that it only seems to work as punishment when it is used within close relationships (like parents and kids), where punishment is balanced by reward and (hopefully) encapsulated in a loving relationship. (Even here there's a fermenting miasma of confusing academic debate, so take the above as true at your own risk, as have I.) This loving relationship (happy thought) is a key factor in our integration of morality in the first place and also (as it turns out) helps build those bits of you that actually make the decisions the conscious you only thinks it does.

But when the human mind encounters pain from sources beyond these close relationships (like, say, random accidents and incidents, or the consequences of a legal system), it can have much more interesting results.

Enough pain won't just change the behaviour the punishment intended. It can (and very frequently does) do a whole lot more (and by more I mean worse).

Even a novice neuroscientist will tell you that enough pain can significantly change how the brain senses, prioritises, stores, and uses information. Doctors, therapists, and counsellors (and Secret Service interrogators) of various ilk will eagerly concur. Victims of all kinds of pain (accident, illness, war, abuse, etc.) will attest the same. Pain can change, almost entirely, your mind. The problem is, we don't always know what it will change your mind to (although the balance of evidence-based research will tell you where crime and punishment is concerned, it's going to be something bad).

So.

Not only does the brain have to make 'right,' 'good,' and 'legal' decisions based on the changing internalised models of the above that do not always agree, while using the free will it doesn't really have, in balancing personal needs with external (potentially biased) laws and regulations buffeted by an uncertain socio-economic context defined by political agendas that may be far from fair (while also not necessarily being able to distinguish what it wants from what it needs, assuming of course that this outcome is contextually possible and the brain involved is also sane).

It needs to do it perfectly, forever.

Otherwise, the pain resulting from criminal punishment will likely make it even harder to get it right next time. Harder still the time after that. And so on. (Ever wonder why reformed criminals are so rare?)

So what, you may wonder, is my point? (Difficult to say, I'm not really in control of me anyway.)

But I'd like it if my point was something along the lines of the following:

1. Don't judge people too fast. It's a lot harder for some than for you.
2. It's probably time to bring back the death penalty. It'd be less cruel.
3. When are we going to stop listening to old men? They're clearly a problem.